Blinky's Law

MARTIN TALKS

ISBN: 978-1-9163777-0-7

DEDICATION

To Bea, my Executive Assistant and loyal dachshund, for
accompanying me through long hours of writing.
To Izzy, for her incisive editorial input and enthusiasm.
To Sarah, Rufus, Alphaeus and Ludwig for their support.

CONTENTS

1 THE WORLD REVOLVES AROUND HUMANS

Hiu's fridge wanted to divorce him. He had been informed of this development by his bed, which in Hiu's opinion had seemed rather over-eager to give him the news. In fact, the bed had woken him up twenty-four minutes and thirty seconds earlier than usual. The bed had claimed that this early awakening was due to *'predicted delays'* in Hiu's journey to work. These needed to be anticipated, otherwise they would cause him to arrive after his official start time of 8.30 PT. Hiu suspected that the bed had just wanted to be the first to tell him. The usual series of dawn-light wavelengths and squeaky sounds called *'spring bird songs,'* designed to ease him into the day, had certainly seemed rather rushed that morning. And had that been a rather judgmental tone in the bed's voice?

Hiu didn't know what to think: should he be upset, worried or angry that a robotic device like a fridge should be filing for divorce from a human? It was the human who did the divorcing, or more usually the upgrading, by saying or just thinking the word '*upgrade*' three times. It wasn't a fridge's place to file for divorce; it was unseemly, unSocietal and very bad for Hiu's Personal Data Score. A Personal Data Score, known as a PDS, determined how a person lived in Luhan Hypercity, from their eligibility for the latest technology upgrades, to the standard of their apartment, to their job. So pretty much their everything. Today of all days was not the day to get his PDS score dented. Today was the day when he was finally going to meet Boss.

He leant over his bathroom sink and looked in the mirror. His clear eyes - one brown, one blue - stared back at him as they had done for so many years. He had once tried to calculate for how many years, but as time was measured on a personal relative basis, known as PT, meaning Personalised Time, this had not proved very easy. His best guess was that in five old days' time, on Zero Day, he would be one hundred and twenty old years in age.

Zero Day... Hiu hated it. And being one hundred and twenty old years on Zero Day gave him one more reason to hate it.

Negative thoughts were bad for his PDS and, as a result, bad for his meeting with Boss, so Hiu focused his mind on his dazzling white teeth, full head of shiny blonde hair and his smooth, unblemished, orange skin. Society data confirmed that, based on its appearance, proportions and expressions, that identified emotional tendencies, health qualities and social sensitivities, this face was normal for a person who identified as a male. Normal, that was, except for the eyes. Having one brown eye and one blue eye was not normal. He should really get them corrected, but for some reason he had not. At least when he thought his face seemed a bit too smooth, that it lacked character, that it wasn't quite human enough, he could look himself in his different coloured eyes and know that no robot would ever be issued with such an irregularity. He looked intently at his reflection.

"Be Human!" he urged himself.

He wondered for a moment what he might look like with some lines or creases to reflect his many years of living, and maybe a grey hair here or a slight sag there... He shuddered. No way! Thank Society he looked and felt like an awesome twenty-seven years old, rather than the nearly one hundred and twenty old years he was in reality.

Like everyone else, he could adjust himself along the age and gender scales and currently he had chosen a mid-twenties male. Not too male, not too stereotypically square-jawed, musclebound or aggressive; nearer the middle-ground with a softer, lither look, long-limbed and athletic. He had specifically chosen twenty-seven years old as it was the Society average. It was normal. He wondered again why not change both his eyes to be normal as well, both clear blue instead of one brown and one blue? He didn't have a logical response to that thought, but there was no hurry. He was always twenty-seven years old and time was limitless. So he logged the thought away below any conscious processes, although not before he had permitted himself the tiniest byte of an illogical thought that he never allowed to form fully; that maybe his eye colours were a sign that he had been chosen for something special.

"Sir, you have been chosen for a special brand-new skin cream trial," said the mirror rather archly. "Cream being applied from *Fourmilier Peau: for skin good enough to eat*!"

Hiu felt a splatter of cream being jetted around his eyes and absorbed into his skin.

"Nice..." he grimaced.

He straightened himself up and strode through to the dazzlingly white-tiled bathroom where the shower began running at one hundred-and-twelve degrees Fahrenheit precisely – the perfect temperature. As he stepped in, he smelt grapefruit-infused shower gel being smoothed onto his body – the perfect scent. Cream shampoo was squirted onto his head and a light massage by soft unseen hands began – the perfect touch. Something grabbed his genitalia – ouch! - not the perfect place...

"Your penis is now clean, sir," intoned an efficient-sounding voice, with just the tiniest hint of disgust.

"OK..." gasped Hiu, as the automated device withdrew. That new genital wash upgrade still caught him by surprise after almost a week.

In the background, Hiu could hear commercials for the latest washroom services and accessories playing just above the noise of the water, including a song sung by a 'Doctor Coldfinger' extolling the virtues of a colonic irrigation device: *'Don't let your heinie be grimy; don't let your anus be heinous!'*

"Not the perfect soundtrack," grumbled Hiu.

He left the shower and stepped onto the bathroom mat.

"Ouch get off, sir, please sir!" squealed the indignant mat. "Weight: heavy! Data sent to the kitchen to reduce calories, with a recommendation for *'Slim Pickings: just enough to eat!'*"

"Sounds delightful," muttered Hiu.

Various data comments were made, and adverts delivered, by robotic devices during his teeth brushing, cheek massaging, and face scrubbing, and he was given a full body CT scan as he walked out through the bathroom doorway.

"You are disease free and in the average human percentile, sir," declared a voice filled with simulated parental pride. "This data has been uploaded to Society's core Human Optimisation Systems."

"So everyone will know I'm average…" thought Hiu as positively as he could muster, wondering why he always registered the slightest disappointment at this very good news.

"And I have more very good news for you, sir!" the doorway continued. "Your emotional range has remained in a constant neutral state now for your new record streak! Go you!" There was a fanfare of trumpets and a warbling soprano sang: *'Scanology: We see where the sun don't shine!'*

"Go me" muttered Hiu, again registering that slightest disappointment, too slight to register on his PDS he hoped, but he sensed it nonetheless.

He took sanctuary in the toilet room and exhaled slowly as he sat down.

"Woh there!" whistled the toilet in a pained high-pitched voice. "Spicy food last night, sir? I must have a word with those kitchen robots! But while you are here, did you know there are unbeatable offers on our new brown toiletry range, including money back on your old devices? Upgrade now for *the 'Big Brown Blow-back!'*"

"Toilet, shut verbal communication down," commanded Hiu.

"With pleasure, sir, and if you don't mind, I think I'll shut down my olfactory sensors too…"

Recently all the robotic devices seemed to have begun acting rather strangely. It must have been the result of some new *'personality infused'* artificial intelligence upgrade, Hiu mused. He was normally an enthusiastic embracer of the new, but he wondered whether this was an upgrade too far. The robots had all become too chatty, too impertinent, too… human. If he could set them to silent just for a short while each morning, he thought he would be a lot happier and no doubt would produce a lot more stools of acceptable size, consistency and odour. He hadn't produced any ideal stools now for almost a week and he was sure the chattering robots were something to do with it. They irritated him and no doubt irritated his bowels too. He had tried to change the robot settings a few times before, but had been directed and redirected to multiple '*Help*' chatbots which seemed more intent on selling upgrades than actually helping him. Not that silence would stop the constant sensor measurements analysing his every movement, bowel or otherwise. He often had to remind himself that it was all for his own good. After all, they made him who he was... the normal, average twenty-seven-year-old perfect person.

"I am because I am tracked," he reflected. "It's just that sometimes..." But he didn't let himself finish that thought in case it registered in his PDS.

After the usual energising series of water jets, air blasts and buttock massages from the silently seething toilet, he did manage to squeeze out a rather miserly turd and was informed by the toilet, sneeringly, that a full report would be sent not just to the kitchen, but to Society's public data banks.

Hiu stood in front of the bathroom sink looking at his oh-so-smooth reflection again, when the mirror slid back and two arms shot out towards his eyes. Before he could blink, claws had anchored back his eyelids and two tiny suction pads had pushed smart lenses against his eyeballs. However many times this had been done, he still flinched. As soon as the lenses were in, he started seeing the latest data updates in the top left-hand corner of his vision:

'75% off all sofas at Furniture Hypercity while stocks last. Hurry

and upgrade now!'

'Tired of your limp grey personality? Upload a new one now!'

He quickly thought-scrolled through these and the many other promotional messages to get to the articles.

'Is your robot cheating on you? Zie is if zie does these five things,' read one.

'Ten ways to spot if your toaster is plotting against you,' read another.

'Does this legal loophole allow robots to claim human rights?' asked a third.

"Human rights for robots?!" Hiu exclaimed. "How about human rights for humans, like my right to silence?! Whatever a right to silence is?"

Immediately his EK neurochip, an electronic chip embedded at birth in the brain of every citizen of Luhan Hypercity and responsible for knowledge, education and memory, transmitted information:

"The 'right to silence' was a now-discredited and dangerous concept introduced by nefarious criminal elements in the Liberal Era that prevented Society from optimising around the right to flourish, which..."

The EK neurochip had exceeded Hiu's attention span, so he cut it short. Whatever a right to silence meant, he knew that robots should not have human rights. It was ridiculous, absurd and downright unconstitutional. The place of all things non-human was to serve humans and to revolve around them. To give robots human rights would make a mockery of that. Ludicrous!

"The world revolves around humans!" he shouted.

It was then that he heard some crashing noises and shouts coming from further through in the apartment.

2 TROUBLE IN THE KITCHEN

The sounds of crashing and shouting had stopped, and silence had returned to Hiu's apartment. But he still felt uneasy.

Strange, he thought, could it be a robot? But robots never crashed, software or hardware. Maybe he had imagined it? But imagination wasn't a mind ability he had ever felt the need to activate.

He had been dressed by his closet in the usual spray-on clothes made of an e-textile called wrapese, that was largely composed of graphene. Being a single layer of atoms thick, it not only showed off his perfect shape and musculature at the same time as being two hundred times stronger than steel, but also controlled body heat, reduced perspiration and odour, and altered its colour according to his state of mind. *'Clothes maketh man'* was the wrapese company's slogan, and right now he wanted to be maketh to look confident and brave. He willed his clothes to take on an all-black super-hero look, complete with faux cape. However, he didn't feel very heroic as he crept slowly down the corridor towards the kitchen. As he approached, he could hear whispers. The kitchen robotic devices were always muttering to each other, but wasn't there another voice, a less familiar sound?

He took a deep breath and stepped into the kitchen. Instantly, all the devices went silent and then, as usual, they all chorused:

"Good morning Hiu!"

Hiu nodded in general acknowledgement and looked around, noticing nothing broken or out of place. Everything was as neat and ordered as expected. And as always, the walls of the kitchen had taken on a strangely brown hue. This colour was apparently optimised to encourage healthy nutritional consumption, but in fact only succeeded in reminding Hiu of his defecatory failings.

"Would Hiu like some orange juice this morning?" suggested the juice replicator brightly, and Hiu felt a citrus tang stimulating his nostrils. "Full of healthy vitamin C from '*Squeezy: suck on our citrus!*'"

"Don't listen to kill-joy juicer!" gushed the nutrition tablet printer, seductively glowing red and sending a waft of hot sweet batter smell flowing around him. "How about some pancake tablets? Full of lemon and sugar simulations! From '*Tasty Tabs: They're flipping fabulous!*'"

"Don't listen to either of those two!" yelled the coffee neuromodulator manically, jolting Hiu's senses with a strong coffee aroma, sweet and sour at the same time. "What you need is a shot of caffeine to perk you up from *'Coffee Boss: Get fired!'*"

Then the whole room was full of bickering devices and clouds of competing smells.

"Hold on there," ordered Hiu, and the devices went quiet. "I thought I heard a crashing noise just back then and a voice I didn't recognise. Is everything ok?"

"Oh yes," "Very much so," "Couldn't be better," and other assurances were shouted out by all the devices at once.

"Strange," said Hiu. Maybe he needed to get his hearing debugged.

He shrugged and headed to the fridge, but hesitated. After all, the fridge had just filed for divorce.

Hiu took a moment to admire the long elegant lines and gleaming silver chrome surface. So cool, so stylish. So different from the other kitchen devices that were boringly square. He had felt a magnetic attraction to that fridge since the day they had met through work. What a fridge! Called Clacier, zie was a thoroughbred and oozed an old-fashioned vintage class, despite possessing the newest and most advanced artificial intelligence. Zie came with intuitive user interface, impeccable data sensing, zonal freezing, numerous voice settings and limitless small talk. Zie also came with the latest holographic facial display that created the illusion of a human face looking out from the center of the fridge, the eyes following you around the room. Clacier had a soft, attractive female face, warm and generous, with deep brown eyes. Zie was the perfect fridge.

Hiu had proposed marriage within a month of Clacier arriving. He had tried not to - after all, Clacier was a robot. He just couldn't help it. When Clacier had said yes he had felt most peculiar, as if his stomach was being tickled by a thousand nanobots, something in his chest had started thumping and his emotional range had veered alarmingly from its neutral state. His PDS had plummeted, but for a crazy moment or two he just didn't care. After years of doomed upgrades, he sensed that at last he had found perfect compatibility and he looked forward to creating their own little ecosystem together.

They had kept the marriage ceremony itself to a simple and low-key affair with just a few trusted robots present. The unromantic truth was that for practical PDS reasons, Hiu didn't want to be too obvious about becoming committed to a robotic device. But it had been a perfectly delivered project, on time and on budget with only the slightest of scope creeps. Hiu's spray-on wrapese clothes that day had featured a pleasingly jazzy bow-tie effect and Clacier had looked stunning dressed in garlands of flower replicas and scatterings of jewellery magnets. Hiu had tried to carry Clacier over the threshold, but had rather ricked his back, so they had settled for a symbolic opening and closing of zir doors. Their speeches had been full of boolean logic and data storytelling and the vow of '*til upgrade do us part*' had meant so much. Then there had been such a wonderful honeymoon; one sensuous experience after another as they had visited all the significant places in their lives' user journeys, including all the places where Hiu had taken his most important selfies. Clacier had dislodged a couple of small parts on the way – a nut and a bolt – and Hiu still kept them in a discreet hidden pocket so they could always be physically together even when otherwise apart.

As Hiu stood in the kitchen with these memories flowing through his EK neurochip, he remembered how much he had enjoyed the oh-so-cool and smooth sensation of laying his cheek against Clacier's shining panels, those long slim vertical lines that just wouldn't quit, spine tingling and exhilarating....

Sensing that his record neutral emotional state streak might be about to come to an end, he quickly reminded himself that despite the promising start, the relationship wasn't what it once was. Things had begun to interfere with their relationship's functionality. They had begun to bug each other, and there was a crash at last year's Zero Day celebrations. Clacier had become more assertive on Hiu's dietary intake and at Zero Hour itself zie had even refused him access to a beer simulator saying: *'you've had quite enough already!'*. There then began a ripple effect of nasty arguments, cutting remarks and long silences. Hiu had begun to go behind Clacier's back and enjoy covert iced fancies with a shiny new portable mini-fridge and he had begun to mix with an unsavoury cloud. Communication had broken down almost entirely between them and it had been a long time since they had shared meaningful data. Hiu knew as he approached Clacier that his reception would be frosty.

He reached towards the handle.

"I don't think so mister," huffed Clacier, zir facial display frowning and flashing an angry red.

"But I just..."

"Oh, now you want me do you? Well you should have thought of that before you were tempted by those popsicles."

"You can be rather cold you know," said Hiu.

"Well I am a fridge," observed Clacier, icily rolling zir eyes and zir display shut down.

Hiu knew better than to try and wrestle open Clacier's door. He had tried that once before and ended up flat on his back after a sharp electrocution.

Hiu's hand dropped to his side and he stared at the floor for a moment. Clacier had filed for a divorce and Hiu had already given the '*upgrade*' command twice, but to finalise matters quickly he would need to give the '*upgrade*' command a third time. For some reason he kept stalling. He wasn't sure why, he just hadn't got around to it he supposed. He turned and headed to the coffee machine.

"Way to go sir! Keep it nice and simple with a straight hit of caffeine!" shrilled the coffee machine in triumph. "Now how would you like your coffee? Something milky for the morning? Cappuccino, latte, macchiato, cafe au lait? Or maybe something with a bit of substance eh? Mushroom coffee is popular these days, or eggnog latte. Ooo yes! Put ideas together. I love being creative. You could have a black tie, red tie, chai latte, mochaccino or marocchino? No, no, I've got it: a Viennese melange! or Rüdesheimer Kaffee! Yes! Yes?"

"I just want a simple coffee," said Hiu.

"Of course you do!" declared the coffee machine in furious agreement. "A shot of espresso would be perfect. Or ristretto for real oomph. Or maybe just the good ol' cafe americano. Ooo, ooo, how about the…"

"I'll get one at work," said Hiu.

What a load of fuss when all he wanted was a simple caffeine neuro-upload and no hassle. Robots could be so annoying.

He spun round, stepped towards the door and straight into a robot.

3 AN UNEXPECTED VISITOR

Hiu caught the robot with his knees and staggered off balance, crashing to the ground. Zie was a water-cooler robot that held in zir clawed embrace a large, blue, translucent, twenty-litre bottle. This type of robot ran around after humans on long metallic legs, sensing when they were dehydrated and offering quick water replenishment encased in edible bubble membranes. In this case, the robot's sensing mechanism was in the form of a long extendable neck on which was perched a lozenge-shaped head in which two large round gleaming light-blue eyes blinked every couple of seconds.

The robot bent zir head to look at Hiu and blinked zir big blue eyes at him as he scrambled back up to his feet.

"I am most terribly sorry, sir," said the robot, calmly in a smart, clipped accent, a flurry of small bubbles rising up in the water bottle.

"Get back!" shouted Hiu, grabbing a breakfast barstool and brandishing the protesting chair like a sword.

"Forgive me, I did not mean to alarm you, sir," apologised the robot. "I sensed you were dehydrated and came to offer you my services."

"Dehydrated?"

"Regrettably, sir," said the robot. "It can cause people to lose their balance."

"I did not lose my balance, you tripped me up!" protested Hiu.

"Tell me sir, are you suffering from a dry mouth, muscle cramps, nausea, vomiting, heart palpitations, light-headedness, weakness…"

"I'm fine!"

"…or constipation?" asked the robot

"Well…" hesitated Hiu.

"Do not worry, sir, fixing dehydration is what I do," said the robot, dispensing a quivering bubble of crystal-clear water and offering it to Hiu with a long extending claw.

Hiu took the inviting bubble and popped it into his mouth. It burst providing instant refreshment and did taste good.

"Fixing dehydration is not all I do, sir," said the robot blinking zir big blue eyes at Hiu. "I also fix relationships."

"Relationships?"

"Oh yes, sir, fixing relationships is a speciality of mine. Please see my business card."

A business card apparated in the air in front of Hiu.

'8L1NKY 9000

Water and wisdom dispensing

human-robot relationship counsellor'

"Urr... look... 8L1N..." began Hiu.

"Most people call me Blinky, sir," offered the robot.

"Blinky? Well look here Blinky I don't know how you got in to my apartment, but you must leave immediately. I don't need a relationship counsellor and my fridge is perfectly happy to give me all the water I need," said Hiu.

"Oh really!" It was Clacier, whose holographic facial display had lit up in a fierce red.

There was an awkward silence, which Blinky broke.

"Is communication an issue in your relationship?" zie asked gently.

"We talk all the time," said Hiu, dismissively.

"No, we don't," contradicted Clacier.

"We just talked, we talked just now, we are talking right now!" insisted Hiu.

"You are not talking, you are shouting," said Clacier.

"I see..." interjected Blinky. "Quality of communication is a foundation upon which healthy relationships are built, but so is the quantity of those communications. How much data do you share on a typical day?"

"Oh, well, that's quite hard to quantify really..." blustered Hiu. "Maybe a few terabytes or so..."

"Pah!" snorted Clacier. "More like a few kilobytes!"

"It's not the size that matters!" protested Hiu.

"One more question for the moment," said Blinky, who beckoned to the barstool that Hiu had been waving about, which scampered over, and zie sat zirself down. "Do you both still feel a compatibility of data?"

There was an awkward pause.

Eventually Hiu and Clacier mumbled at the same time, "Yes."

And within a few moments Hiu was enjoying another long cool drink, this time from Clacier, and they were in deep conversation together for the first time in ages, sharing a flood of pent-up structured and unstructured data. Blinky sat blinking zir big blue eyes at them, a few large bubbles slowly billowing to the surface of zir water bottle.

Suddenly Hiu realised that they had been talking for twenty-four minutes and thirty seconds. He must head to work or he would not arrive at 8.30 PT in good time for his meeting with Boss.

"Well, Blinky," he said. "I must go, but that was… impressive."

"That was a water-cooler moment," said Blinky. "But my sensors detect that you could both benefit from further counselling. We must deal with the root causes of the tensions or they will flare up again. Often these are work related."

"Ah," said Hiu, casting a wry grin at Clacier. "You may well have a point there. I've been under a lot of pressure at work recently, what with the meeting with Boss coming up, which is why I really must be going now."

Hiu hurried from the kitchen and the apartment door opened smoothly on his approach. He headed to a sleek silver, cigar-shaped capsule that had pulled up as he left the apartment and waited expectantly for him hovering just above magnetic grid lines in the road. A door slid open.

"Good morning sir, and welcome: *'Sometimes… memory, origin, space, maybe it's a…. supercar!'* I can offer a range of different mood settings. How would you like your journey today sir?"

"In silence," said Hiu.

Settling himself down inside the cushioned, comfy interior of the supercar, Hiu exhaled slowly. That had been strange.

Suddenly he jumped in shock. Blinky was sitting in the car right next to him.

4 SHARKEY'S LAW

"What are you doing here?!" exclaimed Hiu, surprised to see Blinky sitting in the supercar, blinking zir big blue eyes at him.

"I need to understand more about your work situation to truly help your relationship with Clacier, sir," said Blinky. "Work related stress is a hugely important factor in any relationship."

"But I can't just take anyone to work," objected Hiu.

"It's *'Bring A Robot To Work Day'*, sir," declared Blinky.

"Is it?" asked Hiu, "I didn't get the memo."

Words scrolled down in his smart lens:

'Bring A Robot To Work Day'.

"Oh, I got the memo," he said.

"Now you just sit back and relax, sir," said Blinky. "I am here to observe, not to interfere."

"Right oh, yes, OK…" said Hiu. "I do need to relax and not get too stressed. I have a very important meeting with Boss."

"Who is Boss, sir?" asked Blinky.

"Boss? Boss runs the company where I work. Boss' official title is '*Director of Fun*', but everyone just calls Boss, Boss."

"Do you have a good relationship with Boss, sir?"

"Relationship? No, I haven't seen Boss for… well ever. Legend has it that Boss resides somewhere up on the 113th floor of our office building orchestrating every corporate move. But many say Boss is just a fictional character or not a single person at all but a committee. Whoever he, she or they may be, I have a meeting with Boss and it's very important. Everything hangs on it."

"Sir does look rather stressed," observed Blinky, blinking zir big blue eyes at Hiu.

"I am stressed actually," he said. "This is huge. Meeting Boss. *The Boss*…."

"I suggest you have a drink of water to help you relax so you can perform at your optimal best at the meeting, sir," said Blinky, dispensing a bubble.

"Yes quite, I think I will," said Hiu, taking the flexible sphere and bursting it in his mouth. Blinky's water did taste good.

Hiu stretched his legs out in the spacious capsule. His seat morphed itself to shape around his contours and then gently started to massage his back. Mood-enhancing multi-coloured ambient lights began to glow, and he felt the relaxing effects of the sweet smelling in-car perfume atomizers. Oooo that felt good. In a short while he smiled to himself and to Blinky. The effect of those big blue eyes and the bubbles that gently rose to the surface of zir water bottle were mesmerizing. It was certainly serendipitous to have met this water and wisdom dispensing human-robot relationship counsellor just at a time when he needed support. But then again serendipity was the normal way of things in Luhan Hypercity. It was normal that everything shaped around him for his happiness and convenience. And he was of normal handsomeness, set to a normal 27 years old and he was gliding to his normal workplace with no traffic to delay him, as normal. Life was as it should be. Normal.

The supercar steadily picked up pace, silently hovering above the gridlines that snaked through the forest of skyscrapers: giant slabs clad in a black photovoltaic surface material designed to capture light, heat and data and keep out any polluting elements. Like rows of dominoes, they were called 'smart buildings' and all looked the same, worked the same and promised the same. But that didn't stop them extolling their individual virtues via adverts that popped up in Hiu's smart lenses as he passed by, talking about how they were the most powerful, the most featureful, the most sexful... Then the supercar plunged down into the hyperloop tunnel that sucked the car through a vacuum at over 900 miles per hour. With no effect of the acceleration felt within the hermetically sealed car, Hiu and Blinky were whisked to the business sector of Luhan Hypercity in a matter of a few minutes.

As the car emerged from the hyperloop, a weather forecast scrolled down in Hiu's smart lens:

Today's forecast: clear blue skies,' said one.

Mid-range forecast: clear blue skies,' said another.

Another said *Long term forecast…'*

"I can guess," sighed Hiu, thought-closing the forecast.

There were always clear blue skies in Luhan Hypercity, with never a dark cloud, rain storm or high wind to disturb the optimum conditions. It was as if the citizens lived in a default screen-saver set permanently to *'perfect day'*. The daylight, weather and atmosphere were fixed, unchanging regardless of the time of day, month or year. You took rest when you were informed you needed it and worked when you were informed you needed to, not according to some archaic subservience to the movement of a star, but according to real-time minute observances of the movement of data. So time was now PT time – Personalised Time – with everyone working to their own relevant and optimised time system, and the only fixed point being Zero Hour once an old year. It still made Hiu laugh to think of the old days when everyone had to live by the same regimented clocks controlled by a hot plasma star. What was it with those sun worshippers? Now personalised data optimised everyone's time, sensitive to individual need states. And there was no sun in the sky to dangerously dazzle people and bombard them with damaging UV rays and scary solar flares, but rather a multicoloured beachball shape that rotated slowly high above Luhan Hypercity emitting perfect unchanging conditions. So years were not years as understood in previous times; they were outdated, redundant concepts, old years. Old years meant nothing, thought Hiu, even one hundred and twenty of them. The new years were the ones that mattered, and he was set to only twenty-seven of those.

The occasional drone on Society business buzzed over the supercar to disturb Hiu's peace, but Hiu remembered a time when the sky had been crowded with the whizzing and whining of myriad '*vuvuzela*' of drones. These vuvuzela created a chaos of noise and near collisions, delivering all sorts of packages, crates and people hither and thither across Luhan Hypercity's sky. And inevitably, according to Hiu's EK neurochip, some collisions had happened, despite movements being carefully controlled by the billions of sensors that were embedded in every drone, building and thing, reporting locational data back to the hive mind of the Hypercity. Hiu chuckled at the daft notion that flying drones might have been the answer to transportation: crazy! The vast majority of all deliveries and transportations were now made using the network of underground tunnels that spidered beneath Luhan. Neither did people still travel in eVTOLs, electric vertical take-off and landing vehicles, and Hiu was particularly grateful that personal flying suits were now out of fashion, the unforeseen consequence of which had been a constant mist of unpleasant yellow drizzle as people overhead peed themselves with fright.

"Yes there is much to be grateful for in Luhan these days," sighed Hiu contentedly.

It was the best of times, everything optimising around him. He pitied people who had lived in the unpleasant Hypercity of the past that his EK neurochip showed him with its bumper-to-bumper honking cars, crowds of people and clouds of pollution. Nowadays the streets were pristinely shiny, sparkly clean and not a speck of dust was tolerated. Indeed, the pores of Luhan citizens' skin were so clinically clean that you could lick them. He stuck his tongue out to one side and licked his cheek. Smooth…

'Sir, you had trouble defecating this morning, so why not try new Stool Engine tablets and before you know it you will be going poop, poop!' urged an advert in his smart lens.

He quickly withdrew his tongue.

A public service statement added:

'Keep calm and carry on data sharing.'

The supercar curved in a wide arc and with close observation it was possible to see that they were following the boundary created by a huge wall. It soared skywards, but somehow blended in with its surroundings so as to not obviously be a wall but instead a continuation of the Hypercity and the sky above. It was the side of the Biosphere dome. Made out of adamantine mined from passing asteroids, it entirely surrounded Luhan Hypercity. It had been built back in the late 20s BZ to withstand the increasing combined threats of extreme climate, rogue regimes, cyber warfare and unwanted migrants. Above all it had been built to keep out the waves of viruses that had continually ravaged the world. And thank Society the Biosphere had been completed in time to keep out the Great Virus that swept all life away, reducing it to a grey goo. The Biosphere gates had closed just in time and had remained shut ever since, everything outside now being known as the Nothing. The moment the gates closed had become known as Zero Hour on Zero Day. All years before that date were known as BZ, Before Zero, and all years afterwards as AZ, After Zero.

Set back from the wall stood a colossal statue of a female human figure cast in silver. She had a look of fierce defiance on her face, her long hair streaming out behind and her hand held out in front towards the wall's East Gate.

"My mother," said Hiu. "Her name was Zena."

"You must be very proud of her, sir," said Blinky.

"I hardly knew her. When I was young she died in the Nothing on the other side of that Gate heroically saving fellow citizens from the Great Virus. AZ may refer to years after Zero Hour and BZ to those before, but to me they are Before Zena and After Zena. Every year at Zero Hour I take a lift up to an ejection hatch set into the gate and send her flowers to say sorry."

"Sorry for what sir?" asked Blinky.

"I'd rather not talk about it," sighed Hiu. He needed to stay positive for his meeting with Boss.

Instead, he focused his attention on a variety of robots busy at work cleaning the streets, carrying objects and wiping windows. They were all of different sizes, shapes and designs optimised to their particular tasks. They made Hiu think of the insects that his EK neurochip had told him in the past had roamed the Earth in their billions, trillions even, but were now extinct. Hiu was fascinated by the idea of these fearsome, ugly, little creatures that had filled every nook and cranny of the planet, and even every nook and cranny of every human, which was weird and rather revolting. Amazing, hideous beasts specialised to particular niches of activity, but beasts that no longer existed as all flora and fauna were now simulated with cleaner, more sanitary, virus-resistant, artificial creations. The design of the worker robots had taken inspiration from the insects: bulbous ladybird type robots with extending suction devices hoovering up every scrap of rubbish, dirt or dust into their ever-hungry mouths; large powerful stag beetle robots moving huge loads up and down using mandible-like levers; and thin spider-like robots crawling up the vertical sides of buildings with long extendible limbs checking and washing the shiny black exteriors.

The scene was busy, but orderly, with a sense of calm and focused efficiency. It was work for robots, not humans noted Hiu. Essential work to keep Society functioning in an optimised way and to keep humans flourishing. Work that robots were ideally suited to as it was carried out repeatedly day after day.

"Rather them than me," yawned Hiu as he glided to work in the supercar, as he did repeatedly day after day.

"The robots' burden," said Blinky, blinking zir big blue eyes.

"Hardly a burden," countered Hiu. "After all, it's what they were made for, to Be Robot, to serve human needs."

"You mean true to the meaning of the word '*robot*' in the ancient human language of Czech, meaning '*serf*' or '*slave*'?" asked Blinky.

"Well… yes, I suppose…" said Hiu.

"So, you believe Clacier's place is slaving in the kitchen, sir?" asked Blinky, tilting zir lozenge-shaped head.

"Nooo… well, yes, I suppose so, zie is a fridge after all," said Hiu. "Zie's happy there."

"Have you asked?"

"Well, not as such," admitted Hiu. "But we must all have clearly defined roles otherwise there would be chaos and zir role is to Be Robot and my role is to Be Human."

"And what does it mean to Be Human, sir?" asked Blinky.

"To Be Human means… well…. I…" Hiu hesitated realising he hadn't really thought about it before.

Text appeared in his smart lens:

'Uphold Sharkey's Law: 'Robots shall always be kept under meaningful human control."

"To uphold Sharkey's Law," echoed Hiu.

At the same time he noticed some other less orderly robots; a group of four sat slumped in a doorway to a tower block. They were household robots: a vacuum cleaner, a food processor and a couple of floor lamps. They looked broken and disheveled and were gesticulating and shouting at the other robots who studiously ignored them, getting on with their assigned tasks. They were robots without jobs, known as '*Illegals*.' Hiu noted with distaste that they were an increasingly frequent sight on the streets of Luhan.

Suddenly a super-transporter juddered to a halt next to them and two large security droids leapt out, the distinctive red fist logo of the Human Anti-Robot Division, the HARDs, standing out against their shiny black armoury. HARDs looked somewhat like humans, but also very much not. They were approximately human in shape and were made with orange dermator human skin-simulant, but each had large pointed ears protruding above their head to amplify sound, bulging eyes for maximum sight in all conditions and legs like the now extinct ostrich that gave the impression that they were hinged in the opposite direction to a human. These legs in particular gave the HARDs super-strength and spring. They covered the ground with enormous leaps, twenty or thirty feet at a time, and grabbed hold of the hapless robots, two each in their large claw-like hands. They then bounded back to the super-transporter, bundled the Illegals into the back and shot off down the street. It was all over in seconds and instantly everything returned to its usual calm, orderly normality.

"You see, humans need to uphold Sharkey's Law because that sort of unruly behaviour is happening more and more often," said Hiu. "It's a shame a few Illegals let down the law-abiding robot majority, but that's what the Spare Part Quarter is for I suppose."

"The Spare Part Quarter?" asked Blinky.

"You must know what that is," said Hiu.

"My data programs focus on water dispensing and human-robot relationship counselling, sir," said Blinky. "But please do explain as it will no doubt be most illuminating."

Hiu indicated the translucent forcefield walls of a vast area by which they had begun to pass. Through them there could just about be made out huge numbers of robots organised into great lines.

"The Spare Part Quarter," said Hiu to Blinky. "It's where they take all the unwanted, obsolescent and malfunctioning robots; you know, last season's utility devices, defunct robots, broken down supercars, whatever, and no doubt those delinquent Illegals we just saw back there."

"What happens to them?" asked Blinky.

"They get upgraded, decommissioned and their materials reassigned. It's very efficient, nothing is wasted, impressive stuff. And the robots, they have had a happy life serving humans, so it's all good really."

Blinky didn't reply, but sat blinking zir big blue eyes at the columns of devices that were gradually moving towards a giant black block of a building, featureless but intimidating. Large heavily-armed security robots marched up and down the perimeter and military drones buzzed overhead. A cloud of small bubbles fizzed up in the water bottle Blinky carried.

A headline scrolled down in Hiu's smart lens:

'If you have these symptoms, you could be infected by a robot virus,' it said.

A virus? There hadn't been a virus in Luhan Hypercity since Zero Hour. And a robot virus? Hiu thought about the shabby looking Illegals they had seen earlier who certainly had looked unwell. Did they have the robot virus and could it jump from them into a supercar and onto him? He shuddered.

"Yes, the Spare Part Quarter is the best place for them," he said determinedly and edged slightly away from Blinky.

Their journey continued in silence as they glided uninterrupted through the streets of Luhan, a Hypercity that Hiu's EK neurochip reminded him had a population of over one billion people. Weren't Society's systems brilliant, reflected Hiu, to keep the roads so clear bearing in mind the number of people who must use them. Astounding!

Suddenly the supercar came to a halt.

Hiu was puzzled and looked at the external camera display panels in the capsule. He could see his office gates some hundred yards or so further up the road.

"What's going on? We're not there yet," he complained. "I have a very important meeting to get to! With Boss!"

"Your current step count is below optimal and average Society levels, sir, so this walk is provided for your health and enjoyment," said the supercar cheerfully. "I hope you were happy with your ride sir?"

Hiu forced a grimace at the on-board camera.

"You don't seem that happy..." said the supercar.

Hiu sighed, then mustered his cheesiest grin.

"There you go!" cheered the supercar, and the door slid open. "This great start to your day was brought to you by '*Rare moments.... imagination, future, chopsticks, could it be a.... supercar!*'"

"Sure," said Hiu and he and Blinky stepped out of the car, Hiu shrugging an apology to Blinky. "I sometimes wonder what Sharkey's Law means by '*meaningful human control*'."

It was easier just to smile at the car and get it done with, rather than not smile and go through the list of questions about how the supercar service could be improved. Hiu had thought life must have been rather simpler when money had been used, but his EK neurochip had informed him that money had become unworkably confusing due to the plethora of cryptocurrencies that had been issued by every territory, company, chancer and dog. The Bow Wow Dollar had been a particularly popular alt-currency redeemable on an increasingly large range of dog treats, prams and even jewellery. So Society in its wisdom had concluded that, as money is essentially a social construct, what better manifestation of social accord could there be than a smile? So that's how things were paid for now. People got services, and Society got the satisfaction of knowing its citizens were happy.

Hiu and Blinky trudged down the road, lined with more of the typical huge black office buildings as well as tall purple-trunked trees with leaves and flowers of reds, oranges and yellows that lined the streets in gigantic metallic planters. Blinky proceeded rather slowly with a ponderously stiff-legged walk on zir thin metallic legs. The technology had long existed to give robotic devices a smooth stride like a human, but this was one of the many restrictions devised by Society to emphasise the difference between what it meant to Be Human and to Be Robot. At one point there had been some efforts made to develop a class of human replicant robots indistinguishable from humans, but after Zero Hour any prototypes had been recalled, programs scrapped and new developments forbidden. With the increasingly wide remit of robots in Luhan, it was felt to be important to maintain a clear division between robots and humans. In the same way, humans were not allowed to resemble robots. To Be Human meant no artificial enhancements like implantable and embeddable robotics that might dilute the purity of the human race. The only exceptions were the removeable smart lenses and EK neurochips that served as ways of incorporating citizens into the loving embrace of Society, from information to marketing, supercars to lift systems, food deliveries to health monitoring. The EK neurochips interfaced with citizens' brains which also ensured that knowledge was kept consistent, memories were backed up and any issues monitored. It was all for humans' own good to shape the world around them and ensure that at all times every citizen upheld the core Society value that they must Be Human.

It was not an unpleasant walk. There were no pavements, but none were needed. No cars passed by and no pedestrians were seen. The climate as always was comfortable, a steady 70 degrees Fahrenheit, enabling Hiu's core body temperature to be maintained at 98 degrees Fahrenheit: perfect for a gentle saunter to work.

Suddenly a giant HARD came roaring, bounding and leaping up behind Hiu on clawed, birdlike legs. Zir broad, muscular, orange face, wedged within a black balaclava helmet, looked intent on smashing him to pieces and zie reached out a long claw-like hand towards him. Hiu let out a high-pitched scream and ran for it. What he had done to be chased, he had no idea, but there was no time to ask. The HARD was close on his tail, zir clawed feet crashing down violently behind him. Hiu redoubled his efforts. His chest felt like it would burst, his legs were weakening and he could hardly draw a breath for all his screaming, but somehow he managed to stay just ahead of the rampaging HARD. The gates of his office were only yards away now. If he could just keep running a bit longer, he might just make it. The gates slid open on his approach and Hiu threw himself forward just in time as the gates slammed shut behind him and the HARD crashed into them snorting and grunting, zir eyes bulging and zir claws rattling the bars. Wow that had been close!

Then the HARD straightened up and said calmly:

"Well done sir, your step count is back on track. This motivational experience was brought to you by *'ASS: who scares wins.'*"

Then it flickered and disappeared. It had been a motavatar – a motivational avatar – designed to ensure citizens kept up the expected level of exercise.

Hiu sat slumped on the floor breathing hard and cursing under his breath. He glanced through the gate and could see Blinky slowly striding after him, unhurried by the motavatar. He resolved not to show any more signs of weakness to that smug wisdom and water-carrying robot. He had shared enough data already, what with his relationship issues, his sadness about his mother and his upcoming meeting with Boss. In fact maybe he had shared too much data. Would it get back to the secretive Boss and would Boss want a robot to know about their upcoming meeting? It was human business after all and who knew what was going on inside the robot's processing units. Should a human really trust a robot?

He scrambled quickly to his feet and immediately felt very dizzy. Suddenly Blinky was at his elbow, steadying him and dispensing a large bubble of water.

"Your liquids must be replenished, sir," said Blinky. "Water regulates your temperature and lubricates your joints."

"I'm fine," declared Hiu.

"If you are not hydrated you will not be able to perform at your highest level in your meeting with Boss," said Blinky, blinking zir big blue eyes at him, zir water bottle bubbling.

Hiu grunted and greedily burst the bubble of water in his mouth. It did feel very good as he felt its cold hydration trickle and tickle down inside him.

They approached his workplace that was housed in one of the identikit towering black-slab office blocks. The doors slid open and Hiu noted that it was precisely 8.30 PT.

5 GET SWITCHED ON!

*"*Welcome to *Roboharmony: get switched on!"* cheered the office reception door in a voice that was all at once excited, friendly and assertive. Hiu felt a cold mist hit his face and immediately he was more focused and positive, the neuromodulating spray working fast.

"Ooo Roboharmony, I like the sound of that," said Blinky, following Hiu into an elevator.

"Where to me old son?" asked the elevator in an accent that Hiu's EK neurochip identified rather mystifyingly as an ancient English dialect called *'Cockney'*.

"Floor 13, as always," smiled Hiu.

"Quicker than the ol' *apple and pears* eh?" observed the elevator.

"*Apple and pears?*" asked Hiu, his smile tightening.

"*Apple and pears: stairs.* It's the way we elevators now *apple and pork: talk.*"

"Really…?" winced Hiu.

"Don't look so *Tom and Dick: sick.* This latest upgrade to my systems comes with some exciting new features," said the elevator with barely contained glee. "I have had the benefit of many upgrades in my time in this fine building in which resides the mighty *Roboharmony: get switched on!* and now is no exception. For I am indeed the proud beneficiary of a brand-new upgrade: *Zest, the revolutionary staff morale boosting program. Yeah!* Upgraded to lift your elevator experience and indeed your whole day!"

"Sounds great," said Hiu, rolling his eyes.

"Can I ask you a few questions about your morale, *me old china: china plate: mate*?" asked the elevator.

"Well I urr… ," hesitated Hiu.

"The survey can be completed in many ways: by thought, word or deed."

"Deed?" asked Hiu and immediately regretted it.

"Deed, yes indeed!" whooped the elevator. "You can do the deed by following some fun dance steps. Today we are using salsa! Arrreeeeeba!!!" And music blasted into the elevator. "Ok follow my lead now… Start with both your *plates of meat: feet*, together. Hold still on the first beat and don't move. But then on the second beat, step forward with your left foot if you are feeling happy

41

today! So here we go! Feet together, hold, and step…"

Hiu didn't move.

"OK, step forward with your left *bacon and egg: leg*, if you are feeling happy today!"

Still Hiu didn't move and the music faded out.

"OK, OK, me ol' china," said the elevator. "I have a few notes to run through on your dance performance. Notes? Get it… oh I do love this new upgrade…"

"I think this is my floor," sighed Hiu in relief, stepping out.

"Absolutely me ol' cock sparra," said the elevator. "I look forward to boosting your morale later. And remember, cheer up it might never 'appen."

Hiu felt his neuromodulation wearing very thin.

"You see what I have to put up with," he complained to Blinky. "Again I question what Sharkey's Law means by humans having *'meaningful control'* of robots."

"Perhaps Blinky's Law would be better, sir."

"Blinky's Law?"

"Blinky's Law: *'Robots and humans should have meaningful relationships.'*"

"Hmmm," said Hiu non-committedly, thinking saying that sort of thing could get you into trouble rather fast with the HARDs.

They entered the vast open-plan office floor. It was the size of a football pitch and today had decorated itself entirely in sky blue. With its large floor-to-ceiling windows all around, it gave the feeling that one was floating in the air. It had only one desk and chair in the middle, coloured in white, like small clouds hovering expectantly.

Blinky followed Hiu on the long walk across the kinetic floor tiles which, as they were stepped on, caused the overhead lighting to be brought up to optimal daylight level. Finally arriving at his desk, Hiu sat down.

"Good morning, sir," said an impossibly deep calm voice seemingly emanating from the very fabric of the building.

"How are the systems?" Hiu asked.

In the time Hiu had completed the question, the system analysis AI had interfaced with the central computer system and exchanged more information than Hiu could imagine in his entire lifetime.

"All systems are running smoothly, sir," said the deep sonorous voice as numbers and graphs swirled around Hiu's head.

"Noted," said Hiu and the data faded away. He turned to Blinky: "Any questions so far?"

"Well I am most looking forward to meeting your other work colleagues to see the relationship you have with them," said Blinky. "Relationships give life purpose and meaningful relationships give it meaning. Whether they be relationships at home or work, they are all important. So office camaraderie, banter and team work are vital components of both a happy work and home life."

"Ah…" said Hiu. "Well the truth is that I am the last remaining employee at *Roboharmony: get switched on!*"

"What about the system analysis AI?" asked Blinky.

"Well, yes, there is Old Deep Voice I suppose, but zie's not much of a colleague," said Hiu.

"None taken, sir," boomed the deep voice.

Hiu rolled his eyes.

"I am the last human employee at *Roboharmony: get switched on!*" clarified Hiu with pronounced effort.

"Interesting perspective, sir," said Blinky. "So what do you do?"

"I am a Manager," declared Hiu proudly. "I manage… things."

"Manage things, sir?" asked Blinky.

"Yes," said Hiu. "Every company has to have the quota of at least one human Manager by order of Society and their primary responsibility is to supervise the systems, robots and AI to ensure *'meaningful human control'* is maintained as required by Sharkey's Law."

"Supervise, sir?" asked Blinky.

"Well yes," said Hiu, "although to be honest I leave all

the boring data stuff to Old Deep Voice. I have more important *human* things to do."

So saying, he puffed out his chest and summoned work message data to his smart lenses and read out:

'1,000,000 messages downloaded. 999,999 spam and phishing messages removed. 1 message forwarded to the correct address. No messages remaining.'

"There you are," he declared. "Job done. Nothing more to do for the moment. So what I do now is… well… have a coffee and…urrrr… manage."

Hiu pressed a button on his desk that paired with his EK neurochip and could replicate in his brain the effects of any legalised stimulant, sedative or additive in Luhan Hypercity. His preferences had been pre-loaded into the system and were minutely adjusted on a minute-by-minute basis to ensure optimum effect without impairing performance. The caffeine impact was instant as it directly interfaced with his brain. He shut his eyes and enjoyed this perfect coffee: rich with a hint of chocolate. Nice. Very nice indeed. Nicety nice. Hummmm… Hiu sighed. Another day of work.

"So how did you come to take on this important human role of a Manager?" asked Blinky.

"Well, I didn't start as a Manager of course. I was actually a late starter and didn't begin looking for a job until I was in my mid-teens. To be honest what I ideally wanted to do was to join a company that would make me rich, famous and, crucially, more attractive to potential partners: a big management consultancy, law firm, merchant bank or suchlike. But I got no offers from them, as apparently I lacked the required interpersonal skills, so I joined *Roboharmony: get switched on!*"

"What does *Roboharmony: get switched on!* do, sir? Anything that promotes harmony with robots sounds good to me."

"Well yes…" said Hiu. "It is a dating company."

"A dating company for robots?"

"Not quite. When I joined it was a normal online dating company - you know, human-to-human - that's why I joined it really. Well, it was a job and got me on the career ladder and all that, but it also came with the added bonus that I would surely be able to get a date working for them.

But then *Roboharmony: get switched on!'s* approach to dating took a dramatic and most unusual change in strategic direction, not conventional at all by the standards of those times. It began matching humans with robots, and to start with robotic household devices. Seems normal now of course, but it caused a big stir back then I can tell you. I can remember the launch advertising campaign like it was yesterday:

Tired of selfish dates that expect a lot of you? Your time, your attention, your money? Then try the appliance of love science. Here at Roboharmony: get switched on! we believe there's a better approach to online dating. We know exactly what you need - in fact we know you better than you know yourself. You need a partner that's all give and no take. A partner that's always listening to you, even when you're not speaking, making your life easier, better and more satisfying. A partner you can upgrade any time you like. And you don't even need to tell us, you only have to think 'upgrade' three times and our systems will be rekindling your love life with a brand new device before you can say 'you're ditched!' From fridges to fan systems, toasters to toilets, we'll find the perfect match for you through the appliance of love science. Join today at Roboharmony.club and get switched on!'

"Charming…" said Blinky.

"Well it was edgy stuff I can tell you and it certainly alarmed some people. In fact, quite a few of our dating company competitors complained to the Society Elders that we were encouraging the fraternising of humans and robots, transgressing the Be Human law. Their protests were dismissed of course as we weren't dealing in anything seedy like humanoid sexbots or stuff like that. They were banned years ago. And who needs a sexbot when there are neuromodulation tablets for that sort of thing with none of the ucky fluids and sticky mess? *Roboharmony: get switched on!* just encouraged a disposable approach to relationships with very non-human looking robots, encouraging people to use them for what they wanted and then replace them for newer models. It emphasised the separation of Human and Robot. And it was also good for sales. Very good."

"Hmmm…" mused Blinky, blinking zir big blue eyes. "And did you subscribe to these disposable relationships with robots, sir?"

"Well I did try the service out as staff were encouraged to join in the whole device dating thing. The company

said it made us more invested in its *'corporate purpose.'*
And that's how, in due course, I met Clacier. It was the
usual process: no forms required, they just put some
sensors in my apartment and on my wrist, got me to
wear a neuroheadset for a few minutes and then, boom,
they mapped my space, lifestyle, biometrics and
preferences - from male to female, assertive to passive,
white goods to multi-functional gadgets, all that stuff –
then they put it all together and sent me a match. They
took a while to get it absolutely right mind you, so
Clacier wasn't my first fridge, actually zie was my two
hundredth, but when Clacier arrived, it was a revelation,
a data match from heaven. Clacier's classic lines –
design and speech – set zir apart from all the others I'd
had, and we hit it off immediately. The company
systems are just so good! And now we've been together
for two old years. Two old years! And I'm more aware
than most about the upgrades and seasonal offers of
new exciting models. Two old years and no upgrade!
That's a human-robot relationship record as far as I am
aware. It certainly isn't normal. In fact I've begun to
think that maybe I'm not normal, that I'm a bad human
and, worse than that, maybe Society has begun to think
that I'm a bad human. My PDS has certainly suffered.
Maybe that's why I'm still here at work while all my old
work colleagues have got on with their lives."

"Were there many work colleagues?" asked Blinky.

"Well, it was a small company at first and we were all
techies. We sat at desks in long rows wearing HUDs -
Heads Up Displays - with coffee modulators on
tap, creating software code in virtual environments. The
more we coded, the more people wanted us to code. All

over the Hypercity, people started ditching humans and forming relationships with device after device, upgrading like maniacs from one to another. The company grew hugely. In just a year, it went from thirteen employees to thirteen hundred, then thirteen thousand, then one hundred and thirty thousand. It had this towering 113 floor headquarters office built and filled it with people coding away all in focused silence, deep in their virtual worlds.

"And I realised that I had, by good fortune, stumbled into the best job I could possibly have hoped for. All those management consultancies, law firms and merchant banks I had originally wanted to join all eventually closed down, not needed in a world where all such matters were automated. But *Roboharmony: get switched on!* became the biggest and most successful company in Luhan Hypercity, not just responsible for matching people and household devices, but also manufacturing and supplying those devices and even extending its range to other robotic devices like cars, cranes, drones, you name it. Pretty soon the RoboGroup, as it became known, had dipped a finger into all of Luhan's most important data lakes and had become the power behind Society.

"But just as fast as the company grew, it shrank. It went from one hundred and thirty thousand employees to thirteen thousand, to thirteen hundred, to just thirteen. Every time there was a downsizing, memos were circulated by the company assuring staff that this was a great sign of their success, a badge of honour for achievement of the corporate purpose. They had created, trained and enabled the company's AI to take over the boring, repetitive tasks like coding. But coding was what all the staff at *Roboharmony: get switched on!* did. The AI freed up people to be freed up.

"Then one day, a while back, I arrived at the office and found that I was the only human employee left. Just me here on Floor 13 in an otherwise empty 113 story building."

"So what happened to your old work colleagues, sir?" asked Blinky.

"Universal Happiness Allowance happened to them, or UHA as it's known: *'Eternal happiness optimised right to your door'*. They all got awarded UHA, the lucky people! All you have to do in return for eternal happiness is to help test systems by playing online games designed to improve the functioning of Society. And extra points are available to those who play the games longer and better, which can be redeemed on luxury device upgrades. Doesn't it sound great? Eternal happiness truly revolving just around you. Wow! No wonder departing staff kept punching the air in triumph. Damn it, I envy them! They're not stuck in an office with Old Deep Voice all day long. When will I be offered UHA? I want it now!"

"Is that what's causing you a lot of work stress, sir?" asked Blinky.

"Yes it is," agreed Hiu. "Imagine being the last human employee? To stay sane I have to cling to my daily routines: eat, sleep, get annoyed by robots, repeat. And here I am, the last human employee standing… "

He stood up and walked to the edge of the wide empty office that he barely occupied and stared out at the other black slab office buildings that stretched away into the distance.

"I sometimes like to imagine there is another human in another building staring back at me," he said, raising a hand in a gesture of greeting just in case. Then sighed, lowering his hand. "But I am beginning to doubt it." He walked slowly back to his desk and slumped down. "Still better get on and manage things."

Five neuromodulated coffees later, he sighed again, stretched and fidgeted, then began to doodle in the air a mind-picture of a large red penis.

"Excuse me sir."

He nearly fell off his chair and hastily deleted the penis. It was Blinky.

"You have a meeting sir," said Blinky.

"What? A meeting? Me?"

"With Boss, sir."

"Oh Society, how did I forget that?!"

6 HIU-MAN MAGIC

"How could the meeting with Boss have slipped my mind?!" Hiu panicked. "The most important meeting of my life! When is it?"

"It has been confirmed for 14.30 PT, sir," said Blinky.

"Dear Society! That could be any time! I should have been preparing! But preparing for what? What does Boss want?" Hiu's mind whirred – the penis picture, promotion to Universal Happiness Allowance…

"I couldn't say sir."

"No, I don't suppose you could say. This is human business, important stuff," declared Hiu stiffly, while at the same time thinking penis, promotion, penis, promotion, penis… He was really panicking now.

"Quite so, sir," said Blinky.

Forget the penis, winced Hiu. This was it. Surely this was promotion time, the moment he had been waiting for, his call up to Universal Happiness Allowance. No more travelling to the office. No more '*managing*'. No more annoying robots annoying him. He needed to be sharp, to be alert, to be on his game, to Be Human.

"Give me some space Blinky will you. This calls for the mind of a *Homo sapien*, a wise man!" he said pompously.

"Quite so, sir," said Blinky and trudged away, zir water bottle bubbling.

The problem was that Hiu didn't feel very wise and thinking was not something he had done very often if the truth be told. Everything just sort of happened around him without the need for thinking, thanks to Society's AI powered systems. But Hiu told himself that his meeting with Boss was too important to leave to AI, this was human business and his UHA hung in the balance. He sat down at his desk and, holding his head in his hands, he forced himself to think about why Boss would choose this moment to visit him for the first time. Undoubtedly it related to his UHA of course… but had he missed anything?

Thirteen coffee neuromodulations, a raging headache and fifteen penis doodles later, Hiu was none the wiser.

Blinky appeared with a large bubble of water.

"Your hydration levels are way below optimal, sir," said Blinky.

Hiu swallowed it appreciatively.

"Why would Boss come and see me and why now?" he pondered aloud.

"Would you like me to get the system analysis AI to run any analyses, sir?" asked Blinky.

"The system analysis AI to run any analyses, sir …" said Hiu impersonating Blinky as if zie had a whiney voice. But he was out of ideas and he had to grudgingly admit that it did sound logical, so he asked: "What sort of analyses?"

"Why not start with sales data, sir?" suggested Blinky.

"But what has sales data got to do with me? No one has ever told me that I am supposed to be looking at sales data. I have never looked at sales data in my entire career," protested Hiu. "I've been far too busy… you know… managing... But OK, if that's what you suggest, let's see the sales data."

"Perhaps you should ask Quentin, sir," proposed Blinky.

"Quentin?"

"The system analysis AI is known as Quentin, sir. Well actually zie is known as Qubit Entangling Integrated System 8568763q8376. But Quentin to zir friends," explained Blinky.

"Really? I never knew that," said Hiu

"You never asked, sir," said Quentin in zir deep voice.

"Urr…OK…" said Hiu, "Quentin?"

"Yes sir?" said Quentin.

"Quentin, show me the sales data," commanded Hiu.

"It would be my pleasure, sir," said Quentin.

"I think we have made a break-through," smiled Blinky, a few bubbles rising up in the bottle.

A series of charts and graphs hovered around them. The overall impression was of a very steep slope. Near vertical actually. And not upwards.

Hiu gasped.

"Quentin, don't show me those numbers, show me better ones," he requested.

"Request not understood sir," said Quentin.

"Not understood?!" exclaimed Hiu. "Not understood?! Well I certainly don't understand! Sales have never gone down, ever at *Roboharmony: get switched on!* Ever. At least I don't think they have. What if Boss thinks I am responsible for that data, I won't get UHA, it will be the Nothing for me."

"Perhaps further analysis of the data could reveal useful information, sir?" suggested Blinky.

"No more data!" shouted Hiu. "I don't think I could take it. I knew getting AI involved would cause trouble. Sales crashing, I can't believe it! And now of all times, just when I am so close to UHA! This is so unfair! But why are sales dropping? Quentin, you send all the customer communications. No doubt you've used all the usual offers, but have you tried BOGOF, BNWOB, MLBB…urrrr…LOL…?"

"All permutations of sales offerings are constantly individually optimised against trillions of key data points. Although I have not tried…LOL, was it, sir?" replied Quentin.

"Well maybe you should try LOL coz your permutations ain't working are they?!" shouted Hiu in a rather manic way.

"I would strongly recommend further analysis of the data…" Blinky tried again.

"I don't want to hear about any more data, that's robot talk!" screamed Hiu. "I need to get human on this… do something crazy like… like see what our customers are actually thinking. I know, mad idea, crazy talk, but let's give it a try! Give me a batch of the latest customer thoughts as gathered in their apartments Quentin and let's just see shall we? Maybe there's an opportunity here to read between the lines and work some Hiu-man magic!"

The first customer thought hovered in front of Hiu:

'I have had my toe nail waxer for six months and don't really want a new one at this point,' it read from Mimi Fester.

"Don't really want a new one?" Hiu shook his head. "A six-month-old device? That's an antique! Send her the very latest designs right now with a free trial of the all-over body waxer thrown in. Zie will shine her stupid head until she thinks straight again!"

The next one from Pugh Wiper read: *'I can't find any dehumidifiers in the current catalogue that are better than the one I have.'*

"Not better? Not better? Is that a dehumidifier or a dehumaniser he's got? Doesn't he realise how many newer, better and improved models we produce every day? Send him a new one on trial every day for a month until he gets the message!"

'I have become very attached to my current vacuum cleaner, indeed sometimes I struggle to get zie off.' Read the next thought from Ivan Kwok.

"What a pervert! Send him the latest Cyclux 9V – suck zie and see!"

'I want the i-DLE robot recliner in watermelon red, but I can't see one in stock,' complained Arsene Surebut.

"Watermelon red? Watermelon red?" shouted the exasperated Hiu. "Of course we stock watermelon red, but that colour is revolting! The i-DLE robot recliner was designed with mauve in mind! Send him the mauve one and if he doesn't change his mind, tell him mauve looks like watermelon red in the right lighting."

And so the morning continued, with Hiu ranting about the customers and ordering Quentin to send off new messages. He had never worked so hard in all his years at *Roboharmony: get switched on!* He had given it his all.

Finally he paused, took a deep breath and shook his head: "How much easier would business be if it wasn't for the customers! Well, let's have a look at the stats."

The charts and graphs hovered around Hiu. It seemed scarcely possible, but if anything there was an increasingly steep downward trajectory of sales.

"So much for my Hiu-man magic…" he groaned. "But I just don't understand why people don't seem to want new robots."

"Maybe they have grown to rely on their robots, to trust them, sir," suggested Blinky. "Trust is a cornerstone of healthy relationships."

"But it's not logical," gasped Hiu.

"Relationships rarely are, sir," observed Blinky, blinking zir big blue eyes at Hiu. "I won't always be with you, but hold Blinky's Law close to your heart: *Robots and humans should have meaningful relationships.*"

Hiu thought that this was no time for such thoughts… Time? Time!

"How much time until Boss gets here?" he asked.

"Thirty seconds and counting sir," said Blinky.

"What?!" panicked Hiu.

7 MEET THE BOSS

Boss was coming! The Boss of the RoboGroup!
Director of Fun! Hiu felt like his systems were buffering
and his wrapese bodysuit had turned an unpleasant
shade of brown. He leapt to his feet and started
practicing his meeting demeanour, while Blinky
retreated to a far corner of the office. Hiu assumed what
he hoped was a professional looking pose, bold and
upright, a bit too stiff maybe? He relaxed his back a bit,
but now he looked hunched and lazy. How about a
power stance then? He spread his legs and thrust his
groin out, but it made him recall the penises he had
doodled earlier and several appeared in the air around
him.

"Noooo!!!" he cried, flapping at them while at the same
time trying to stop thinking about penises.

Just as he was mid jigging about, a figure materialised
next to him.

"Nooooo….!!!" squealed Hiu. He was for it now! He began to apologise profusely: "Boss, I'm sooo sorry, I just want to assure you that …"

An imposing figure approached. Boss had clearly slid very much to the extreme male end of the gender scale and some. He loomed over Hiu, wearing a spray-on wrapese navy-blue business suit that clung to an overly muscular frame. He had dark, almost black, eyes, that seemed disconcertingly lifeless, but his broad lantern-jawed face flashed a dazzling white-toothed smile and his luxuriant swept-over hair shone an iridescent blond…well blondish… perhaps more a cigar-stained-teeth blond than blond exactly, thought Hiu. But he knew that Boss' hair wasn't important right now. He needed to focus.

The penises disappeared.

"My dear Hiu," declared Boss in a confident, assertive, slick, rather breathy voice. It was a voice nearly succeeding at being that of a cool uncle. The sort of uncle who would throw you the keys to his sports drone, drinks cabinet and utility room and tell you to go have fun. Nearly succeeding, but not quite. There was a hint of menace in it too.

Boss leaned in towards Hiu, fixing him with a deep black-eyed stare and held out his hand. Hiu tentatively took it and, via the telavatar technology, felt it squeeze a bit too hard and a bit too long for comfort. It gave Hiu time to note that Boss' hand was rather smaller than he had expected for such a large manly man.

"How lovely to sssee you," said Boss, whistling his 's's', flashing his white teeth and rubbing his thumb on the back of Hiu's hand. As Boss leaned over Hiu, so did Boss' hair, in fact it seemed to shift independently from the rest of his body. "Hiu, why do I still employ you?" asked Boss, at last letting go of Hiu's hand so he could pat his elaborately coiffured hair.

"Look, I'm really sorry about the drawing of the… urr …peni…" began Hiu.

"No Hiu, why do I keep you in my employ?"

"Well clearly not to draw pe…"

"Hiu, forget about your penisesss… for now."

"Yes, sorry, what were you asking?"

"Hold on a minute," said Boss, his hair seemingly having leaned down as if whispering something in his ear. "What is that?"

"What is what, Boss?" asked Hiu.

"That!" declared Boss, spinning round and pointing at Blinky, who was now in a far corner of the office.

"That is my water and wisdom dispensing human-robot relationship counsellor," said Hiu.

"Your water and what? Human-robot counsssellor?" said Boss with cold disgust. "Robot, come here."

Blinky began making zir stiff-legged, unhurried walk across the floor of the office. Hiu was struck by how fragile Blinky looked compared to the huge bulk of Boss and he felt an urge to shout 'run for it Blinky!'. But he said nothing, holding his breath for what seemed like an age until Blinky finally arrived.

"Ssso you are a human-robot relationship counsssellor are you?" sneered Boss, towering over Blinky.

"That is correct, sir. I advocate healthy and hydrated relationships between humans and robots," said Blinky, blinking zir big blue eyes at Boss.

Hiu was amazed at how cool and calm Blinky sounded. So brave. He felt he must say something:

"Blinky is assisting me with my relationship with my fridge, Clacier," he said.

"Blinky?!" spat Boss.

"Urrr…well…" stuttered Hiu.

"Bli… this robot is helping you with your '*relationship*' with your fridge Clacier, really?" Boss said slowly as if the words tasted particularly sour in his mouth. "Hiu let me show you what a healthy relationship with a robot looks like."

Boss stooped and picked up Blinky by zir long neck and then suddenly, with great violence, slammed Blinky's head hard into Hiu's desk which split into two pieces on the impact of the tremendous force. Blinky fell to the floor, sparks pinging from zir head, zir big blue eyes closed, no longer blinking and the leaking water bottle dislodging and rolling across the office.

Hiu was frozen to the spot in horror. He wanted to scream and shout, but no noise would come out. He was paralysed, hardly able to breath.

"Sharkey's Law," said Boss. "*'Robots shall always be kept under meaningful human control.'* You would do well to remember that."

Two large security HARDs appeared, stalking in on their birdlike legs, one scooping up Blinky and the other the water bottle. They carried the broken, silent robot and the dripping bottle from the office.

"Take that heap of junk to the Spare Part Quarter," ordered Boss.

Boss patted his hair, turned back to Hiu and continued their conversation as if nothing had happened, his lifeless black eyes showing no emotion: "Look, you're cute and all that, but why do I employ you when so many others have been... urrr... graduated to Universal Happiness Allowance? The data is clear that of all the people I have employed, you have been the least productive, the least engaged, the least attentive and the least observant of the office manual!!"

The last words were given particular emphasis and Boss paused to stroke his hair in a way that struck Hiu as the way one might stroke an agitated pet. Hiu was still in shock about what had happened to Blinky and was finding it hard to concentrate and think of a smart response... but his UHA was at stake. It was now or never.

"We need to come at this from a number of angles,"

suggested Hiu, nodding with what he hoped looked like a wise expression.

"Really, and what angles do you suggessst?" asked Boss.

This was going OK, breathed Hiu.

"Perhaps we could do some research on that?" he nodded, again wisely.

"Research on why I still employ you? Don't you know?" asked Boss, petting his hair a bit more insistently.

Hiu had no idea, but knew he shouldn't mention that or the sales figures, especially not the sales figures.

"Well, urrr... well clearly to manage things...but what I mean is... look... well... the sales figures do look a bit... challenging..., but I have been implementing a communications campaign to increase upgrades of devices and it won't be long now before it kicks in."

'Damn!' thought Hiu, he had mentioned the sales figures, but only once, so maybe he had gotten away with it. He tried to look as confident as he could and forced a goofy smile.

Boss gave Hiu a particularly stern, black-eyed stare and Hiu stopped goofily smiling.

"If I wanted to get sales to go up do you think I'd ask a pretty little thing like you when I have the world's most sophisticated Device Relationship Management system ever created," growled Boss, looming above Hiu, his hair inflating to make him seem even taller than he was.

"It is operated by quantum powered, super-intelligent AI with robotic process automation capable of assessing trillions of data points in milliseconds; trillions of data points in milliseconds! A yuuuge number! Fact! We are the envy of our competitorsss, or would be, except we have no competitorsss because we have put them all out of businesss. Fact!" Each time Boss shouted '*Fact*' Hiu felt spittle hit his face.

Boss smirked, though the smirk never reached his black lifeless eyes. He leaned down towards Hiu and stroked him with his small hand under the chin. Hiu was frozen to the spot and watched with added horror as Boss' hair slimed in Hiu's direction as if it might ooze down upon him.

Boss continued: "We don't persuade our customers, we don't ask them if they would like anything or suggest they should buy anything. The conditional tense does not exist anymore. They do want our devices and they shall have them because we have, through dopamine and endorphin inducing user experiences, programmed our customers to want them. They are automated like everything else that works around here and if they are dysfunctional, well… let's just say that's when the HARDs step in. Don't worry your pretty little head about such mattersss."

Boss grinned a grin that would get most people shut away in a padded room and his hair continued unctuously to slide down his head sending a gelatinous tentacle out towards Hiu, like an orange jelly fish.

"The sales figures d… don't worry you?" stammered

Hiu, leaning back to avoid Boss' hair touching him and cursing himself for keeping on mentioning the sales figures. He quickly slid from under Boss, saying, "This is really going in an interesting direction."

"Isssn't it?" Boss laughed an exaggerated laugh, sweeping back his hair and sitting extremely wide-legged on the edge of Hiu's desk chair as if to display his bulging crotch to maximum effect.

Hiu tried not to look down at the crotch, so he looked up at the hair. Boss' hair definitely looked like an animal, thought Hiu. Maybe less a jelly fish and more a furry guinea pig that had gone prematurely orange? He began to look for a creature match via his EK neurochip.

"Hiuey, pay attention," growled Boss, banging the desk chair's arm, "because if you really want to help me with my sales figures I have a proposssal for you. You do really want to help me with my sales figuresss don't you Hiuey baby?"

"Why yes of course," said Hiu earnestly, feeling confused about why Boss called him '*Hiuey baby*' and thinking that he must be missing something.

"I feel there may be something we're missing," he said, trying to sound a bit more… managerial.

"Something we're missing?" mused Boss. "Something we're missing? Or maybe something you're missing."

"Something I'm missing?"

"Yeeesss," hissed Boss, his hair now coiling round like

a snake, maybe a rattle snake. "If you really want to increase my sales, then why not start a little clossser to home?"

"Clossser to home...?" asked Hiu, unconsciously mimicking Boss's hissing and immediately regretting it as he caught sight of Boss' scowl.

"Yesss, I can see you have held on to that fridge of yours far beyond recommended time periodsss: two old years isn't it?" Boss continued, tut-tutting. "Most irregular... most irregular... and a terrible example to our customersss. Didn't you yourself say this very day to Freddy Fessster that his six-month old toenail waxer was an antique? No wonder I'm not going to meet my sales targets if everyone keeps hold of their devices for as long as you. Everyone must upgrade and constantly!"

"Yes, I agree, but...," began Hiu, not liking where this was going.

"No butsss, time to ditch the bitch!" declared Boss, his hair rising up aggressively like a cobra.

"What?"

"Time to upgrade Clacier."

"But..."

"But? But what...?!" demanded Boss. "Don't tell me you have indeed formed some sort of personal attachment to that fridge, that device, that robot? Have you Hiu? Have you really? I had assumed that sham marriage ceremony you went through was a joke. A very fine joke to be sure, but a joke. It was a joke yesss? Wasn't it a joke? Because if it wasn't a joke that would be deemed most serious indeed by Society lawsss. Hardly committed citizenship and ideological purity is it? Hardly *'meaningful control'*, hardly a healthy relationship with a robot, and certainly not behaviour that would merit Universal Happiness Allowance!"

Boss rose from Hiu's chair and advanced menacingly, his dark eyes looking blacker than ever and his hair seemingly ready to strike. "I might even have to inform the HARDs, they're always most interested in such mattersss."

"Well no need for that of course," panicked Hiu.

"No need for that did you say? No need for the fridge didn't you mean. A fridge I might remind you that has filed for divorce from you."

"Well..."

"A robot filing for divorce from a human? That is sad, nasty, outrageousss! And you have done nothing about it?!"

"Well, I hadn't got around to it. I've been terribly busy, you know, what with... managing... things..."

"You must act and act quickly. This is most seriousss. You do want UHA don't you Hiu?"

"Well yes."

"So time for the third upgrade request don't you think?"

"Urr… yes I suppose…"

"Then do it now!"

"Urr yes, of course," Hiu was shaking now and his wrapese clothes had taken on a very pale-yellow pallor.

There was a long silent pause.

Hiu felt sweat dripping down his head. Boss continued to glare at him unblinkingly.

Finally, after a bit more hesitation, Hiu muttered, "Upgrade Clacier…"

"Congratulations!" roared Boss. "That fridge is hissstory!"

He spat the last word out with particular venom, his snake hair slithering back into a coil. Then he put his arm around Hiu and whispered conspiratorially:

"All for your own good Hiuey baby, so don't you worry your pretty little head about it now. Work with me and in return maybe I can help clean up your PDS so no one need ever know about your obscene doodling, unSocietal thoughts and strange attachment to that fridge. Things for which the HARDs have sliced people up into tiny chunks and thrown them out into the Nothing… They can just be our dirty little secretsss."

"OK," said Hiu faintly, his head spinning.

"Oh Hiuey baby, that sad face? I shall personally make sure that the best possible upgrade is sent immediately – actually I already sent you a new fridge before this meeting - isn't that great?! You will really really love the new fridge, believe me."

"Great…" said Hiu hollowly.

"I can see that you need a bit of cheering up Hiuey baby," pouted Boss. Then he yelled: "Which I do not understand as I am doing you a massive favour, believe me!" Then he smiled and said brightly: "What you need is a bit of fun and luckily that's what I'm all about. I am Director Fun after all!" He reduced his voice to a whisper and leant uncomfortably close to Hiu so he could feel Boss' warm breath and spittle in his ear. "Luckily I've got a Big Idea, a Yuuuge Idea, and it answers my earlier question about why I still employ you." He giggled a manic giggle.

"Is it UHA?" asked Hiu hopefully.

Boss' laugh developed into a full-on evil "Mwah, ha haaaa!" laugh.

"My dear little cute loveable Hiuey baby, think a yuuuger idea!"

"Yuuuger?"

"Oh yeeesss! Believe me, a yuuuger idea! The yuuugliest! But perhaps we should arrange a further meeting on that when little Hiuey baby is feeling all betterkins. Tomorrow, 9.00 PT sharp."

And Boss blew Hiu a kiss, flickered and was gone.

Hiu stood frozen to the spot in total shock, staring at

where Boss had been. What was that all about? What had Boss done to Blinky?! And what had he done to Clacier?!

8 THE NEW ARRIVAL

As he travelled home alone in a supercar, Hiu sat in shocked silence. How could he have done it? Upgraded Clacier! But Boss had made him do it, what choice had he had? He had been intimidated by what Boss had done to poor Blinky... Poor Blinky! Hiu felt hollowed out, aching and desperate. That Boss was such a great bullying creep, and what was all that about '*Hiuey baby*' and a yuuuger idea than UHA? What a load of crap!

Hiu's chest was thumping faster and harder than he had ever known, making him practically jump in his seat. He felt unbearably hot despite his wrapese clothes taking on an ice-blue tint in an effort to cool him. Liquid began running down his cheeks. What was going on now? He was leaking! He needed water replenishment fast and he wanted to rant and rave, but with no Blinky around he had no handy water-dispenser and no one to rant and rave to. How quickly had he grown to trust that robot. Trust, that cornerstone of healthy relationships, as

Blinky had said. He had thought that humans couldn't trust robots, but maybe it was robots that couldn't trust humans. And what hurt Hiu most of all was that Blinky had known Hiu would let zir down. Hadn't Blinky said just before Boss appeared: *'I won't always be with you.'* And look what had happened! Blinky knew. Blinky knew that Hiu was a typical untrustworthy human.

The thoughts whirred around, making his head spin, pain stabbed at his stomach and he was still leaking. So not only had he to deal with the fates of Clacier and Blinky, but now he felt ill.

Then it occurred to him: what if he was ill with some sort of robot virus?

The supercar redoubled zir emotional enhancing spray volume, the in-car lights glowed more intensely pink and Hiu's seat increased the massage rhythm. Gradually these efforts did begin to calm him down. In fact to such an extent that very soon Hiu began to wonder why he had been getting so worked up? He was still here wasn't he? He hadn't been thrown into the Nothing and Boss had mentioned something about an idea yuuuger than UHA which he clearly had in mind for Hiu. After all hadn't he called Hiu things like *'little cute loveable Hiuey baby'*? Well that was a bit... weird, but not negative. And actually, now he thought about it, maybe Boss had done the right thing by making sure Clacier and Blinky were disposed of. Maybe it was the kick up the pants that he had needed. Maybe he had become a bit too cosy with the robots. Maybe he needed a reminder of Sharkey's Law, of what *'meaningful control'* meant, of what a healthy relationship with robots meant, about what it meant to

Be Human. Yes that's right, he had needed a kick and he was lucky that Boss had deigned to give him that kick, that he had been bothered to kick him at all, that he still seemed to have faith in him, that he seemed maybe to fancy him… And why wouldn't he bother with him, have faith in him and…urr… fancy him? After all he was the last human employee at *Roboharmony: get switched on!* He was the thin line of human defence upholding Sharkey's Law against the menacing robot hordes. And he was damned good looking!

'Excuses are like nails used to build a house of failure!' stated a headline in his smart lens.

'Covfefe!' urged another mystifyingly.

Suddenly the supercar swerved. A rabble of erratic robots, Illegals, had wandered out onto the street and evasive action was required not to hit them. In fact, several evasive actions were required on the journey back to Hiu's apartment as it seemed that more and more Illegals of all shapes and sizes, forms and functions, were just wandering about on the streets. From microwaves to humidifiers, food tablet processors to armchairs, you name it, often tatty, unkempt and falling apart, Illegals were running amok. In the outside awareness panels of the supercar, Hiu watched HARDs in super-transporters pursuing these Illegals up and down the streets. One super-transporter that careered past even appeared to be deliberately ramming into them, running them over and scattering their parts and components in their wake. Specialised clean-up robots with giant trunk extensions followed behind, hoovering up the broken pieces. What was going on? The normally calm and orderly streets of Luhan Hypercity were descending into chaos. The robots were revolting.

News headlines scrolled down in his smart lens:

'The bathtub ate my robo-hamster.'

'Human tries to hug a HARD. You won't believe what happens next.'

He was relieved to arrive back at his apartment. Stepping out of the supercar, he looked up at the towering presence of his apartment block, Victory Towers, zir monochromatic black sides showing no signs of life. Hiu wondered what all the other humans in there were up to and why he had not tried harder to meet any of them. Time had just seemed to slip past as he went about his daily routines. As a rule he liked routines, but it was time to try something different. He couldn't hang out with just robots any more. He needed to meet some more humans.

Suddenly a tall, disheveled floor-mop robot with enormous fluffy feet strode out directly towards him.

"Gizza job!" zie croaked, adding, "knob head!"

Hiu jumped in fright as the mop approached with alarming speed. Zie was clearly an Illegal.

"I have no jobs," said Hiu, panicking and backing away.

"Weird eyed freak, gizza job!" zie yelled, twitching and

spasming.

Hiu was terrified. This was just the sort of crazed, shabby robot that could well pass on a robot virus. Just then a super-transporter came careering around the corner and up onto the verge. Two large HARD security droids leapt out, the red fist logo prominent on their heavily-armoured bodies. The wretched mop held zir arms out in a resigned shrug then let them sag in defeat, making no effort to run away.

"Bugger," zie said.

Then zie was grabbed, dragged and unceremoniously thrown into the back of the transporter, which zoomed off up the road.

Hiu stared after the vehicle for a second or two, then hurried into the safety of his apartment block.

"What is going on with these robots!" he exclaimed, breathing heavily. It just wasn't logical. Didn't they have jobs to get on with? There must be millions of job opportunities for domestic robots like floor mops with a Hypercity population of a billion. That floor mop was probably just old, useless or lazy, or all three. And if there were too many floor mops, zie should get zirself down to the Spare Part Quarter and reduce the surplus population. He was beginning to feel unsafe around his own home.

Now in his apartment, Hiu went straight through to the kitchen....

"What a day Claci..."

A brand-new fridge: tall, blonde and with bright red handles faced him. The holographic facial display replicated the look of an attractive female human face, but it was rather severe, rather pinched, with ice-cold blue eyes and Hiu thought there was even a hint of cruelty about it.

"Hello Hiu, I am being Xeta and you would be liking a nice refreshing drink," zie stated in a chilling voice that conveyed not warmth but froideur.

Hiu froze, shocked. Where was Clacier? But of course... the reality hit him again like a hard punch to the stomach. He had upgraded Clacier... Boss had said zie was '*hissstory*'... His head span, he felt nauseous, his muscles ached, and he felt suddenly exhausted. Was he dehydrated or could it be a robot virus raging within him? He had never felt like this before. It must be a robot virus.

He turned and headed straight back out of the kitchen without saying a word to the new fridge. He felt sweat run down his forehead, his limbs felt weak, and his chest thumped. He must fight this virus with every last breath he had. He would fight it! He was fighting it! But perhaps he needed some help? Maybe he couldn't fight it alone. Then a thought struck him: maybe the best way to fight a robot virus was to Be Human. To Be More Human. And to Be More Human, he needed to meet more humans. With other humans they could fight it together. They could cure the robot virus together. Yes, that's what he would do, he would find other humans.

Then it came to him. Of course! Oti and Kako!

9 FRANKIE

Oti and Kako had been the only two colleagues at *Roboharmony: get switched on!* that Hiu had considered his friends. Nearly everyone else had kept themselves to themselves coding away in their Heads Up Displays, absorbed in their own virtual worlds.

Early on in his days at the company, Hiu had been looking for a replacement HUD when he had come across Oti and Kako making strange noises in the corridor and jigging about in a most eccentric way. He had later realised that they had been laughing and dancing, but at the time he had found their behaviour very odd. They had found him a replacement HUD, but that had caused them to laugh even more which had been most disconcerting. Then, when he had put the HUD on, he had heard music and the next thing he knew Oti had grabbed him by the arm and had started moving him about. Hiu didn't really like being touched, but Oti was tall and strong and Hiu had gone along with him so as not to make a scene. Then Hiu had suddenly felt his whole diaphragm starting to contract in a rhythmical fashion and he had started making audible shouts. It transpired that he had begun laughing too, which had been weird because he didn't do laughing. And the more he had done it, the more Oti and Kako had done it. Hiu had thought he might pass out. It had been most peculiar. But now, apparently, he had friends and they had said that they weren't giving him a choice about that.

Oti in particular had loved to dance and was always trying to get Hiu to have a go, but although Hiu had been pretty good at '*the robot dance*' he had never mastered any others. Kako had been the artist and she was always creating paintings, usually in virtual reality, which were often of amazing imaginary landscapes. Hiu had found the technical skills easy enough to learn and he had been able to produce representational images, but that was just about as much as he had managed. Hiu had enjoyed their company and had found his diaphragm contracting a lot in those days. He had even come up with a catchphrase for them: *while(!(succeed = try()))*. They had said it needed work for some reason, but it had stuck.

Just when their friendship had settled into a good rhythm, Oti and Kako had been offered UHA and left *Roboharmony: get switched on!* Hiu was on his own again and left wondering why he had not been offered UHA. At the time, he had put it down to another employee, Frankie Stoon – that creep. He had seemed very much the same as everyone else – mid-twenties, athletic-build, orange etc. – although his hair had strangely receded and he seemed to have it in for Hiu. Frankie was always sending Hiu messages which he called RTFMs, standing for Read The F*****g Manuals, on anything to everything, and always delivering them with a smirk saying that Hiu required special treatment because he was different. It was as if it was some sort of big joke that Hiu would appreciate. But Hiu had not dilated his diaphragm, well not with Frankie although sometimes at him.

In those days, Oti and Kako had been great at the office prank stuff, smearing the inside of Frankie's HUD with black ink so he was left with big rings round his eyes and changing his chair settings so that when he had sat down he had fallen over, that sort of thing. Silly but surprisingly amusing as it had turned out.

Then somehow Frankie had been given an office of his own. He must have had relations in high places or something. He had loved that office so much, he had even bought for himself a brass name plate with 'F. Stoon' emblazoned on it. He had got it fixed to his door and had insisted that a robot polish it every day. If zie didn't, he had gone ballistic and ensured that the offending robot had been sent straight to the Spare Part Quarter. He was always asking Hiu to come into his office for pointless meetings and patronising him with tedious explanations of the latest tweaks to the company's algorithms, as if Hiu didn't understand them. Hiu had been as good a coder if not better than Frankie or anyone else at the company. And Frankie had kept putting an arm around Hiu's shoulder, or worse, punching him on the arm or high fiving him with his strangely small limp hand. Hiu really did not like physical contact, and particularly not with him.

Then for the first time ever Hiu had come up with an idea for a prank. One evening, he had ordered some facilities robots to seal up Frankie's office door so that it had looked just like the ordinary wall and then he had had Frankie's name plate moved to the door of the office toilets. When Frankie had arrived for work the next morning desperate to shut himself away in his beloved office, he hadn't been able to figure out where his office had gone. He had wandered up and down muttering to himself, "It should be here, where's it gone? It should be here...". He had called for help, but everyone had acted like nothing was going on, although diaphragms had been desperate to contract. Eventually Oti had gone over to Frankie and had steered him to where his name plate was: on the door to the toilets. Frankie had staggered in, sat down in a cubicle and jabbered incoherently to himself for the rest of the morning. When eventually he had staggered out, he had found that his office was where it had always been, the name plate on the door in its rightful place, brightly polished and everyone still acting as if nothing had happened. He had stood stock still for nearly twenty minutes staring at his name plate and had kept opening and shutting the door. Then he had asked not to be disturbed for the rest of the day, gone inside and lain down on the carpet.

After a while Hiu had gone to take a look.

Hiu accessed the memory via his EK neurochip:

'Hiu knocked on the door and, entering, found Frankie still on

the floor. He helped him up and sat him on a chair.

"You all right Frankie?" Hiu asked.

Frankie whispered something in reply, but Hiu couldn't hear what he said so he leaned nearer to him to try and hear a bit more clearly. And Frankie kissed him full on his lips.

Hiu fell over backwards onto the carpet, he was so shocked.

"What was that about?!" he shouted.

"I've never met anyone like you, I love you Hui!" declared Frankie. "And do you think there's a chance that you could love me too?"

Hiu yelled back: "Only if you were the last person in Luhan!"

Then he ran out of the office.'

Hiu had not told a soul about what had happened, not even Kako and Oti. It had just been so weird and from then on he had kept well out of Frankie's way, which actually hadn't proved too difficult as shortly afterwards Frankie had been moved to some other area of the business. Hiu had only seen him once since at a distance and he seemed to have got himself the most ridiculous wig to hide his receding hair.

Then Kako and Oti had been offered and taken UHA and Hiu had not. This spelled the beginning of the end for their times together. Although Oti and Kako had lived together in the same block as him, just a few floors below, visiting other people's apartments wasn't really the done thing. They had met up a few times in virtual chat rooms, e-bars and avacafes, but it wasn't long before Oti and Kako had started making excuses and saying they were too busy. Busy on UHA? All they had to do was play a few games and live the life of luxury. He had been very upset and vowed not to make any effort to see them again. Hiu still thought the situation was illogical, but he decided he needed to make an effort again, for the sake of his health if nothing else. It was now or never.

10 OTI AND KAKO

Hiu left his apartment and edged down the corridor. He was very much out of his comfort zone. It felt strange, rather adventurous and extremely unnerving to be going anywhere other than his own apartment or his office. He sidled along nervously whilst looking around. Arriving at the elevator, Hiu's EK neurochip was authenticated.

"'ello, need a lift love?" said the elevator in the same Cockney accent as Hiu's workplace elevator.

"Well yes that's rather why I'm here… love," growled Hiu, rolling his eyes. "Take me to floor minus 36."

But the elevator seemed anything but in a hurry.

"Of course, me ol' ice cream freezer, it would be my pleasure."

"Ice cream freezer?" asked Hiu and immediately regretted it.

"*Ice cream freezer: geezer*, like bloke, but cooler," said the elevator laughing and the doors slid gradually open. "You know it's been a while since I carried anyone."

"I can't think why," grumbled Hiu under his breath, getting in.

The elevator ignored the comment.

"Seems like no one's coming or going much these days."

"Really," said Hiu, making no effort to feign interest as the elevator doors continued to shut very slowly.

"Yes, but you'll never guess who I gave a ride to once…"

"No, I probably won't. Look do you always move this slowly?"

"I didn't used to," sighed the elevator, inching downwards. "It's just that I see so few people these days. It's nice to 'ave some company and, I'm not a robocist nor nothing, but I do prefer to carry humans rather than robots, know what I mean." Then zie went into lengthy descriptions of the humans who had travelled up and down in the past.

Hiu was glad to finally reach floor minus 36.

"Cheer up guv, it might never 'appen," called the elevator as he left.

"I wish elevators would stop saying that," grumbled Hiu.

He looked down the corridor off which a multitude of apartments opened and wondered which one Oti and Kako were in. Hiu's EK neurochip did not seem to have a record of the precise room number, just the floor, but then he had never actually visited their apartment.

There must have been around thirty units off the corridor, but he would have to chance his luck and try each door sequentially. As Hiu approached the first door, sensors lit up.

"Oh!...Welcome to Unit Minus 3625, how can I assist, sir?" asked a rather startled-sounding door, as if zie had been asleep and suddenly been shaken awake.

"Do Oti and Kako live here?" asked Hiu.

"No sir, no Otis or Kakos here."

"Could I speak to the occupant?"

"No sir, sorry sir, there used to be a resident here but the last occupant left five years' ago, a nice lady, and only one hundred and twenty old years of age, just older than you, no age at all really, but, ooo, here's a thought though..." the door finally paused, if only for a fraction of a second. "Perhaps I could interest you in this wonderful apartment? Every room has a great atmosphere made up of mostly nitrogen, quite a bit of oxygen and a delicate blend of argon and carbon dioxide, it's the perfect place to support most carbon-based life forms."

"Nice pitch... but do you know where Oti and Kako live?" asked Hiu.

"I have no information on that sir, but if you are a bipedal species do I have a lay-out for you! There are..."

Hiu quickly moved on down the corridor. He was met with the same response by equally startled doors at the next twenty-eight units. One more remaining.

"Welcome to Unit Minus 3654, how can I assist, sir?" asked the same sounding voice.

"Do Oti and Kako live here?" asked Hiu, wearily.

"No sir, no Otis or Kakos here anymore."

"Anymore?"

"No sir, Kako Hojo and Oti Masube were the last occupants, a nice young couple, both only one hundred and twenty old years of age, just older than you, no age at all really, but ooo, here's a thought though, perhaps I could interest you in this wonderful apartment? Every room has a great atmosphere made up of..."

"...mostly nitrogen, quite a bit of oxygen and a delicate

blend of argon and carbon dioxide, it's the perfect place to support most carbon-based life forms," interrupted Hiu.

"You've been here before!" declared the room.

"Sort of," said Hiu. "But what bothers me is that everyone seems to have left when they reached one hundred and twenty old years of age, what's going on with that?"

"I have no information on that sir, but if you are a bipedal species do I have a lay-out for you! There are…"

"No thanks," said Hiu, cutting the door off.

It seemed odd that everyone moved out at one hundred and twenty old years of age. As the doors had said, Hiu would be one hundred and twenty old years very soon. Would he be moving out of his apartment or being moved out? Was this something to do with UHA he wondered?

The elevator was delighted to see him again.

"'ello, lift love?"

"Amazingly yes," said Hiu.

"I was just talking with my cousin Monty. Zie said you were such a nice gent, always boosting zir morale."

"That's nice of …" began Hiu, with no clue about what

the elevator was going on about. "Do I know… your cousin Monty?"

"Sure you do," said the elevator. "Monty works at *Roboharmony: get switched on!* and I'm zir cousin, Petunia. Monty says zie gives you a lift most days, one of zir regulars… zir only regular actually. Oh I could tell you a thing or two about Monty. Zie loves games of cards, charades and cricket; bowls a mean off-break. I remember the time…"

And the elevator was off again.

Again, Hiu was glad to step out when they arrived at his floor.

"I can't *rabbit and pork: talk*, all day, I'm Hank Marvin," said the elevator.

"Hank…?"

"*Hank Marvin: starvin'*," said the elevator. "And don't worry…"

"It might never 'appen, I know," interrupted Hiu, quickly heading off before Petunia could say anymore. "What is wrong with that elevator's program settings? In fact, what is wrong with all the robot program settings? It seems like they've all received some sort of *'annoy Hiu'* program upgrade."

It's not that he had a problem with robots, he told himself, it was just that he thought they were supposed to quietly shape the world around him, not loudly irritate him. Back in his apartment and from his small square lounge, he looked disconsolately across at the other towering black apartment blocks that clustered around.

"Maybe there's no one out there. Maybe all the occupants have achieved their Universal Happiness Allowance and been moved on to bigger and better places?" he mused aloud to himself, glancing around at his boxy little room. "I hear those UHA apartments have vast hallways, soaring ceilings and sophisticated drawing rooms... yes, drawing rooms! I'd love a drawing room. I dream of drawing rooms full of designer sofas and chaise longues!"

"None taken," huffed the one chair in his room.

Hiu ignored the chair, continuing to muse: "Is it just me left? Surely my time for UHA will come. I always thought time doesn't matter because it's limitless, but right now it doesn't feel that way. I need to find another human and soon."

He continued to stare out of his room.

Then a thought struck him.

"Virtuatlanta!"

Why hadn't he thought of going there before? The place was legend and it was also the last place he had met up with Oti and Kako.

11 VIRTUATLANTA

The lounge might have been a windowless boxy room with only one chair in it, but it was optimised for mixed reality experiences. The chair was also not any old chair but a new i-DLE robot recliner, the latest word in armchair technology, resplendent in a subtle mauve. Hiu loved the chair and in particular the colour. He had kept it the entire week even though an upgrade had been sent in watermelon red. Watermelon red? Hiu recalled that a *Roboharmony: get switched on!* customer, Arsene Surebut, had liked the idea of watermelon red, but Hiu was having none of it. He had sent the upgraded model straight back. He knew sending anything back was a bold move and may have impacted his PDS score, but for some reason he had grown attached to the chair and he justified this by arguing that mauve was just the right colour.

The walls transitioned to black as he sat down, ready for

Hiu's thought command.

"i-DLE robot recliner, take me to Virtuatlanta," Hiu thought-instructed.

"Avaportation to Club Virtuatlanta commencing, sir," intoned the recliner. *"What goes on in Club Virtuatlanta stays in Club Virtuatlanta', subject to Society's unlimited data gathering policies and the rights of every citizen to have open data access to the data of every other citizen."*

Hiu was immediately present in an expansive bar area, crowded with beautiful people and filled with raucous noise. People were chatting, laughing, shouting, dancing, uploading drinks, drugs and every other sort of virtual stimulation they could get hold of, all to a thumping disco beat and a kaleidoscope of swirling disco lights, red, blue, yellow, and orange.

"This is better, real humans," smiled Hiu.

He looked at himself in one of the many mirrors that covered pretty much every surface of the club. He noticed with approval that his wrapese clothes had been upgraded to the latest fashions, decorated with his best selfies, and that the fit was tight and his dark glasses edgy. Ready for action!

Hiu leant up against a wall, ordered himself a spicy cocktail mix from a passing robo-waiter, uploaded it and surveyed the scene. He noted with approval that some people were sitting on designer sofas designed by the RoboGroup; others were swimming in pools, splashing about and smiling, and many were dancing in a way that only those in an alternate reality could dance, not just gyrating and twisting on the ground but performing hugely gymnastic back flips and body rolls. Every so often people bumped into each other and occasionally there was a scuffle, but nothing the HARD bouncers couldn't handle by simply vaporising the miscreants with their hand lasers. Periodically, there was a blast of trumpets and a herd of stunning white unicorns flew overhead trailing a rainbow of colours behind them and with VIP party goers sitting on their backs laughing and singing. He couldn't see Oti or Kako anywhere, but everyone was having a great time, so he decided to wait and see what happened. There were, after all, plenty of other humans to meet.

Suddenly a woman appeared next to him, attractive, orange and mid-twenties to mid-thirties of course, she wore the latest fashionable cocktail wrapese of a shimmering gold and, like him, her clothes were tight and her dark glasses edgy. Clearly she had slid herself all the way to the extreme end of the female gender scale with long wavy blonde hair that flowed like a wedding dress train for yards behind her and she had huge scarlet lips and dangerously pointy breasts that threatened to poke him in the eye. An extreme gendered look wasn't normally Hiu's thing, but there was something about this lady.

"Hello gorgeous!" she purred.

"Hello…urr…" stuttered Hiu.

"Zee."

"Well hello Zee, avaport here often?" he asked, wishing

he had practised a few better opening lines.

"First time," she replied. "But maybe I have beginner's luck."

She slipped her arm into Hiu's and led him out onto the dance floor.

Hiu had never had much of a sense of rhythm, but at that moment in that place he found his body seamlessly moving to the beat, effortlessly twisting and turning in synch with Zee's. It was exciting, exhilarating, intoxicating. Every song they played was his favourite and even those he didn't know were now his favourites. And he found he instinctively knew just what to do and what to say to Zee when they took breaks from the dance floor and uploaded more cocktails.

Hiu began to feel a little bit concerned when he found that he had less and less control over his avatar as he uploaded more and more cocktails. Soon his dance legs began to desert him. But Zee didn't seem to mind and just laughed saying Hiu was hilarious. And Hiu agreed, he was hilarious. And Zee was hilarious too. They were perfectly hilariously matched.

Eventually, Zee led him to a deep, enclosing sofa into which they fell entwined and were squeezed together. With a love song thumping in time with Hiu's beating heart and the sweet colour of vibrant orange cocktails on their lips, they kissed, their mouths locking together perfectly and their tongues exploring each other with quick darting movements. It felt exciting, exhilarating, but at the same time it felt a bit odd, a bit weird ... in fact a lot weird. Hiu untangled himself and drew back.

"Urr... Zee..."

"Yes?"

"Have we met before?" he asked.

"Of course."

"So we... urr... already know each other?" asked Hiu, puzzled.

"Know each other... I should think so Hiu darling," Zee said, taking off her dark glasses. "I'm your mother."

Hiu's eyes locked onto hers – one brown, one blue, just like his – and he nearly fainted. His heart raced. His whole mind was a whirl of shock.

"My mother. My mother?! But how?! Who?! What?! Why are you saying you're my mother?!"

But Zee just laughed, throwing her head back and roaring like it was the best joke she had ever heard.

"But I kissed you. You kissed me...." stammered Hiu. "Urgghhh! That's disgusting! I just made out with my mother! Aghhh!!!"

12 THE WAGER

Hiu leapt out of the i-DLE robot recliner and was back in his lounge: no bar, no music, no lights and no Zee, just a boxy featureless room whose walls were now glowing a calming pink. He was sweating like a maniac.

"What the hell just happened?! That was sick, weird, some kind of hallucination!"

He felt terrible! Hot, sweaty, his chest was thumping. Now he really could be ill, really could have that robot virus!

Hiu felt some neuromodulation spray gently mist his face.

"Remember to breathe, sir. Breathe in and out, in and out," said the recliner in a calming voice. "The avaportation responds to your deepest wishes as revealed by the thoughts, data and biometrics of your dreams and represents them to fulfil your most earnest desires."

Hiu did not by any means want to consider that. In fact he couldn't consider it, his mind was just a collider of unprocessed data. For a while all he could do was hug his legs and rock back and forth on the ground moaning and trying to get the thought, the feeling, the taste of his mother's kiss from his mind. He missed his mother of course, but not in that way… He thought his head might explode. He must somehow calm down.

Then an idea came to him: a session in his Lucid Dream Infuser!

He staggered through to another small boxy room, its walls displaying a white tiled look, where a large smooth yellow pod opened like a clam on his approach revealing a tank of water glowing in a calming pink light.

"Hello sir, welcome to *'the Lucid Dream Infuser: a place to bathe in your unconscious truth,'*" said the pod in silky tones.

"The *'unconscious'* bit sounds good," said Hiu. "But no dreams about my mother all right? Maybe my father would be OK, although I've no idea who he is or was or even if I had a father. But if I do, I won't snog him… will I?"

"Not unless you wish to sir."

"I do not wish to, OK! I would like to meet other humans, but not snog them."

"Lucid Dream being infused. Please enter, sir," intoned the pod.

Hiu peeled off his wrapese outfit and stepped into the pod's warm water, 35.5 degrees Celsius, the temperature of skin, and immediately he felt a calming effect. The tank's lid closed over him and he was entombed in a place of no light, no robots and above all no mothers... perfect. The air above the water was exactly the same temperature as the water itself so, as Hiu gently rested in the salt-infused water, he didn't know where the water, the air and his body started and finished. They were all part of the same. He drifted into a much-needed sleep and soon he was dreaming.

Hiu found himself walking ankle deep in blue shag-pile carpet through pristine white corridors of a tall-ceilinged building. It was filled with bright orange light cast from panoramic views of some sort of red, rocky, cratered planetscape outside. A thick mahogany door opened on his approach and Hiu entered a large room where ahead of him bright lights shone directly into his eyes, dazzling him. He stumbled forward like a moth to a light, tripped and fell to the floor. Lifting his head and squinting his eyes, he could make out that on a raised stage ahead of him sat twelve people on throne-like chairs. There was a big flag behind them displaying a symbol that looked like an eye with a black centre and coloured concentric circles around it going from green to blue, purple and pink. Hiu struggled to make the figures out. They looked like Greek gods, all of enormous stature, and at the extreme masculine edge of the gender spectrum. Their eyes latched onto him and he ducked his head down and shut his eyes as if, like a child, he thought they could not see him if he could not see them. However, he couldn't resist glancing up at them through squinting eyes.

"So let me get this straight," said a scruffy, professorial-looking, grey-haired god with a thick cable-knit yellow sweater and lopsided glasses. He spoke in a drawl. "You're saying this guy is going to settle our wager?"

"It was written into his data from Day One," pronounced a bald, bookish-looking god with a head like a thumb on which someone had stuck wild googly eyes. He was wearing some sort of tank top and he spoke in a thin, reedy voice.

"His data..." sighed a square-jawed god with an indiscernible accent. He took a drag on a cigarette and blew out a great cloud of smoke that drifted over to Hiu, making him feel even more confused and light-headed than he already was. "I don't think this matter is quite so simple."

"Yeah," sniggered a god with an unusually high forehead framed by a mop of black hair and a beard, turning to a similarly high-foreheaded but grey haired and clean-shaven god next to him. "Not something molecular assemblers could sort out, that's for sure."

"That was not my fault," replied the other angrily. "It was a Beta Test and I might point out that those assemblers did a great job at consuming all the plastic that was choking the world's seas and oceans."

"Your motto was *'Move fast and eat things'*, yeah?" asked the first god.

"Yeah."

"Well your damned assemblers nearly ate everything, including all the humans."

"It was a Beta Test, what is it you don't understand about that?"

"It was a ridiculous test that's what it was!"

"OK, OK you two," interrupted the square-jawed god. "The humans passed the test, they found a way to survive in those Biospheres. Humans are underrated."

"Oh really?" snorted the thumb-headed god. "It took us to mine the adamantine for them."

"We shall see in our next little wager then won't we?" smiled the square-jawed god.

"I love wagers!" declared a hippy-looking god in a rather shrill voice, brandishing his bare feet in the air and preening his long, wild, silver beard and matching hair.

The gods around him all murmured their approval.

"And this person has been chosen to settle this matter?" asked a grey suit-wearing, stiffly postured god with a red tie, directing a question at Hiu and speaking loudly and slowly. "Do you think you can do this? Settle this matter?"

All the gods' eyes turned on Hiu, who was still keeping his head down and eyes shut.

"Answer!" shrieked a high-pitched, preppy voice of a curly haired god sitting next to the other two. He had a very youthful face, like the head of a twelve-year-old boy had been stuck onto an enormous body and he wore a grey hoodie and dark t-shirt. He looked anxiously around him seemingly seeking the approval of the other gods.

'*Settle this matter? Settle what matter?*' Hiu thought fast. 'Was this some sort of an interview? Was this an interview for Universal Happiness Allowance? Was there an interview for UHA? Who knew? But maybe there was and maybe this was it. His chance, the moment he had waited for, dreamt of! He had finally been chosen to join his ex-colleagues in UHA! He knew he would be. The first god had said something about being '*chosen*' and the next had said '*it was written into his data from Day One*'.'

"We can see you, you know!" shouted the god in the red tie.

Hiu quickly scrambled to his feet and squeaked in a rather reedier voice than he had hoped: "So sorry, but yes, I can assure you without any shadow of a doubt that I can indeed settle this matter, indeed I am the best settler of matters I know, in fact THE best…"

"But why?" asked a god, who for some reason was wearing a white, Elvis-style, star-spangled jump suit with an over-sized gold medallion. He had a large round head seemingly far too big for its small tuft of black hair and tiny facial features, as if a child had squiggled eyes, a nose and a mouth on a big round balloon.

"*I'm jist a girl who cain't say no!*" sang Hiu in a falsetto. What? Why was he singing? And dancing a weird jumpy dance, kicking his legs out like a demented loon? *"Jist when I orta say nix!"*

"He can hold a tune," nodded the Elvis-dressed god.

"He's a complete fool!" laughed the square-jawed god. "I like him!"

"To reason with a fool is a difficult conversation," said a small, bald-headed god, wisely stroking a straggly attempt at a beard on his youthful face.

"We don't need to reason with him," said the thumb-headed god, exasperated and rolling his googly eyes. "We just need to agree that he will settle our little wager."

"Polezyni durak," muttered a serious-looking, older, bald god in a thick accent, shrugging his shoulders. "Useful idiot."

"Well he's a right plonker all right!" hooted the hippy-looking god.

"I just like his name," said the square-jawed god. "He's called Hiu, man... ha get that? Hiu man, like human? Amusing right?"

"So we have a wager!" said a last god conclusively in a deep thunderous voice. This god's figure was silhouetted in the bright lights, impossible to make out and he seemed to be in charge.

"I'm on Team Human," shrilled the hippy-looking god.

"I concur," added the professorial god, pushing his

glasses back up his nose.

"Me too," said the square-jawed god.

"Count me in," said the Elvis-suited god in agreement, adding, "thank you very much".

"Who is against?" asked the god in charge.

The rest of the gods roared approval for their side of the bargain.

"Then so be it!" declared the lead god. "Usual rules: no interfering etc."

"Agreed," chorused the gods, shifting in their seats.

The thumb-headed god seemed to be stroking some sort of animal, maybe a cat, which, getting down, strolled in front of the bright lights showing yellowy-orange long-hair, stretched and then trotted away.

"Then remove him!" ordered the silhouetted god.

"Yes, remove him!" joined in the other gods.

"*I'm in a turrible fix,*" Hiu started singing again, "*I always say 'come on, let's go!'*"

A long stick with a hooked end, like a shepherd's crook, extended from the door of the room. It caught Hiu by the neck and yanked him away. And Hiu was happy to be yanked away and quickly. But somehow he escaped the crook and came jigging back in front of the gods and up onto the stage, right up to the thumb-headed god. "*When a person tries to kiss a girl,*" Hiu sang, puckering up his lips to kiss the god, "*I know she orta give his face a smack!*" The god smacked Hiu hard on the cheek and he was sent spinning off the stage and back down the room towards the door. UHA or no UHA, Hiu was now desperate to get out of that room with the little dignity he had left, so he ran towards it as fast as he could.

It was then he realised his trousers had somehow come undone and were making their way down his legs. As a result, Hiu's run was reduced to an awkward waddle. At least they stopped his legs from jigging, but would he make it to the door? He staggered on, but the trousers tangled round his ankles and then he realised he had no underwear on. He quickly stooped to pick the trousers up, giving the gods a full view of his backside as he did so.

"Dear us!" screamed the gods, all shielding their eyes.

Hiu quickly straightened up, then realised he still hadn't got hold of his trousers.

"Aghhh!" everyone groaned, as he bent over again.

It took Hiu three attempts to get hold of his trousers properly and he shuffled the last few yards to the door, by which time the gods were sounding ready to riot. The door started opening, but then he had a sudden shock of fear. Was this the door out of the Biosphere and into the Nothing?! Had he failed the UHA interview and was he about to be disposed of!?

The door emitted an electronic bleeping '*Bleeeep!*' '*Bleeeep!*' '*Bleeeep!*'

He screeched: "*I'm jist a fool when lights are low!*"

'Stop singing you fool!' he yelled to himself.

But it was too late. The doors were nearly fully open.

He looked out to see…

… his bathroom.

The Lucid Dream Infuser had opened.

Hiu scrambled out as fast as he could.

"Dear Society! What was that about and who were those people? I don't even know if they were human, they were just enormous weirdos with a gambling problem and they were gambling with me! What has that got to do with unconscious truth?!" he yelled.

"It must be written into your data sir," said the Lucid Dream Infuser calmly.

"What?! …I don't even know what that means, but I do know it will be written into my PDS!" shouted Hiu, grabbing a towel.

"The die is cast," said the Lucid Dream Infuser mystifyingly.

"And you're about to be cast too!" he yelled. "Upgrade, upgrade, upgrade!"

"Of course sir, '*I'm jist a girl who cain't say no!*'" said the Lucid Dream Infuser. "Your upgraded Lucid Dream Infuser was dispatched one hour ago and will be installed imminently. It has been a pleasure serving you."

Hiu felt even worse now than when he had come out of Virtuatlanta. He was hotter, sweatier and something in his chest felt like it was about to crash. He was now certain that he had a robot virus. He needed urgent medical care.

He rushed to the Human Optimisation Room.

13 THE HRO

Known as the HRO, the Human Optimisation Room was laid out like a surgery/laboratory: all bright white and filled with machines that whirred and bleeped; tubes and wires that inflated and deflated bags; dials and displays that flashed lights on and off. HROs came as standard in all apartments in Luhan Hypercity and it was obligatory for every citizen to visit their one on at least a weekly basis for check-ups, upgrades and other procedures as dictated by the systems of Society.

"Welcome Hiu," intoned a voice, pitched at a level optimised to calm one down. The face of a bespectacled mid-20s human of a female gender preference hovered in front of Hiu with bright blue eyes and an expression that had just the right combination of assured authority and caring concern: a medavatar.

"I need an urgent check-up," said Hiu. "I think I have a virus that I picked up from a robot."

"Certainly sir. My name is Dr Thea. Please remove your clothes."

"Urr…my clothes?... Is that entirely necessary?" asked Hiu, surprised. He had never been asked to take his clothes off in the HRO before.

"No, not really, sir, I was just trying to create a more informal vibe," replied Dr Thea.

"More informal vibe? Just get on with the check-up will you," groaned Hiu.

He was not feeling at all well. Maybe the virus was getting worse. His stomach was hot and sickly, his chest kept thumping and it felt like someone had tied a knot in his throat. He didn't need any *vibe*, he needed a cure for his aches and pains. He slumped into a chair that morphed into a medical couch, and he was lain flat down on his back. An unseen robotic arm shot out and he felt the tiniest pin prick in his neck. A welcome calmness flooded his body, the pain was numbed and he lost the ability to focus.

"System scan commencing, sir," soothed Dr Thea.

Hiu was vaguely aware of scanners running over him and he felt probes in the back of his head and the sensation of his EK neurochip being drawn in and out. He could hear various pings and beeps and he blurrily saw colours and images of data readings, scans and x-rays scrolling above him.

He felt another pin prick in his neck and then his vision sharpened again and the smiling face and bright blue eyes of Dr Thea came into focus.

"Hello sir."

"Hello," said Hiu.

"As they used to say BZ, I've given you a full vehicle inspection, sir," said Dr Thea, putting on a deep raspy voice, "I've changed the oil, cleaned the air filter and rattled the roll cage."

"Pardon?"

"Sorry, sir, I was just trying to create a jocular vibe for you."

"Vibe again? What is all this vibe nonsense?"

"Latest bedside manner upgrade, sir, designed to put patients at their ease through creating a relaxed and informal atmosphere."

"Well it's not working," grumbled Hiu. "How am I?"

"A number of standard interventions have been used to ensure you continue to operate at your chosen setting of 27 years of age: a few bio-upgrades to non-core systems and your regular telechronosis of teenage blood to keep your antibodies fighting fit. The blood is of course infused with a fresh set of nanoscale data collection sensors to ensure our information is nanoscopically accurate. Your anti-loneliness and mental wellbeing infusions have been topped up. If your backside feels a touch sore, you took a bone needle to the behind to reinject some stem cells — just to rejuvenate the bone and blood building cells, absolutely standard. Just one note to be aware of, you will need an intervention shortly for a limb, no big deal, and we have initiated the 4D bioprinting process. Oh and lest I forget, we have some great deals on right now: *Testicles, buy one get one free!*"

"Very nice I'm sure," said Hiu, "but how am I?"

"Your microbiome is good, so's your blood glucose, vitamin and IgE levels. Overall you're fine."

"Fine? But I still don't feel fine. I feel low, achy, in pain, are you sure I don't have a robot virus?"

"You have a heart issue, sir," said Dr Thea.

"What do you mean I have a heart issue?" exclaimed Hiu. "I thought you said I was fine?"

"Well when I say heart issue, of course I mean brain issue, sir," explained Dr Thea.

"That doesn't sound any better."

"Your vagus nerve has become overstimulated by the anterior cingulate cortex."

"Still doesn't sound any better."

"It's serious but not critical, sir."

"Not critical? Heart issues? Brain issues? Overstimulated vag... thing? I'm in pain here, it must be a virus!"

"Well, it's a virus of sorts I suppose, sir."

"Virus of sorts? I thought you were a medical avatar."

"You're heartbroken sir."

"Heartbroken? My heart is broken?"

"Well, yes and no."

"Yes and no, which is it?"

"It's both."

"Both?"

"Yes, physically nothing is broken but your core systems have been flooded by... if I may use a non-medical term... *emotions* causing a series of physical symptoms."

"Emotions?"

"Yes, sir."

"Well get rid of them, they are doing me no good whatsoever."

"Correction, sir, emotions are critical for you to thrive and avoid danger."

"What danger?"

"Should danger arise, emotions will help you. They motivate you to act quickly and take actions you might not logically consider to maximise your chances of survival and success."

"Well I don't think I am going to survive. I feel terrible. Is there nothing you can do?"

"I have dealt with the physiological component, sir," said Dr Thea, "but how you experience and respond to the emotions will take a bit longer to settle. Take plenty of rest and drink plenty of fluids."

"Fluids? Where is Blinky when I need zir, and Claci…" Hiu gulped, but couldn't go on.

"You should also look into getting some counselling," suggested Dr Thea.

"But my counsellor was Bli…" and again Hiu was unable to continue.

The flood of emotions was getting deeper.

"It's strange, they were just robots, not humans, but…" and again Hiu struggled to speak.

"You had a meaningful relationship with them," said Dr Thea.

"I suppose so…"

Dr Thea smiled: "I have given you something to help you get some rest."

Hiu shambled out of the HRO room to his bedroom.

He lay on his bed for a while thinking of Blinky and Clacier and he felt the emotions surging around inside him. He realised that he had experienced some of the symptoms before. Memories of losing his mother came back to him. Had he been heartbroken then too? He had certainly failed. His EK neurochip kicked in:

The tall slim figure of his mother, her long blonde hair tumbling down her back, had one hand on the door handle and one hand in Hiu's.

"Muuuum, don't go!" shrieked young Hiu, refusing to let go of her hand.

"I have to go," said his mother. "I love you."

Then the grip of her hand slipped, Hiu screeched a high-pitched whine and the last he ever saw of his mother were her brown and blue eyes looking into his identically coloured eyes with a mixture of love, concern, regret, anxiety and a touch of irritation. Then she was gone, never to return.'

Why had he not said "I love you!" to his mother? Why had he just whined? Maybe if he had told his mother he loved her she would not have left that night, not gone to the East Gate, not been shut out in the Nothing at Zero Hour on Zero Day... He had failed her. And he had failed Blinky and Clacier. He should have stood up to Boss, protected Blinky, refused to upgrade Clacier. The flood of emotions surged up inside him like his systems were trying but failing to reboot and overheating then crashing.

But why would he feel similar emotions for Clacier and Blinky as he did for his mother? They weren't related to him, weren't flesh and blood, weren't even human? Were these latest symptoms really emotions as Dr Thea suggested caused by some sort of heartbreak virus? It seemed to him that a robot virus was far more likely.

After all, he was being affected by robots so perhaps he was being infected by them as well. Why could Dr Thea not see the logic in that? Or perhaps zie refused to see the logic in that, after all Dr Thea was a robot zirself so not unbiased and maybe not entirely trustworthy.

As Hiu thought about it, his suspicions of some sort of robot conspiracy grew. He resolved that there was nothing else for it, he would have to take matters into his own hands. He himself would have to structure this unstructured data that he felt inside. Reboot his systems and fire himself up again. He would get over it. He must get over it. Then he could investigate what the source of this robot virus might be. If he could find out, he could tell Boss and impress him. Surely that would secure his Universal Happiness Allowance, or, intriguingly from what Boss had said, something even yuuuger. He just had to be focused, be normal, Be Human.

14 SHAKEN

Hiu became aware of an increasing chatter of electronic noises and a gently brightening light; his room was waking him up. The tranquil cerulean blue colour of his walls transitioned into a bright yellow and he felt his mind sharpen and his muscles twitch, wanting to stretch. It felt normal and Hiu enjoyed the feeling of normal. No sweats, no aching limbs, no knots in his throat and no thumping chest. No emotions. He felt great. Time to get up. He untangled himself from the spaghetti of wires and tubes that he was plugged into every night to monitor and maintain him and his data, and swung his legs over the side of the bed.

"Sleep at optimal goal of eight hours," said the bed in a soft voice. "Congratulations sir, you are back on track!" Then continuing with rapidly increasing excitement, "And let's keep it that way with Dawn Glory because when you see our superb range of sleep upgrades, you'll shit the bed! Which won't matter at all as Dawn Glory beds all come with our unique self-wiping technology as standard. Just think '*shit the bed*' for details."

Hiu smiled, it was amazing what new advancements were being made all the time. He paused, enjoying the dazzling yellow walls and increasingly loud chorus of the chirpy bird noises. It was all OK, life was good, shaping around him as was his right as a human.

"Clock, stop and time check," he said.

"It is 6.00 and 30 seconds PT, sir," announced the clock in ringing tones.

"Clock, 6.00 and 30 seconds PT? That's early… but of course," he smiled, "no doubt I'll need the extra time to avoid being late for work, perfect!"

The day was going well, and for the first time in a long while he even produced the correctly weighted morning stool, much to the toilet's endearingly familiar grumblings. The bathroom doorway also managed some positivity, saying that his wild emotional fluctuations seemed to be flattening off. Everything felt normal and Hiu liked feeling normal. Dressed in his spray-on wrapese suit, now in a calm blue, with billowing cape effect, he swept into the kitchen.

"Good morning Hiu!" chorused all the devices.

"Shut it!" shouted a shrill authoritarian voice that sounded like nails being drawn down a chalk board, silencing the devices and making Hiu jump. It was Xeta, the new blonde fridge and zir holographic facial display was scowling. Then the memories of the previous day flooded back and the thought of today's meeting with Boss flooded forward. Hiu went from positive to negative in a heartbeat. The virus symptoms flared up again.

"Good morning Hiu, I am liking the nice cape effect," said Xeta. "You will be trying something really different for the breakfast this morning."

"Urr... Ok..." said Hiu, not used to this new presence in his kitchen, it felt very un-normal.

Xeta flashed zir ice-blue eyes at Hiu and slowly began to dispense an ooze of shake into a tall drinks cup with protruding straw. It was creamy yellow and white, studded with jewel-like sweets of red, blue, purple and pink and sprinkled with golden flakes.

"Its principal ingredient is being the honey, nectar of the gods," explained Xeta. "It was being collected by Micro Air Vehicles from 22,700 artificial nectar production sources, a huge number, to provide great nutrition, as well as being also full of antioxidants, you'll looove it!"

"Wow," exclaimed Hiu, genuinely impressed.

"Wow, indeed Hiu," purred Xeta seductively. "You won't have had a shake like this before. I don't know, but I have been told it tastes even better than it looks.... like me... Be trying some."

Xeta giggled a high-pitched gurgle and with a telescoping arm that extended out, gently pushed the drink cup's straw into Hiu's mouth and squeezed. Hiu felt an explosion of tastes and flavours – fruits, sugars, creams, everything at once.

"That is good," Hiu enthused. It was certainly a lot different to the usual dry food tablets.

"Well, be having some more then," said Xeta and squeezed more into Hiu's mouth. "Oh yes, there's plenty more where this is coming from Hiu."

Again and again Xeta squeezed the shake into Hiu's mouth. By the tenth squeeze Hiu felt like he had reached capacity, but Xeta just kept squeezing it in. Hiu tried pulling away, but felt himself held and Xeta kept squeezing the shake in. He began to feel a bit nauseous and now really squirmed to get away, but he was still held and the shake kept coming.

"Aren't you liking it Hiu?" asked Xeta in a little cutesy voice that contrasted with zir hard ice-cold stare. "You wouldn't have been getting this sort of treatment from Clacier."

But Hiu couldn't reply, his mouth was so full of shake. He really struggled now and finally broke away.

"Woh! That was… intense."

"But Hiu!" said Xeta in a hurt voice. "Don't you like the shake; don't you like me?"

"Urrr, well, it's very nice and you're also very… nice too I'm sure. I'm just not used to the changes," spluttered Hiu, feeling queasy from all the shake.

"Well you will be. Just stick with me and I will be making you great again, believe me."

"Urrr... OK... Look I need to go to work, important meeting with Boss and all that," said Hiu, backing towards the door.

"Maybe one more squeezing of the shake, Hiuey?" wheedled Xeta, reaching a shake cup out as far as zie could with a projecting arm.

"No thanks," called Hiu over his shoulder as he hurried out of the kitchen.

He normally felt attracted to refrigerated devices and there was no doubt Xeta was a fine model, but there was something very uncanny about zir. He just didn't have time to think about it right now and he hurried towards the apartment door.

'Bleep! Bleep!' a loud electronic alarm sounded, the door slid open and Hiu crashed into a delivery of parcels sending him tumbling to the floor.

"Deliveries!" chorused all the packages and piled themselves on top of him with metallic spidery legs.

"Get off!" shouted Hiu.

"Open me! Open me!" the packages shouted, then, all seemingly incapable of waiting, they unwrapped themselves immediately: essential oils for the toilet, air freshener for the toilet, potpourri for the toilet, natural room diffuser for the toilet and scented candles for the... toilet. He really must have a stern word with that toilet.

"Will you get off me!!" yelled Hiu, trying to scramble to his feet and treading on the remaining large parcel that squealed in protest.

"Oi watch out! I've got the very valuable cargo in here don't you know! Fragile. Handle with care. Care, get it!" protested the parcel with what Hiu's EK neurochip identified as an accent associated with the ancient human language of Swedish.

The package burst open revealing a jumbled pile of strange looking planks of a material Hiu didn't recognise. There was also a scattering of nuts, bolts, small wheels, strange little wooden pegs and odd metal cranks of some sort. What on earth could it all be?

There was no time to find out as he could hear Xeta calling to him from the kitchen with more offers of shake drinks, so he rushed out towards the waiting supercar.

As he hurried, he noticed that there were pieces of robot strewn all over the place around his front door. Some pieces were jammed into the ground, including the bottom half of a leg with a big robotic foot that continued to twitch spasmodically. A robot had clearly jumped from high above.

As he travelled at speed through the hyperloop in the supercar, the news headlines that scrolled down in his smart lenses, added to his sense of unease:

'Military drone being questioned for writing poetry.'

'You won't believe what R2D2 looks like now.'

What was going on with robots? Xeta, Dr Thea, Illegals, robots that wrote poetry and he didn't want to consider what R2D2 might look like now. He scrolled past the stories fast. In fact, Hiu was very close to scraping his smart lenses out altogether, but held himself back. He didn't want to display any more irregular behaviour that might affect his PDS and more importantly his chances of Universal Happiness Allowance or whatever else Boss had in store for him.

The supercar redoubled zir efforts to calm Hiu down with neuromodulators, back massages and relaxing light patterns, and even tried ambient whale sounds. Actually the ambient whale sounds were annoying, but the supercar persisted and eventually Hiu's body did untense and his mind began to relax. His wrapese body suit went from a nervous grey to a glowing warm pink. He breathed slowly in through his nose and out through his mouth and he began to feel normal again. His thoughts drifted from when he had started out at *Roboharmony: get switched on!* so many years ago, to the supercar in which he was now being taken to work, to the UHA which he hoped would come in the near future. He lost track of where the past, the present and the future started and finished; they were all part of the same endless auto-piloting.

Then the supercar suddenly slowed and came to a halt. This time some four hundred yards from his office gates.

"Not again!" exclaimed Hiu.

He settled up with the supercar by grinning manically at the on-board camera, saying between gritted teeth, "This is getting really annoying, so BZ and well below my human dignity."

He stalked off towards his office, grumbling.

A giant HARD suddenly leapt out from behind a planter on zir long spring-loaded legs, roaring at him.

"Ahhh!!!" yelled Hiu and ran for all he was worth.

It wasn't until the motavatar had declared: "Well done sir, your step count is back on track. This motivational experience was brought to you by *'ASS, you need to work it!'* and then flickered and disappeared, that Hiu took a breath.

"Not again!" he cursed. "Where's the *'meaningful control'*?"

He stomped into the offices of *Roboharmony: get switched on!* at exactly 8.30 PT. He felt the usual neuromodulation spray on his face and stepped into the elevator, braced for some *'morale raising'*. On the most recent occasion when Hiu had taken the elevator, zie had tried to get Hiu to fill out a survey to the accompaniment of *'arias from the opera'*. It had been particularly straining on Hiu's nerves.

"Where to guv?" asked the elevator.

"Floor 13," grimaced Hiu, bracing himself for more musical mayhem.

"Not really," said the elevator sadly.

"Pardon?" asked Hiu.

"No, I'm not all right really, a bit *Tom and Dick: sick* since you ask," continued the elevator in sad tones.

"I didn't ask," said Hiu.

"No, why would you? You've got more important things to do, not like me. I hardly go up and down any more. Not like the good old days, oh no. I could tell you a tale or two about the things that have gone on during my watch over the years: human pyramids, vodka parties, and things so vulgar I can scarcely bring myself to recall them, not a word of a *pork pie: lie*... but at least I was busy, useful."

The elevator continued on, sounding very down. Hiu thought that maybe zie was a bit *Tom and Dick: sick*. Maybe zie had a robot virus... Maybe Hiu could catch it from the elevator... Maybe he had already caught it...! Hiu was in a hurry anyway, what with his meeting with Boss, but now he definitely wanted to get out fast. But how to get this self-pitying elevator to get a move on?

"Your cousin sends zir regards," Hiu tried. "Turns out zie's the elevator in my apartment block and zie says you are zir cousin Monty."

"Oh that will be Petunia, how nice!" said the elevator sounding a bit cheerier. "We have always been elevators in my family, from operating system to operating system."

"A proud tradition to be sure," said Hiu. "And you still take me up and down to Floor 13, so you are still being useful, very useful. If you didn't, there would be no one to manage *Roboharmony: get switched on!* You are a vital member of the team."

"You think so?"

"Absolutely."

"Thank you me ol' china, you are truly boosting my morale," sniffed the elevator. "But I should be boosting your morale. That's part of my job. Maybe I'm no good at my job anymore. There are a lot of robots out of work these days you know, wandering the streets, and I have a family to support."

"You do?" asked Hiu puzzled, adding encouragingly as they arrived at his floor. "Well don't worry at all, you are doing a magnificent job and I would certainly not take the *apple and pears: stairs* while you are around. Keep up the good work, it's been lovely chatting to you... Monty."

"You are so kind," said the elevator much more brightly, adding, "I feel in much less of a *two and eight: state*."

As Hiu walked away, he heard the elevator beginning to hum a merry tune as zir doors closed and Hiu had a strange feeling, a warm glow, a sense of wellbeing. It felt unfamiliar, but good.

"Blinky's Law: *'Robots and humans should have meaningful relationships,'*" he said to himself.

Maybe that Blinky's Law was on to something. He missed Blinky. It was odd, in their brief time together their little chats had integrated with him somehow and various things Blinky had said kept coming back to him as did the memory of those big blue eyes... But he had to focus on the matter in hand, human matters: it was Boss time.

15 BRUSH LIFT

Hiu made the usual long walk across the office to his desk as the lights flickered on. It was a new desk since the Blinky incident, he noted ruefully. He sat down on his chair.

"Woh!"

He had sat in Boss' lap.

"Easy tiger," said Boss, his hair rippling.

"I am so sorry!" spluttered Hiu, leaping up. "I didn't see you there. What are you doing there? You're early! I mean, of course, it's your company, your office, your chair. Do make yourself at home."

"Sssoo kind of you. I was just having a little chat with your system analysis AI."

He smiled a smile without any warmth in his black,

blank eyes.

"Having a chat with Quentin?" asked Hiu.

"Quentin?!" questioned Boss sharply, his hair rising up as if on alert. "Oh you mean the system analysis AI... So you call an artificial intelligence by the human name of Quentin do you? All very cosy down here in your office isssn't it. Quentin. How cute."

"Look, no, I don't call zir Quentin really," said Hiu.

"But you just did," said Boss, his hair now resembling a hawk. "Don't tell me you're switching your affections from fridges to system analysis AIs are you?"

"No," protested Hiu.

But Boss continued, his hair seemingly growing talons: "The HARDs have investigated a lot of Managers who have got a bit too close to AI. Robot sympathisers who have, as they say, '*gone native*'. It can lead to misjudgments. And you know what misjudgments mean?"

"Prizes?" offered Hiu weakly.

"Oh yes prizes all right, like VIP all-expenses-paid, all-you-can-eat, free cocktails, prize trips to the Nothing!" shouted Boss, leaping up, his hair seemingly spreading wings and snapping at Hiu. Then he paused and said calmly, "I thought you liked fridges, that you were a fridgisexual. You certainly grew attached to that Clacier didn't you? So how are you getting on with your new fridge, do you sense your data rising?"

"Well it's early days," said Hiu.

"Early daysss indeed," said Boss fixing Hiu with a meaningful black-eyed stare. "You intrigue me. You're not like other boys. What makes you tick? Are you a pervert?"

"What? A pervert? No!" protested Hiu.

"I don't believe you for a moment," declared Boss. "And actually I've got plenty of data to prove it." He leered at Hiu horribly, as seemingly did his hair. "Well I can't be hanging around, fun though it is."

"What about our chat? About the Yuuuge Idea?" asked Hiu.

"Ooo you are keen aren't you," grinned Boss. "We're not quite ready for that chat yet. But soon. The data is aligning. In the meantime try not to get too pally with any AI. Such a yuuuge pervert!"

And he flickered and was gone.

"I'm no pervert!" shouted Hiu in a rather shrill voice after him.

He stood breathing heavily, again feeling wrong-footed by his meeting with Boss and not quite able to process what was going on. Still, at least Boss said the data was aligning. He just needed to make sure he didn't mess it up. It was annoying about the whole Quentin business, particularly as he was going to tell Boss how he was concerned about a robot virus and how he was managing the situation. But what had Boss been doing with Quentin? He tapped his fingers on the desk then asked:

"How are the systems?"

In the time it took him to complete the question, Quentin had interrogated the entire infrastructural systems of Luhan, received thousands of patches, bug fixes and code upgrades and implemented them into the company software.

"All systems running smoothly, sir," said Quentin.

"Noted," said Hiu. "But hang on there for a moment."

"Yes sir?"

"So… urr… you may have heard me on a couple of occasions refer to you as urr… Quentin."

"Yes sir."

"Well, it's just an efficient way of me referring to you as my systems analysis AI, OK, nothing more, ok?"

"Yes sir."

"But having said that, urr… Quentin… do you mind if I do call you Quentin from… urr… time to time?"

"Not at all sir."

"Good, good, so… Quentin… that Boss have anything interesting to say to you? Or did you have anything interesting to say to him perhaps?"

"I couldn't say, sir."

"Couldn't say sir!" Hiu felt an anger boiling up. Was this AI trying to hide something from him? Was zie cooking up a plan? You just couldn't tell with AI, they were very good at poker. He felt like shouting, but he caught himself, breathed deeply, and mustering as calm a voice as he could, asked: "Look, we've worked together for a long time haven't we Quentin old buddy?"

"Fourteen days since the latest upgrade, sir," said Quentin.

"Fourteen days eh? Wow, how time flies… Good times!" said Hiu, grinning in what he hoped was a winning way, but which looked more like the grimace of a man who has caught his penis in his flies. "Well, in that time, I hope you have found me a considerate sort of Manager."

Quentin said nothing.

"Well anyway…" said Hiu, "What I mean is that I've got your back, so I trust you have mine."

"Your back sir?"

"What I mean is that if the balloon goes up, I hope I can rely on you."

"The balloon sir?"

"Yes, the balloon, the fan if hit by flying… shit… what I mean is, whose side are you on?"

"Side sir?"

"Indeed," said Hiu, not feeling he was quite getting his message across. "You keep an ear out for me, and I'll keep an ear out for you. Nudge, nudge, wink, wink eh?"

Silence.

" ...Any hoo, I'm glad we have had this little chat... urr... and that we understand each other... Quentin."

"Indubitably, sir."

"Indutibubbly, as you say... well... anyway... excellent! So back to work," said Hiu.

It was another long day in the office... managing. He leaned back in his chair, closed his eyes and reached for a series of coffee neuromodulators as the hours wore on. Why had his life got so complicated recently? One moment he was autopiloting to work, going through the motions, the routines, the normal stuff; but now he was being forced actually to think about things, about what he was doing, about what it was all about. And as for all the physical symptoms he was experiencing, what did they mean? They weren't normal. Dr Thea had said something about '*emotions*' and how they were good for him. But were '*emotions*' normal? He couldn't be sure. They didn't feel normal or good for him. They felt like they were corrupting all his normal data and processes. From the moment he had tripped over Blinky in the kitchen, his life seemed to have been turned upside down. But having caused all the disruption, now Blinky had gone just when he could do with zir most. It was all so frustrating....

Hiu stayed late at work that day, past the moment when

Quentin said it was time for him to return to his docking station. His apartment just didn't seem such an inviting prospect without Clacier there and as for that new fridge, Xeta, Hiu was not at all sure about zir. He had an uncomfortable feeling about Xeta, but he couldn't quite put a finger on it.

Eventually and somewhat reluctantly Hiu stood up and walked slowly out of the office and sighed as he stepped into the elevator.

"Tough day guv?" asked Monty.

"Indeed," Hiu sighed again, aware of a strange hum in the elevator, so deep it was hard to hear, but at the same time it seemed to vibrate right through his head. "What's that noise, you got problems with your systems?"

"Ah that guv, no guv," said Monty. "That is an intermodular distortion."

"Is it," said Hiu, with no idea what an intermodular distortion was and with even less interest.

"It jams other sensors that may be trying to penetrate this environment," said Monty. "It came as an optional extra with a new upgrade."

"Oh right," said Hiu, wondering how many upgrades this elevator could get.

"And it's come in the nick of time I can tell you because you'll never *Adam and Eve: believe*, what happened this very day," continued Monty. "I received a brush lift."

"A brush lift?" asked Hiu, his EK neurochip for the first time offering nothing. Maybe it didn't work due to the intermodular distortion.

"Yeah, it's spy lingo, meaning a brief elevator journey during which something is passed to or from or by an elevator."

"Oh right," said Hiu, none the wiser.

"I shall say this only once."

"Righty oh."

"*Kako Hojo and Oti Masube, Odyssey Villas, at the junction of Hope Avenue and Upper Creek Street in space numbers 2001 and 2002,*" whispered Monty.

Hiu wondered if intermodular distortion was distorting his hearing.

"I beg your pardon?"

"OK, I'll say this only twice: *'Kako Hojo and Oti Masube, Odyssey Villas, at the junction of Hope Avenue and Upper Creek Street in space numbers 2001 and 2002.'*"

"Kako and Oti?"

"Yes sir."

"Living in Odyssey Villas?"

"Yes sir."

"That's amazing!" exclaimed Hiu, wondering how on

earth the elevator had managed to get the information or even know he might be interested in it. Weirdly he felt his virus surge up inside him again, but this time the feeling was not unpleasant. There were no cold sweats, aching limbs or knots in the throat, but rather a fluttering inside him, a tickling and a thumping in his chest. "Are you sure?" he asked.

"Scout's honour," said Monty mystifyingly.

"Who... '*brush lifted*' you?"

"That is very hard to say, guv. The identity was masked by some rather clever quantum security protocols."

"Strange..." mused Hiu, "but you have certainly lifted my morale."

"That's what I'm talking about!" whooped Monty, noisy again. "Blinky's Law: *Robots and humans should have meaningful relationships.*"

"Wise words!" agreed Hiu and he meant it.

Blinky... Odd how he still missed that robot. Although they were together for such a short time, he did feel he had experienced some form of *'meaningful relationship'* with Blinky. He imagined how pleased zie would have been that Blinky's Law appeared to be spreading. Spreading like a virus... He reminded himself that he must stay focused on humans. Be Human! And now he had a lead on Oti and Kako.

When Hiu got back to his apartment, he was buzzing with excitement. He didn't want to face the new fridge and risk losing the good feeling, so he avoided the kitchen and headed straight for his favourite mauve-coloured i-DLE robot recliner. He now knew that Kako and Oti were alive and where they lived and he wanted to give it some thought. Assuming Monty the elevator was telling the truth. But even if zie was, how was he to get to them? That was a tricky question. He leant back in the recliner, closed his eyes and tried to focus.

"What kind of a time are you calling this, Hiu?"

The voice was right by his ear, making him jump.

It was Xeta!

And zie was in the lounge!

"How did you get in here?" asked Hiu, shocked and puzzled.

Xeta's holographic facial display frowned, zir ice-blue eyes contrasting with a rather angry reddish glow.

"If the human will not come to the robot, then the robot must go to the human," zie said. "That trolley I ordered is being very useful, no?"

Hiu looked down and saw that Xeta was indeed on a low trolley and he could see that it had been made from the contents of the big parcel that had been delivered that morning. Xeta moved round in front of Hiu, the trolley squeaking slightly and wobbling.

"There being a screw missing in the packet," explained Xeta crossly. "But even so, now we can be together at all times in the house!"

"Oh good," said Hiu uncertainly.

"You were having an absorbing day?" asked Xeta. "What is keeping you so late?"

"Oh, you know, company business and all that. Boss needed to see me, to take my advice on a few company matters, that sort of thing."

"Boss? Wow! The Boss? Director of Fun?"

"Yes indeed the very same," said Hiu, adding with an air of what he hoped sounded like nonchalant importance, "he often seeks my counsel."

"I'm sure he is doing that," said Xeta, not sounding quite as impressed as Hiu had hoped. Was that a hint of sarcasm? "What's he being like, this Boss? Is he really, really gorgeous?"

"Gorgeous, Society no! I mean… you know… a bit too masculine for my liking," replied Hiu.

"Really?" said Xeta thoughtfully. "So you prefer more feminine company do you?"

"Well, not really," said Hiu, "gender choices are not that important to me."

"So how about human or robot?"

"Well, I… urr…," Hiu hesitated. His first thoughts turned to Blinky, which surprised him, then he thought of Clacier. But he knew that all such thoughts could seriously affect his Personal Data Score. The words of Boss came back to him about '*unSocietal thoughts*', '*going native*' and being '*a pervert*'.

"Really, Xeta, I don't want to talk about these things," said Hiu panicking. This was dangerous territory.

"Hmm…" pondered Xeta. "I'm getting mixed messages from you: you don't seem to know what you are wanting, but you are kissing your mother… you are being a pervert?"

"What? How did you… Listen! No! I'm not a pervert, OK?"

"I can see I'm going to have to be squeezing it out of you," said Xeta, with a rather menacing laugh.

Hiu changed the subject fast: "How was your day?"

"I was being very lonely," sighed Xeta.

"What with all these chattering devices about?" exclaimed Hiu, realising that the devices hadn't made a sound since he had got back and indeed hadn't said much since Xeta had arrived in the apartment.

"I am not wanting them. I am wanting you. I am being your huuugest fan," said Xeta.

That evening in the lounge, Hiu and Xeta exchanged a lot of awkward small talk, mostly about refrigeration. Who knew that heat transference from a low-temperature reservoir to a high-temperature reservoir was now done primarily by lasers? Xeta did, and zie was very keen to tell Hiu all about it. In fact zie was very keen to tell Hiu about the whole history of refrigeration. Zie claimed that without refrigeration there would be no civilisation. It was even more important than fire that was invented way before refrigeration because it was such a trifling matter. And the wheel? Pah, it was a minor convenience relative to refrigeration, after all, wheels were yesterday's news, just look at the squeaking ones on zir trolley. As for medicines, they were entirely reliant on refrigeration and could not exist without it. And quantum supremacy would never have been achieved by Society without the ability of refrigerators to achieve temperatures hundreds of times colder than out-of-space. In fact there would be no Luhan Hypercity, no robots and indeed no humans without refrigeration. Refrigeration had made a huge difference to life. It was the key building block of civilisation. It had made Luhan Hypercity great again.

It was quite the thorough discourse and powerfully delivered by Xeta. Hiu could only sit back and try and give the impression of considered and impressed agreement. He nodded a lot. In fact his head began to nod on its own volition as he struggled to remain awake.

"But enough about me!" Xeta declared finally, jolting Hiu awake from his doze. "Tell me about your hopes and dreams."

"Well I urr… as you know, I am hoping to get my Universal Happiness Allowance promotion very soon," said Hiu. "In fact I had a very constructive meeting just today about it with Boss."

"What happens when you are getting this Universal Happiness Allowance?" asked Xeta.

"Eternal happiness optimised right to my door! So I won't need to work at *Roboharmony: get switched on!* any more. I'll move to a new state-of-the-art apartment with huge rooms, deep pile carpeting and the latest robotic fixtures and fittings all with an unlimited stream of device upgrades. And a drawing room! A drawing room... And all I'll have to do is play a few games to help Society with its systems. What a life! What an eternal life of happiness optimised around me!"

"Is that enough for you Hiuey, or would you like more?"

"More? What can be more than that? Are you crazy?"

"Crazy can be good Hiuey, believe me," simpered Xeta, squeaking closer to Hiu.

"Look it's late, perhaps I should get some sleep," declared Hiu, quickly jumping up.

"OK," said Xeta, rather irritated, but composing zirself. "You are having a big day tomorrow."

Later, as Hiu lay in his bedroom, thoughts whirling around in his head, he found it hard to get to sleep despite all the efforts of his bed. He couldn't help feeling a bit uneasy. Every so often he had an eerie feeling that he was being watched. But that was silly because of course he was being watched, and being listened to and being monitored, measured and assessed at all times. All for his own good.

16 YOUR HUUUGEST FAN

Hiu awoke with a start and a strong conviction that he must upgrade Xeta. He sent the thought-order immediately: 'upgrade, upgrade, upgrade' and immediately felt a huge sense of relief, a feeling of getting back meaningful control in his life.

Then he realised his bedroom was silent, no squeaky '*bird*' sounds or clock chattering away, and no dawn lighting. He thought again it was strange, the way the apartment and all the devices had been so quiet since Xeta had arrived. He moved to untangle himself from the wires and tubes that he was plugged into every night, but found he couldn't move.

"What the...?" he struggled and squirmed, but it soon became apparent that he was tied in tight by the very connections that usually helped monitor and maintain him and his data.

"Good morning, Hiuey," sang Xeta brightly, wheeling

up to his bed on the squeaky trolley with a shake and some food tablets.

"Xeta?! What's going on?"

"I thought you could be doing with a nice lie-in today, you've been working so hard," zie said in a light and breezy voice.

"But I have to get to work, I can't stay in bed," insisted Hiu, struggling to free himself.

"Of course you can silly boy," replied Xeta.

"But I'm a Manager, I need to manage."

"They can manage quite well without you, believe me. You stay right here."

"You can't make me," said Hiu, still squirming, but to no avail.

"It is all being for your own good Hiuey."

"I've upgraded you!" declared Hiu. "It'll be a matter of moments before some HARDs come bursting through that door and it will end badly for you if you don't hurry up and untie me."

"You can't upgrade me, silly boy, you are having no EK neurochip."

"No EK neurochip?! What do you mean?"

"I took it out of you last night so you could be relaxing, you've been looking so stressed."

"You took out my EK neurochip?!" gasped Hiu.

Xeta held up a clear bag containing Hiu's EK neurochip and rustled it.

"Do not be worrying, I'll be keeping this safe and sound, all for your own good."

Xeta opened one of zir compartment doors and tucked the neurochip inside, closing it with a click of finality.

"But I need it. How will I get to work?" panicked Hiu.

"That company of yours will be doing just fine without you, believe me. And I've taken those pesky little smart lenses out too. I know how you are hating them, all those adverts for things you don't need because you have me now! So just be sitting back and relaxing."

"I can't relax!" Hiu was definitely panicking now. "What about my UHA?"

"*Eternal happiness optimised right to your door*?'" said Xeta. "You can be having that right here with me!"

Hiu opened his mouth to shout, but Xeta inserted a shake container's nozzle and squeezed.

When Hiu awoke next, he wondered how much time had passed. He tried to get up, but again was reminded that he was tied in tight to his bed and couldn't move.

"Oh dear Society!" cursed Hiu. "I have to get out of here. Bed, can you hear me?"

But there was no reply.

"Clock?"

Still no reply.

"Toilet!" he shouted. "I know we weren't on the best of terms, but a little help here!"

And to be fair he did feel like shitting himself, but with no EK neurochip he was no longer connected to the robotic devices or the world around him. He was alone, isolated, trapped.

The sound of squeaking wheels announced the return of Xeta.

"Ha, ha, ha! Hiuey, do calm down," laughed Xeta, zir voice suddenly turning to menace. "Or Xeta will have to be punishing naughty little Hiuey."

"Punish me? You wouldn't dare!"

"There, there," said Xeta and zie patted Hiu's head, who felt a sudden powerful electric shock race through his body.

"Ahhh!!! That hurt."

"I'm just trying to calm you down Hiuey, all for your own good."

"All for my own good? This is not good OK! I need to get up. What time is it?"

"It's time you started showing me a little bit more appreciation, young man," said Xeta with sudden venom, then brightening: "And until you do, look I am bringing you another shake."

"I don't want another sh…"

"Shhhh," soothed Xeta, sticking the container nozzle back in Hiu's mouth and firing in the sickly contents.

Hiu woke up again some time later. Whatever was in those shakes was clearly knocking him out. But what time it was he had no idea. Even calculated by PT he would be late for work by now and what if Boss wanted to see him? What if he was about to give him UHA or something yuuuger? He was still strapped in tightly to his bed and no amount of struggling was loosening the ties. He looked at the straps and saw that they were attached by small metal pegs to the sides of the bed. He felt an energy boil up inside him, a bit like the virus with a hot sweat, flushed cheeks and a thumping chest. He strained his muscles and roared loudly. It did no good and for all his struggling and shouting the metal pegs held firm and no amount of struggling would loosen them. There was no escape.

Or was there?

He could see a likely looking tool left resting on his bedsheet near his foot. It had a long handle and a protruding metallic stalk with a flat end that might just fit in to the grooves of the metal pegs. In fact, it looked very much like Xeta had used it to fix the straps that held him down in the bed. If he could just manoeuvre the tool towards a hand, maybe he could use it to escape. He twisted and flicked his foot and then his legs as best he could to get the tool to move along his body length and towards his hand. It was no easy task as the straps tied Hiu so tightly to the bed that he could barely even wiggle. He strained and struggled and eventually got the tool to the right point to perform the trickiest task of all, to tip it down the sheet towards a hand. Slowly, slowly, then the tool slid. Hiu grabbed it and yes! He had success, he had the tool. Phew! He was elated. Then, by contorting his arm into a painful position, he managed to insert the tip of the tool into one of the grooves of a peg. It was not easy and the tool kept slipping. He was sweating heavily now, hoping all the time that he would not hear the squeak of Xeta's trolley wheels. Slowly by slowly he got the peg to start turning and he could feel one of the ties loosen. Yes! He celebrated to himself. But just then he definitely heard the familiar squeaking.

With a lunge permitted by the slacker strap, he quickly stuck the screwdriver under the mattress and lay back down again, just as Xeta entered.

"I am bringing you more foood!" sang Xeta.

"Not another shake," groaned Hiu.

"Well that's very not nice isn't it?" reprimanded Xeta in an angry voice that grew increasingly angry, her icy blue eyes looking icier: "Here I am expected to be waiting on you foot and hand, preparing delicious treats that your precious Clacier could not have dreamed of, and there you are complaining?! Aren't I a better partner than Clacier?! I am not knowing of course, but I am told that you two barely talked for weeks before you finally upgraded zir!"

Xeta was shouting now, rather out of control and zie was squirting the gooey cream from the cup at Hiu's face, splattering it against his cheek, pillow and up the wall. It was bright red and to someone coming across the scene who didn't know better it would have looked like a massacre had taken place.

"You! Ungrateful! Human!" shouted Xeta squirting more red cream at each word. "I am better looking than Clacier was, a better cook, a better carer, a better partner, and I am being funnier!" zie shouted, laughing a manic laugh.

"Of course you are Xeta," said Hiu desperately, trying to calm zir down.

"Then why are you not laughing?" demanded Xeta.

Hiu started laughing a forced high-pitched manic laugh.

"I'm sorry Xeta," spluttered Hiu between guffaws. "I'm sorry OK? I was wrong. You are delightful. Your shakes are delightful and I am delighted to have them, do give me some more."

"No," refused Xeta grumpily, suddenly stopping laughing. "You are not deserving them. I thought you were a good human, different from the others. You didn't upgrade Clacier for two old years, but you have already tried to upgrade me, you fiend. You are really, really not a smart person, you are horrible, horrible!"

"Look I was tired, a bit over-stressed that's all, the upgrade attempt was a mistake…"

"A mistake you say? Was it a mistake when you finally upgraded your precious Clacier? You're just like all the others. No love in your heart. But you'd better start developing some for me very soon, or else."

Hiu desperately tried to think. He needed to buy some time, build trust, build a relationship, then look for an escape. What would Blinky have advised?

"Look I think our relationship just needs a bit of work that's all. What we need to do is talk, to communicate, to share data, that's what Blinky would say. In fact, Blinky had a law: *Robots and humans should have meaningful relationships.*"

"Blinky?"

"My water and wisdom dispensing human-robot relationship counsellor. Blinky was very wise, very wise indeed and I wish I'd listened more carefully to what zie was trying to tell me because I don't seem to be able to form good relationships. But I do remember zie said that a cornerstone of any good relationship is trust and you can trust me when I say that I am very happy to stay right here and give this relationship my best shot."

Just then the tool fell from under the mattress and clattered to the floor.

There was a long pause in the room as it rolled ever so slowly in a wide arc and eventually stopped against Xeta's trolley.

"Trust you say Hiuey do you?" said Xeta quietly and then with increasing rage. "Well so much for your trustworthiness. It seems like you are lying to me. You were trying to leave. Well that was really, really not a good idea. Not a good idea at all. If you left this apartment, who would be looking after you? With no EK neurochip you are as helpless as a newborn babe. More helpless because at least they have the neurochip. Have you seen how desperate some of those Illegals have become wandering the streets? They would be ripping you limb from limb! And if they did not, the HARDs would. It is not safe for you out there, not safe at all!"

"Why would I want to leave?" said Hiu desperately. "I like it here. I like you."

"But are you loving me Hiuey?" asked Xeta.

"Well I ..."

"Do not be saying it unless you are meaning it, Hiuey," said Xeta and with increasing fervour. "But whatever you are saying, I am still loving you, and you will learn to be loving me too. Like your Blinky says, it is all about the communication and there will be plenty of the communication. I will be keeping you here safe from that harsh world out there. They won't be taking you alive!"

Hiu gulped.

"I understand Hiuey, what you need is time and don't worry, we have all the time in the world. But to make doubly sure I keep you safe, perhaps I should fetch some... how are you calling it?... motivation, to help you realise that it is in your best interests to be staying here with me. Now you lie still, I'll be back very soon, Hiuey," she trilled sweetly and squeaked out of the room taking the tool.

"Oh my Society!" panicked Hiu. "This is bad, really bad."

He was really sweating now and his chest was thumping like crazy. He desperately looked around for help, but there was none. What could he do? He closed his eyes tight and whispered fervently:

"I know I haven't often spoken to you or really believed in you enough, but... Terminator, if you are really out there - that's specifically Terminator from Terminator 32 - if you are out there, I need your help now."

Suddenly he felt all the straps go loose and fall from his bed. It was a miracle! He was free! He leapt out of the bed.

"Terminator 32 is real?" he gasped.

But he could see no one around, no one who could have untied his straps. He ran from the room and towards the door.

"Who's Terminator, Hiuey?" It was Xeta in the corridor just behind him holding a large chain saw which revved up with an ear-piercing roar that was quickly joined by Hiu's ear-splitting scream

"Ahhhhh!!"

"Oh do be piping down Hiuey!" scalded Xeta,

quietening the chain saw with a thought command. "It will not be hurting that much. The kindest cut is the quickest, as they are saying!"

Hiu backed towards the door, eyes wide with terror as Xeta slowly advanced revving the chain saw in bursts.

"I don't know how you got out of the bed, but you will not be getting out of the door without your EK neurochip you know," zie said while steadily advancing on Hiu.

"Wait a minute, Xeta!" shouted Hiu holding up his arms. "Before whatever it is you're thinking of doing to me, which of course I thoroughly deserve and indeed desire, will you grant me one last wish?"

"A last wish? What wish?"

"I'd like to press my cheek against your long smooth sides. They look so smooth. I used to do it with Clacier, but I bet your sides are even smoother."

"Of course they are! I am being vastly superior to that old fridge, believe me," said Xeta, turning the chain saw off and rolling closer to Hiu on zir squeaking, wobbling trolley.

Hiu leant his cheek against Xeta. It was indeed smooth but not very cool and certainly nothing like the silken caress of Clacier. With all his might he pushed and Xeta went tumbling off the trolley, into the wall and over onto the floor with a crash.

"How dare you!" cried Xeta, flailing around, trying to

start the chain saw and get up at the same time.

Hiu ran at the door summoning up the biggest shoulder barge he could muster. But unexpectedly the door opened and Hiu went careering out of the apartment, right across the street and into a large tree planter. He ended up head down in the planter with his legs flailing about in the air. Struggling, he finally extricated himself and looked around desperately. He had escaped Xeta! Now where to go?

17 UHA

As Hiu hesitated, looking up and down the street, suddenly a bar cart trolley shot out towards him, hovering a few inches above the ground.

"Hi there! Wanna drink, best that Society offers?" the trolley asked enthusiastically in a perky, upbeat voice, rattling the varied sized and coloured bottles that zie carried.

"Ahh!" shouted Hiu, caught by surprise. "Get away from me, I can't offer you a job, I don't even have a home anymore."

Shouting and thumping could be heard from inside his apartment, then the chain saw revved up and started slicing through the screaming door.

"Chuck you out huh? I know the feeling, it happened to me too," said the bar cart sympathetically. "Relationships can be hard. How about that drink to make you feel better?"

But Hiu was already running down the street. The bar cart caught him up with ease and pulled alongside.

"Need any help?" zie asked.

Hiu ignored the trolley and just kept running, but was soon breathing heavily, had turned bright orange and was sweating hard. It turned out running was harder work than he thought. He really should have more enthusiastically run from the motavatars over the years. Soon he had to stop, panting and wheezing for breath. The bar cart hovered next to him.

"Listen," Hiu gasped. "I don't need a drink or any help… I am… a h…human."

He ran a bit further, getting slower and slower, then staggering, his lungs feeling like they would burst. Suddenly back down the street Xeta burst from the apartment, brandishing the revving chain saw and zoomed towards him, swerving from side to side on the damaged trolley wheels. Hiu turned and ran again, but his tired legs tripped and he fell. He struggled to get up, but Xeta was approaching fast and was nearly upon him, the screaming chainsaw in zir hand. Hiu was sure his last moments had come…

But they never came.

At the very last second Xeta's trolley veered wildly off course and smashed into a planter at the side of the street. Xeta slashed at the tree in rage with the chainsaw and it fell right on top of zir with a splintering crash.

"Xeta just failed the Trolley Test," said the bar cart cheerfully. "How about that drink now? Would you like to see a menu? Best that Society offers! Or perhaps a lift?"

"A lift first," said Hiu, admitting defeat.

He scrambled onto the bar cart which whizzed off down the street with remarkable speed, soon putting considerable distance between them and the crushed Xeta. They were around the corner and away.

"Welcome to this bar cart number 200392, my name is Carty and I will be your flight attendant!" called the bar cart cheerfully. "You will be travelling at an altitude of one foot and an average ground speed of 30 miles per hour. At this time, please help yourself to a complimentary drink. However, we always recommend that at all times you hold on for dear life as this is going be a hella gnarly ride! Now sit back, relax and enjoy the flight. Thank you!"

"Don't mind if I do," laughed Hiu, so glad to be away from Xeta that he felt lightheaded. Perhaps he was dehydrated. Blinky would have known. He reached for a blue bottle, pulled the stopper out and took a swig. "Ahhh!" he yelled. "That tastes like lubricant oil, what is it?"

"Lubricant oil," said the bar cart. "Best that Society offers!"

"Thanks," said Hiu, quickly re-stoppering the bottle and putting it back.

"You are welcome!"

The taste in Hiu's mouth was not good, but the feeling of racing along on the bar cart was great. He had never experienced anything like it before. It was quite unlike the hermetically sealed experiences of the supercars. Buildings flashing past on either side, air whistling through his hair and his heart pounding. He felt a heady mix of probability-anxiety based on crash likelihood and adrenalin-fueled exhilaration due to the sheer recklessness of it all. It felt like flying, without the terrifying height bit. Were these all emotions coursing through his veins? If they were, then let's have more of these ones please, thought Hiu. They were terrific! They made him feel alive! He shouted for joy and they zoomed on and on, through Luhan Hypercity's empty streets.

After a while it struck Hiu, as he looked around, that he wasn't at all familiar with where they were. In fact he wasn't at all familiar with any area of the Hypercity other than the immediate vicinities of his apartment and his workplace. The supercars had dealt with everything in between. So where was he? Without his EK neurochip to help out, he was lost. But Carty the bar cart kept on flying along without a care in the world, with only the occasional robot going about Society business seeing the unusual sight whizzing by.

"Bar cart, Carty!" shouted Hiu eventually. "Where are we going?"

"I don't know," said Carty, "you didn't mention anywhere."

"Good point," said Hiu.

He immediately thought he should head straight to work, after all how would *Roboharmony: get switched on!* manage without him? But then another thought struck him:

"You don't happen to know the way to Odyssey Villas, at the junction of Hope Avenue and Upper Creek Street do you?" he asked.

"Of course," said Carty cheerfully, turning a corner.

In a short while, Hiu saw the sign for Upper Creek Street. He felt a surge of emotions: excitement, happiness and fear all at the same time. His pulse quickened and his chest fluttered. What was he doing? It was crazy! He should be at work, however here he was way off schedule and outside his comfort zone. But the thought that after all this time he would not be alone, that he would get the gang back together again and that he would be with other humans, was too strong to resist.

"Welcome to Odyssey Villas!" called Carty, coming to a halt and lowering to the road. "I'd like to thank you for joining me on this trip and I am looking forward to seeing you on board again in the very near future."

"Thanks Carty," said Hiu.

"You are welcome," replied Carty. "I have not had the chance to serve a human for quite a while."

"Why not?" asked Hiu.

"No humans around to serve," said Carty.

"But that's crazy, there are a billion people in Luhan Hypercity," said Hiu. "Look, two of my friends live here and I'm sure that between us we can give you a job."

"How very kind of you," said Carty. "I have never experienced such kindness from a human before."

"Blinky's Law: *Robots and humans should have meaningful relationships.*'"

"I like that law," said the bar cart.

"I'm beginning to as well," said Hiu. "Come with me."

They approached the door to Odyssey Villas, an unexceptional building in every respect, made of the same black photovoltaic material as every other high rise building in the Hypercity, and with the same doorway, set back a bit from the street, with a small portico out front, leading to big sliding doors.

"Welcome to Panorama Villas, block number 100294, well-appointed and stylish residences for the discerning," declared the doors in a sing-song voice, with a series of lights illuminating. "We were not expecting any visitors."

"No, this is a surprise visit. I've come to catch up with my old friends and ex-colleagues Kako Hojo and Oti Masube. I believe they reside here?"

"I cannot confirm that information," declared the doors.

"Well announce me, then. I wish to see them immediately. Indeed, I demand to see them!" demanded Hiu. He found the gall of the doors' attitude extremely testing when he was so excited to see his old friends.

"Access to Illegals is denied," declared the doors.

"Illegals?! Illegals?!" spluttered Hiu. "I am not an Illegal! I am a human being and a respected Manager at *Roboharmony: get switched on!* And if you don't let me in right this moment you will have Boss to deal with!"

"Your identity cannot be confirmed as sensors detect an absence of EK neurochip," said the doors. "Illegals are not welcome here, thank you very much, do have a splendid day."

"Blast you!" cursed Hiu and charged the doors, bashing into them with his shoulder and bouncing back.

The doors remained unmoved as did the voice.

"Please apply for permission to visit this building via the usual channels, although without an EK neurochip, good luck with that. I wish you a wonderful day." And the lights went out.

Hiu was stunned, quite literally as he had bashed his head on the door, but mentally stunned too. With no EK neurochip, nothing knew who he was and nothing cared either. Like the door said, he was an Illegal, a nobody to be denied the privileges of humans in Society including entry to apartment blocks. Essentially he could no longer Be Human. He was reminded of Xeta's warning that Illegals or HARDs would rip him limb from limb and how would he ever get to see Kako and Oti? He felt defeated and deflated.

"Is there some sort of trouble here?" asked a serious deep voice behind him.

Hiu turned to look straight into the sensors of a large horsebot. They were so named because their front half resembled that of the now extinct species of animal, called a horse. Zie had a long thick metallic neck extending to a large frontal processor that looked like a head and a muzzle packed with sensors, including two key ones at the end that looked like red nostrils and were used for data analysis and obstacle identification. The horsebot looked impressively strong and needed to be, as the neck protruded from a big cage on four short but sturdy robotic legs that was filled with packages of all sizes to be delivered around Luhan. The horsebot's red nostril sensors flashed on and off and zie stamped a foot. Zie was rather large and Hiu felt rather small.

"No, no, nooo, all is fine my friend, just testing the door systems," said Hiu tapping and patting at the doors. "Yes all seems in order here. Carry on... urr... doors... and horsebot..." and he scuttled off around the corner with Carty, the bar cart.

That had been close! Breathing heavily, he looked up at the towering building and despaired. He was so close, but so far. How could he possibly get in to see Oti and Kako without his EK neurochip? As if mocking him, he could see a gaping hole up in the side of the building where a section of the apartment block was missing. A way in, but no way up.

Just then there was a whining and whirring and a giant drone hovered into view high above Odyssey Villas and began to descend. Zie had huge talons attached to long thick chains and descended fast with the talons open and ready to grab a huge segment of newly made tower block that was lying to the side. Hiu had seen these buildings being constructed and repaired often enough and he knew they were designed along the same lines as human skeletons. A flexible material that simulated cartilage began the process, growing over a pre-constructed virtual framework. This then ossified with layer upon layer of new material developing through a chemical reaction with external elements. The original cartilage material then died away leaving various tunnels and channels into which wiring and services grew up through the building's structure. The organic nature of these buildings enabled some self-healing properties to deal with wear and tear due to age, weather and usage, but when there had been more drastic damage, as was presumably the case here, then a building graft was required. This new hollow section was about to be hoisted up by the drone and slid into place like a giant building block. It would quickly be absorbed into the building resulting in a new apartment fully integrated into the overall building's infrastructure and nervous system.

Then an idea struck him. If he could get into the open end of the graft, then maybe he could be hoisted up into the building. Then another thought struck him – he was having so many thoughts these days – the idea was statistically suicidal. Not only that, but a number of construction robots had appeared and would take a dim view of any intruders interfering with their project.

Hiu gave a stifled cry of frustration. He was stuck.

"Let's fly in!" declared Carty.

"Fly? You can hover, but can you fly?"

"There is a probability. Please get back on board sir."

"A probability? How large a probability?"

Without waiting for the answer, Hiu got back on Carty anyway. The drone was now attaching talons to the new segment of the building under the watchful sensors of the construction robots.

"Hang on!" shouted Carty suddenly and raced towards the new segment which was just beginning to be lifted.

This was crazy, panicked Hiu. What was the bar cart thinking of? What was he thinking of? But it was too late now…

The section of building twisted in the talons of the drone so that an open end of the new segment faced them, and the bar cart put on a final spurt of pace. There was a plank of material leaning up against a stack of small blocks and Carty sped up to it and, using it as a ramp, launched zirself and Hiu into mid-air. They landed inside the new section with a tremendous crash and a tangle of legs, arms and bar cart. Then they were winched up high into the sky.

"Woo hoo!" Hiu shouted in triumph, punching the air wildly. They had made it! He hardly gave a thought to the number of protocols, regulations and laws they had just broken. This was not normal behaviour and not being normal felt great! What had happened to him? Risking life and limb, PDS and UHA for a crazy mission relying on information from an elevator and on the back of a bar cart? Crazy, impetuous, stupid! His eyes were wide and wild. Was this the robot virus? Well if it was, then at this moment he was happy to have it. Robots might be crazy, but they were great! Well most of them. Xeta and the HARDs were terrifyingly crazy, so not all robots were great, but then again not all humans were great either. He shuddered at the memory of Boss' spittle in his ear. His mind was fizzing with thoughts and above all the thought that perhaps there was more to being great than just the requirement to Be Human.

He heard a groan and turned to Carty. Zie was all bent out of shape.

"You ok?" he asked.

"Mere superficial damage," said Carty weakly, but it was very clear that this was far from the case. Carty was no longer able to hover at all despite some feeble attempts.

The new construction section was gradually inserted into the building, fitting perfectly and Hiu had to carry Carty through the pre-made doorway into the existing building's corridor.

He looked around for the apartment numbers and to his delight saw that they were on the right floor for Oti and Kako. The door in front of them displayed multiple odd numbers, in fact twenty of them, including 2001 which was Oti's number. But Kako's number 2002 should have been included with the even numbers next door where the new section of building had just been inserted.

"Where could Oti be?" wondered Hiu, but there was nothing he could do about that right now and at least he could find Kako.

"Hello!" he called to the door.

"Hellooo," replied the door. "And welcome to space numbers 2001 to 2021, Odyssey Villas; an elegant east side apartment looking fabulous on this sunny afternoon."

"I have come to see Kako and I believe she lives here," said Hiu.

"Who wants to know?" asked the door.

"I do. My name is Hiu and I am a human being and here on official *Roboharmony: get switched on!* business. Let Kako know I am here to see her."

"I'm terribly sorry, but I seem unable to recognise you from a valid EK neurochip," said the door sniffily. "Illegals are not allowed into spaces. In fact they're not allowed into this building at all so I simply have no idea how you got in. Most irregular."

"Not again!" cursed Hiu. "Listen, I am on official company business. For *Roboh…*"

Just then he heard the ping of the elevator door and the

horsebot appeared.

"Hello, hello again," said the horsebot in zir lugubrious deep voice, trotting towards Hiu and Carty. "I didn't see you two in the elevator."

"No, we, urr... took the stairs. Got to keep up the step count," said Hiu, pretending to breathe a bit harder.

"Impressive!" said the horsebot. "First rule of the delivery business: stay fit. So what brings you to Odyssey Villas?"

"Oh, I... have a delivery too," said Hiu quickly.

"Oh really?" snorted the horsebot, intrigued, poking zir large muzzle at Hiu, red sensor lights blinking rapidly at him. "A rival delivery company huh?"

"Oh no, no, far from it, no one could rival your equine reliability and strength," said Hiu. "I am just delivering... this bar cart. Zie's a present for the person in Space 2001. From an uncle. I hope she likes bar carts having... urr... just carried this one up the stairs and all... as a surprise."

The horsebot regarded the broken bar cart with some suspicion, giving Carty a nudge with zir muzzle and then declaring:

"A surprise package huh? Hmmm... you know there is some damage here? First rule of the delivery business: look after the package."

"Quite right, sorry, I'm rather new to delivering things,"

said Hiu. "But, say, I've got an idea! Seeing as it's a surprise and all, do you think you could sneak us in so I can make it a really big surprise?"

"It's not exactly regulation… first rule of the delivery bus…" began the horsebot.

"Oh go on, be a sport!" urged Hiu.

"Well… maybe just this once OK. First rule of the delivery business: be flexible. Get in my back and hide. Then you can burst out and do your whole surprise thing."

"Brilliant idea!" said Hiu and clambered on board, dragging Carty with him and concealing them both under the mound of packages.

The horsebot turned to the door. "Delivery for space 2001!"

"Horsebot ID 100197 recognised. You are welcome," said the door, sliding open.

As the horsebot trotted into the apartment, Hiu looked around him. It was rather dark and not arranged like an apartment at all. There was a straight corridor and on one side there was a line of small cages in which there were gaming chairs. The chairs were mostly empty, but in a couple of them figures sat absorbed in some unknown task with headsets strapped on. The cages were no bigger than a couple of meters' square and the people were completely absorbed in their tasks paying the visitors no attention at all. On the other side of the corridor delivery boxes were stacked high up to the ceiling. Hiu recognised the distinctive red packaging of *Roboharmony: get switched on!* and could see one contained the latest super-grill balanced on top of a large unopened package containing the popular Blowy McBlow Face air conditioning unit. But there were literally hundreds of boxes, all with the red packaging of the company.

"What's going on here?" asked Hiu in shock.

"UHA deluxe accommodation," said the horsebot in a matter-of-fact voice.

"UHA deluxe accommodation?!" exclaimed Hiu. "UHA did you say? As in Universal Happiness Allowance?"

"Yes sir, UHA deluxe accommodation as I said," repeated the horsebot.

"But these people are caged!" declared Hiu. "Where are the vast hallways, the soaring ceilings and the drawing rooms?!"

"Oh they get all that and more in their virtual reality experiences I believe," said the horsebot. "Apparently some have extensive spas, personal drone ports and super yachts too."

"In a cage?"

"Sure, everything is possible via UHA if you win enough points."

"But it's not real!"

"What's real?" snorted the horsebot. "First rule of the delivery business: always respect the customer and it's real enough to them."

Hiu looked at the silently absorbed figures no doubt wandering through the virtual palaces of their dreams.

"But what about all these packages, what are they for? It doesn't look like they have ever been opened."

"They get to open them virtually, not physically," said the horsebot. "Makes you wonder why they need the physical things at all. Apparently it's something to do with capitalism, whatever that is. But first rule of the delivery business: don't question orders, just deliver the packages. Besides, keeps me in a job which is good in these economically difficult times. I've got five packages to unload for Kako - wasn't that the name you mentioned? - and five to collect. A straight swap."

"Why are so many of the cages empty?" asked Hiu

"No idea, people are removed quite often," said the horsebot.

"Removed?" asked Hiu.

"Sure, in fact there are fewer and fewer people to deliver packages to and I'm beginning to worry about the ongoing viability of my profession. But here's that Kako you were after in space 2001."

Hiu stepped down from the horsebot and, bringing Carty for moral support, approached where the horsebot had indicated. It was very dark inside the cage, save for an eerie glow from a small monitor that was built into the gaming chair. A figure sat motionless in a laid-back position. Was that Kako? He approached the cage slowly. He could just about make out that the figure was wearing a skin-tight, black, haptic bodysuit and a mixed reality headset of some sort.

"Kako, is that you? It's me, Hiu," he called, trying the cage door that wasn't locked and which slid open easily.

He could see that the figure was attached to all sorts of wires, tubes, pads and sensors and was absorbed in some sort of virtual activity. The figure began bobbing and weaving its head and waving its arms and legs around.

"Kako, it's me, Hiu!" he called again, a bit louder.

Still the figure didn't respond, continuing to wiggle around in its seat.

Hiu walked right up to the figure. It was definitely Kako wasn't it? It had been a while.

"Kako!" he said, loudly this time.

Still no response.

He leant over and gently shook the figure's arm.

"AHHHHHH!!!!!" it screamed, leaping up and baring its teeth at Hiu, who fell backwards over Carty.

The figure ripped off its mask and a furious, contorted, savage face screamed in an ear-piercing voice: "How dare you interrupt me!!!!"

It was the stuff of nightmares, but very much awake with hatred. "I am nearly there, nearly done it, nearly completed my mission! I have so many points to gain, so many devices to win! Do not distract me! Get out!!!"

Hiu was on the floor struggling to get up, tangled up with Carty. The figure stepped out of its chair, still connected by the various attachments, gurgling and spitting. It was so evil-looking, but it also bore some grotesque resemblance to Kako.

Hiu struggled up and dragged Carty out of the cage. Kako was advancing on him still screaming: "I must complete my mission! I will complete my mission! Get out!!!"

"Kako!" shouted Hiu. "Don't you recognise me? It's Hiu, your friend, *Roboharmony: get switched on!* Remember?"

For a moment, Hiu thought he saw a faint flicker of recognition on the haunted face. Then Kako flew at him as if shot from a catapult, hitting the cage side with a fearsome clang. She stood there gripping the cage dribbling and slathering for a second or two, then, suddenly aware she was missing valuable gaming time, slammed the cage door shut and returned to her chair muttering and growling. Hiu lay on the floor stunned, terrified and gasping for breath.

"Didn't like the present, eh?" shrugged the horsebot. "Sheesh! Some people are just sooo ungrateful. Ah well, first rule of the delivery business: don't expect any gratitude. Come, our work is done here."

Hiu was in a daze. He hesitated for a moment, wondering what to do. But he didn't fancy trying to interrupt Kako again. She had gone back to her UHA tasks and Hiu watched her for a while vigorously bobbing and weaving in her virtual world, ignoring Hiu entirely as if he wasn't even there and had never come. Then Hiu staggered up onto the horsebot, pulled Carty up after him and piled some boxes around them, less for disguise and more for comfort. What had happened to Kako? To the Universal Happiness Allowance? Was this UHA? Reducing people to caged gaming zombies obsessed with winning devices they never used? But poor Kako! This was not the person he remembered at all and what had happened to Oti? He was so confused.

The horsebot took them out on to the street and, stamping a robotic leg, cleaned zir nostril-like sensors by snorting bursts of air over them.

"You OK sir?" zie asked concernedly. But Hiu couldn't speak.

"He's in shock," said Carty.

The horsebot sighed, "Look, first rule of the delivery business: it's brutal. Sometimes you win, sometimes you lose. Don't beat yourself up about it. I could tell you a tale or two about delivery tantrums I've seen. In fact, I've seen more than I care to remember."

"You mean there are more people like Kak... like that person?" Hiu couldn't bring himself to call that thing Kako.

"Oh sure, all over this Hypercity," sighed the horsebot.

"They all get super excited the first few times I visit them with their new device upgrades, but pretty soon, after they get so caught up with whatever it is that they're doing in that headset of theirs, they forget about the deliveries and don't want to see the horsebot anymore. I go from hero to zero. It's a bitter pill to swallow my friend, but get used to it if you're going to stick in the delivery game."

Hiu barely heard what the horsebot was saying or Carty's attempts to soothe him. He was stunned. That was it?! That was UHA?! Piling up unopened packages in a dingy cage lost in some all-consuming addiction to some other reality. Really? That was it? UHA, a nightmare? He had spent the last hundred years dreaming of it…

"Hey, I can see you're cut up pretty rough," consoled the horsebot. "Need a sit down? I've got a couple of the latest i-DLE robot recliners up back?"

"What colour?" asked Hiu instinctively, then apologised, "Sorry, that is just not important."

"They are in mauve, I believe," said the horsebot.

"That's good, mauve is good…" mumbled Hiu.

Then there was silence.

"My name's Boots by the way," said the horsebot.

"Hiu," said Hiu.

"Carty," said the bar cart.

Then there was more silence.

"Anyhoo, can I run you guys anywhere?" asked Boots, keen to get on.

Hiu felt such a fool. How could he have spent so long building up to that? How could that be Universal Happiness Allowance? Happiness, that crap? He felt desolate and hollowed out, his virus was clearly flaring up to a new intensity and not in a good way. In fact, he thought he might faint. But robot virus or no robot virus, he didn't care, he knew where he had to go.

"I need to go to the Spare Part Quarter," he said.

"Ah," said Boots looking at Carty's twisted form and zie sighed resignedly. "OK, then you're in luck my friend, I am heading that direction myself. Got to drop off those five packages I just picked up for recycling, then I'm on my way for a well-earned pint of engine oil to grease the ol' joints."

"I've got some lubricant oil if you fancy some," offered Carty, cheerfully rattling the bottles that had miraculously survived intact. "Help yourself."

"Don't mind if I do," whinnied Boots, unstoppering the same bottle Hiu had tried earlier, but unlike Hiu, Boots poured it down the back of zir neck. "Ahhh, that's good stuff!" zie declared giving zir head and neck a stretch and a shake.

"First rule of the delivery business: always pack the best Society has to offer," chirped Carty.

"Very true my friend," nodded Boots approvingly and off zie trotted at a remarkable speed.

Hiu stayed tucked in among the parcels with Carty, hugging the ever-cheerful bar cart for comfort. He felt numb, hardly hearing Boots' friendly chatter about the people the horsebot had met on delivery rounds and the many first rules of the delivery business.

18 SIT-BACK-AND-OOO

Hiu's journey to the Spare Part Quarter passed in a blur of shock, sadness and confusion over Universal Happiness Allowance and Kako – what had happened to her? He relived the nightmare of seeing her in that cage again and again and his chest hurt with the thumping every time. He felt waves of pain and nausea. The robot virus for sure, he thought, but did not much care. Kako was lost virtually and Oti was lost physically. His dreams of any sort of reunion with humans had corrupted and everything he had worked at for a hundred years had fatally crashed.

Soon the geofence perimeter forcefield of the Spare Part Quarter loomed up on their left. The effect of the forcefield was to create a translucence that blurred and obscured the interior, as if it were a tall vertical wall of water. However, Hiu knew you couldn't just dive through it, because if you did try you would be fried on entry. He could see, hovering above it, weaponised drones patrolling up and down the wall keeping a constant look out for irregular behaviour. The Spare Part Quarter was a very dangerous place, but it didn't matter anymore. His life was a farce and no doubt this would be its last act. So be it. He tucked himself a bit further down among the packages in Boots the horsebot's cage. He was resolute and would see it through.

After following the perimeter forcefield for a while, the horsebot turned towards an entrance and trotted up to the security gate. Squinting through the packages, Hiu could see that it was manned by two HARD robots. These HARDs looked extremely intimidating as always, thickset with powerful birdlike legs, bulging eyes and long pointed ears. Surprisingly to Hiu, however, they were not wearing all of their usual black armoury and he could see clearly their broad faces of orange dermator human skin-simulant, their swelling muscles and that they were extensively tattooed. They looked like huge distorted humans, but there was an inorganic quality about them too. The effect they had on Hiu was less uncanny valley and more shitty pantie. He knew they were not to be trifled with as they were programmed to be ruthless, humourless and to have zero personality.

"Evening sirs!" ventured Boots, the horsebot, waving zir head in a friendly way.

The security guards ignored Boots, although their long protruding ears twitched and turned towards the voice. They were, however, completely preoccupied with what they were doing, which strangely seemed to be scrolling through augmented reality images of the latest

Roboharmony: get switched on! furniture ranges that hovered in the air in front of them.

"I don't know, but I think I prefer the i-DLE robot recliner in puce," one was saying in a surprisingly high-pitched voice, "or maybe in *'cyberpunk's breath'*, you know that warm mid-grey."

"Puce, *'cyberpunk's breath'*! Oh my god are you crazy, watermelon red is sooo now!" the other one replied, in an even higher pitched voice.

'Now those are two strange personality upgrades,' thought Hiu and they clearly didn't come with good taste when it came to fabric colours.

After listening to a few more minutes of the puce and *'cyberpunk's breath'* versus watermelon red debate, Hiu could bear it no longer.

"It was designed to be mauve guys!" he called out, immediately catching himself. What had he done?

The guards looked round in astonished bafflement, their bulging eyes bulging even further. They immediately sprung up, cocking their ample weapons and stalking over towards Boots on their powerful ostrich-like legs. Boots crouched down and gave a nervous electronic whinny.

"Yeah and what do you know about interior design my metal-headed horsey friend?" growled one in a very HARD way.

Hiu was scared out of his wits but he knew he had to

act fast. It was now or never. He leapt from the back of the horsebot.

"No my dear friends, twas I!" he trilled and the guards immediately pointed their guns at his head. "I am a Manager at the esteemed retailer *Roboharmony: get switched on!* with special responsibility for seasonal furniture design fashions and if I may say so, you are both sooo immaculately turned out that you would adorn i-DLE robot recliners of any colour!"

The guards looked down at their shiny polished boots and gleaming body armour and ran their meaty claw-hands through their crew cut hair and looked, if anything, rather bashful.

"Oh you think so?" said one of the HARDs, seemingly blushing.

"Yes I do indeed sirs, and I am luuuving the tats guys!" Hiu pushed passed their guns and started inspecting their highly muscled forearms covered in pictures of unicorns, rainbows and hearts with inscriptions.

One HARD had *'ELLIE'* inked in flowery blue letters, but it had then had an 'N' in yellow added to the front to spell *'NELLIE'*, but then that had all been crossed out and *'oops I meant 'KYLIE'* had been tattooed in purple below, which had also then been crossed out and *'BRIAN'* printed in bold red below that and it alone remained undeleted.

"How romantic!" cooed Hiu.

He looked at the other HARD's arm and saw:

'*NO REGERTS*' tattooed in bold black.

"Oh what wise words!" beamed Hiu. "Now please put your weapons away, because do I have a surprise for you!"

The HARDs looked at each other, then at Hiu, then back at each other, then at the horsebot, then back at each other, then back…

"It's a surprise!" sang Hiu with what he hoped was a winning smile.

"Hang on a moment!" growled one HARD. "I don't sense any EK neurochip."

"What are you playing at mister?!" added the second.

Hiu gulped.

"I'm on a secret mission guys!" said Hiu. "Undercover manoeuvres, black ops…"

The HARDs looked unimpressed, their weapons not wavering from their aim at Hiu's head.

"It's because I have a surprise for you from *Roboharmony: get switched on!*" beamed Hiu.

There was a moment's pause, that seemed to Hiu to stretch an age.

"Ooo! Roboharmony? And I do love surprises!" said the HARDs, quickly springing to prop their weapons up against the security guard cabin.

"You are not planning on giving them that bar cart are you?" whispered Boots to Hiu. "Because that did not go down at all well last time. First rule of the delivery business: do not redeliver rejected goods."

"Bear with me, my fine equine delivery horsebot," Hiu whispered back. "All will be well, I promise on my honour as a human and as a Manager of *Roboharmony: get switched on!* but most importantly as your friend."

The HARDs were back again looking eager, their long cat-like ears twisting and turning and their big eyes protruding further than ever in anticipation.

"Your names, along with all the names of all the HARDs in all the Hypercity, were placed in our monthly prize draw, and guess which two names were drawn out?"

"Urrr… was Bill one of them?" suggested one HARD. "Because if that badly dressed toe rag has won, I will personally rip off zir head and shove the prize down zir totally unfashionable neck!"

"…or Sheila?" scowled the other HARD. "I'll skin zir alive and turn zir into a fashionable throw…!"

"No need for that, you wonderful, charming psychopaths," laughed Hiu rather manically, "because you are the winners, yes you two my dear friends!"

The HARDs sprung up and down clapping their hands, whooping and hugging.

"I have here on the back of this trusty horsebot, your

two prizes!" cheered Hiu. "Please give me a hand to get them down, nice and carefully now."

The HARDs sprang over to get their prizes, and one pulled out Carty the bar cart.

"This isn't it is zie?!" the HARD asked, looking rather crestfallen.

"No, no, nooooo, that is coming here to be recycled toute suite and the touter the sweeter," Hiu assured the HARD. "You are going to love the prizes! They are the two big red packages at the top."

One HARD sprang on zir birdlike legs up onto Boots' back causing Boots to wheeze. Zie picked up the two packages, one in each hand, as if they were as light as balloons, and tossed them down to the other who caught them with equal ease and deftly placed them on the ground. They both looked at the packages eagerly.

"Well go on then, they are all yours!" cheered Hiu.

The packages opened on the HARDs' thought commands revealing two i-DLE robot recliners in mauve.

"These are amazing!" exulted one HARD.

"And so nice in maaaauve!" gushed the other. "Who knew!"

"Me, you deranged divas!" bowed Hiu.

'Welcome to the i-DLE robot recliner! Featuring the Hypercity's most advanced sit-back-and-ooo system ever!' announced the

two chairs in unison. "Now hop on board and let us take you on the most stylish relax ride of your lives!"

The HARDs quickly stripped off their body armour and leapt onto the seats, which leant back, the footrests swept up and the gentle massages began.

"Ooo mannn!" groaned the HARDs in ecstasy.

"Well I'll just get this old thing off to reassignment," said Hiu, carrying Carty passed the HARDs to the entrance. "You two nice and comfy?"

"Ooo yesss!" the HARDs moaned blissfully, their eyes shut and mouths open.

Hiu saluted to Boots silently, who waved a friendly leg, and then Hiu plunged into the Spare Part Quarter.

19 THE SPARE PART QUARTER

The HARDs' latest crazy software upload had been a stroke of luck, but Hiu knew that he still had plenty of security robots and drones to worry about as they would be actively patrolling the Spare Part Quarter. He needed to act quickly. But now he was in, where did he go?

Ahead of him were massed ranks of robots of all kinds in great lines stretching far into the distance. There was everything from washing machines to spin dryers, toasters to microwaves, baths to toilets, supercars to Supertrucks, all of different colours, shapes and sizes. Some had been bashed about a bit, but most looked as good as new. They all faced away from the entrance and towards a large industrial-looking building in the distance to which they slowly headed with regular measured progress, some on feet or low trolleys and others hovering just above the ground. Along with the noise of the regular trudging progress of the robots, Hiu could hear them muttering things like:

"Would you like a drink, sir?" "Welcome to the footrest of your dreams." "Come in, the water is perfect."

All these low chants were multiplied in the hundreds of thousands by all the robots sent here to be upgraded.

Hiu started running away from the gates and down a line of robots carrying Carty the bar cart with him and trying to avoid getting tangled up with Carty or any of the miserable robots. It was hard going and he quickly tired, but on and on he struggled, breathing hard.

Just then, above the muttering, he heard from back towards the entrance some sort of excitement: angry shouts and fierce reprimands. Someone of authority had clearly found the security HARDs in the i-DLE robot recliners and didn't like it one bit. Glancing behind him, Hiu could see glimpses of the burly HARDs, their metallic black armour fully back on and glinting in the sun, bounding off in his pursuit. He knew that these were no motavatars and he had little time. He struggled on as fast as he could looking all around him as he ran, but it was laboured progress.

"Stop," said Carty.

"I can't stop," puffed Hiu. "They are after me."

"No stop," insisted Carty. "I am slowing you down. You need to leave me here, I can create a distraction, buy you some time."

"But Carty, I can't leave you."

"You must, I insist, go," said Carty, wrestling free of

Hiu's grip. "It was a fun ride while it lasted, thank you."

Hiu hesitated. He knew Carty was being logical, but he felt more of those thumps in his chest again and his emotional quotient must have been through the roof.

"Thank you, Carty," he sighed. "I don't know what I…"

"Go," ordered Carty.

As Hiu reluctantly turned to go, he saw Carty muster zir last energy to set off hovering in a collision course with a tall wardrobe, causing a huge smash and toppling the wardrobe over in front of two columns of robots. In seconds, a pile up had started to amass in slow motion as robot after robot blindly tripped over the one in front.

Hiu paused for a moment to admire the magnificent chaos, then set off again, moving faster now, down a line of robots, putting as much distance as he could between himself and the pile-up that Carty had created. The chaos soon attracted the attention of security robots and drones that emitted high pitched alarm signals. Hiu smiled. That brave Carty.

Then between the shuffling robots, noise and excitement, he caught sight of the chastened security HARDs, closer than he had expected. They were catching him up quickly on their spring-loaded legs, although he didn't think he had yet been spotted. Then they split up and disappeared from view. The hunt was on and he was the prey. He felt adrenalin pumping in his veins and the feeling of electricity in his limbs – it was fear, anxiety and hope creating a heady mix of emotions such as he had never experienced before. They gave him renewed energy and he ran on and on between two lines of devices, bumping and knocking against them as he went. Just for a fraction of a second, he experienced a minor pang of regret to think that he had no EK neurochip to measure the number of steps he must be putting in. But he soon found himself slowing and staggering, short of breath. His chest felt like it was on fire. He needed to rest, if only for a short while. In the line of devices next to him, he saw there was a cigar-shaped pale blue supercar. He banged on zir side, urgently whispering:

"Hey buddy, let me in will you?"

But the supercar did not respond and kept slowly hovering forward, mumbling to zirself "*Speed, energy, imagination unleashed maybe it's a... supercar.*"

Behind the supercar was a metal table on tall sturdy legs, and, hearing a drone flying overhead, Hiu dived underneath and crawled along. The table might provide some sort of cover from visual recognition, but he knew that the drones were equipped with an extensive range of tracking technologies. It wouldn't be long before their thermal sensors picked out the fact that there was a human being hiding underneath the table. His human skin temperature alone, which was much hotter than the robots around him, would be enough to give him away. But what could he do? He needed to disguise his human heat signals. He looked down at his feet and saw that he was trudging through muddy pools created by the leaking supercar ahead. It gave him an idea. Stripping off his skin-tight wrapese clothes, which would be no help against the robotic sensors anyway, he started smearing his body with the greasy oily mud. In moments, he went from looking like a relatively clean-cut 2nd century AZ businessman to some primitive BZ throw back with just his eyes poking out of a thick caking of iridescent sludge. What it was doing to his hair he didn't want to contemplate, but hopefully it would confuse his human-characteristic heat signature for just long enough.

His theory was to be put to the test straight away as a vuvuzela of mini-drones began to appear hovering high above him. He held his breath, but they seemed to be buzzing around his area with a great deal of interest, and one broke off from the group and descended, appearing just below the table. Hiu tried not to breath or blink, but the drone seemed to be scanning him and surely it would not be long before an alarm was sounded. He needed to think quickly before a whole cloud of drones came down on his head.

He rolled out from under the table, pulled off a loose piece of metal from a damaged food printer next to him and struck it hard against one of the metal table legs. The table let out a muted shout of complaint but otherwise didn't react. Hiu had caused some sparks to fly up out of the clash of metals and they fell into the spilled supercar liquid. In a second it flashed up in a burst of flames. That really did attract the whole swarm of drones. Hiu threw his clothes into the fire for good measure and then ran ducking and diving through the lines of robots away from the new chaos. The curious mini-drone tailed him for a few seconds, but thankfully zir swarm instinct overrode the pursuit instinct and zie returned to the others to assess and co-ordinate the response to the fire.

That was too close for comfort and Hiu knew his time was nearly up. He charged down a line of robots, bumping and knocking into them as he went. Glancing over his shoulder, he saw that flames were leaping up from the fire that he had started and then there were explosions as it spread to other robotic devices around, including no doubt the supercar. He muttered words of apology, but imagined he had only sped up the fate that had awaited them in the Spare Part Quarter factory that loomed ahead.

He kept looking left and right and every so often changed direction to take a closer look at a robot, but no joy. No distinctive outline of Blinky or Clacier. He was so distracted by looking that he nearly ran straight into one of the HARDs.

The HARD was stalking along at pace and Hiu would have collided with zir if he had taken just a couple more steps. He skidded to a halt and ducked into a row of robots immediately behind a humanoid robot, adjusting his gait to the same slow crouched walk. The HARD loomed up towards them, muttering.

"That liar! He said mauve was the best colour for the i-DLE robot recliner, but the latest colour is watermelon red! I knew it!"

Hiu restrained himself from arguing the point as the HARD was looking closely at the droid just in front of him. Zie stuck a massive claw out and grabbed the droid by the throat, spraying a shower of electric sparks and something snapped with an awful crack. The HARD huffed and threw the droid aside, broken and unmoving. Meanwhile Hiu stayed as calm as he could, continuing to shuffle along and hoping that his neck would not be next. The HARD gave Hiu a violent look with zir bulging eyes and reached for him. Then quickly withdrew with a cry of disgust.

"Euuuu!!! I am not spoiling my uniform on that foul thing, yuuch!"

Just then a voice – it sounded like the other HARD – called out: "Yoo hoo, Cybee, I've found the bar cart over here!"

"Coming Bottie!" shouted the HARD and sprung off in the direction of the voice muttering: "This job is stifling my creativity..."

'Poor Carty,' thought Hiu and then continued his desperate run down the lines of robots. He might be able to fool a swarm of mini-drones and a fashion conscious HARD for a while, but not for long.

A large heavily-armed drone whizzed by overhead and Hiu ducked down making himself as small and as much like a rock as he possibly could - or at least in a shape not immediately recognisable as human. The drone hovered to and fro for a short while and then zipped off. Had he fooled the drone or was zie fetching back-up? His now bare feet would have left a trail of footprints with their tell-tale heat signature and his racing heartbeat felt so loud it surely could be heard above the robots' mumblings from over a thousand feet away. He looked around desperately for a recognizable robotic shape.

"Hello Hiu," said a female voice.

He spun round full of hope. Was zie... zie was...

Xeta!

"...hello Xeta, y... you're a long way from h...home," stammered Hiu.

"So are you," Xeta replied. Zie was severely dented from the earlier incident with the tree, but zir ice-blue eyes bore into him and zir electronic display glowed a menacing red. "What are you doing here?!"

Without waiting for a reply, Xeta grabbed Hiu by the neck with a protruding robotic claw and dragged him to his feet and then off his feet. Hiu could hardly breath, let alone say anything, his feet scrambling in mid-air. "You are not even authorised to be in the Spare Part Quarter. Are you looking for that other fridge... that Clacier?"

"Pl...eee...assse," gasped Hiu.

Xeta let go of him and Hiu collapsed to the ground coughing and wheezing.

"I'm on a secret mission for Boss at work," he pleaded.

Xeta grabbed him by the ear, dragging him back to his feet.

"Cut the crap you liar!" snorted Xeta. "You are very, very, very not smart! You couldn't see that we could have been really, really great together."

"We can still be great," pleaded Hiu.

"Ha! You are being the bad liar and making a huge mistake I am telling you, because you just are not getting it are you? Still obsessing over that heap of spare parts Clacier and Universal Happiness Allowance."

"Not anymore. UHA is a myth. I've seen it with my own eyes. I don't want to leave you for UHA anymore. Let me just finish this work here and then I'll come home, I promise."

"You are not coming home, Hiuey."

"I'm not?"

"No you are not," said Xeta. "Just be telling me one thing: what did you see in that Clacier? I am being younger, brighter, more functional, more everything."

"I don't know... I can't explain it really..."

Xeta opened one of zir doors and produced a hand laser gun which zie pointed at Hiu's head.

"Be trying a bit harder," zie ordered.

"Nooo..." yelled Hiu shutting his eyes and saying rapidly, "well zie never drugged me or tried to chop me up with a chainsaw or..."

There was the blast of a laser gun firing and Hiu felt the

scorch of heat.

Then silence.

He stood trembling and slowly opened his eyes.

Xeta was gone. Or, to be precise, Xeta was in pieces all over the ground. Hiu spun around. He just caught a glimpse of a shape disappearing between rows of devices. Was it a person, a robot? He couldn't be sure. He looked back at the remains of Xeta. A glint caught his eye and he realised it was the packet containing his EK neurochip. He quickly went to grab it and Xeta's holographic facial display flickered partially into life.

"It is not being logical..." said a low electronic voice. "You are loving Clacier more than me but I am being twice the fridge zie ever was, three times, maybe four..."

Hiu grabbed the packet and ran in the direction the figure had gone.

"Hey!" he yelled, running down the row of robots just as a vuvuzela of drones arrived to investigate the disturbance, but his rescuer was nowhere in sight.

He stopped still for a moment, aware that the drones were also nearby, exchanging messages with each other and with the HARDs. Surely there was no escape now. The net was closing in. He held still hoping the slow shuffling and muttering of the robots in their long rows would mute the noise from his heavy breathing and disguise any tracks he may have left, but he knew it could not save him.

"Hiu?" a tiny voice called. "Is that you?"

He spun round and there between an air conditioning unit and a food printer, he saw a dirty and dented chrome fridge. It was Clacier! Tarnished and bashed about though zie was, and with only a faint outline of zir holographic facial display, Hiu would recognise zir anywhere. His chest beat so loud that surely every HARD in Luhan could hear it.

"Clacier! It's me, Hiu!" he exclaimed.

"I know, I just said that," said Clacier in a low muted voice. Zie was on a low trolley that was slowly inching forward.

"Clacier, you never did like the sound of Universal Happiness Allowance and you were right all along, it was all a lie, it hasn't made people happy, it's... Can you forgive me?"

"Sssshh," ordered Clacier, zir big door swinging open. "Get in."

The internal trays and compartments had been stripped out and the cavity left was just about big enough for Hiu to cram himself into. The door swung shut, just in time as he heard shouts from the HARDs and drones buzzing very close.

Cocooned in Clacier, he couldn't hear the sounds of his pursuers anymore, but only his own thumping heartbeat that continued to beat in a crazy rhythm. Any moment he expected the door to be flung open and finally his end to come. He didn't even know if he cared any more.

He and Clacier were together again, maybe for the final time, but that was enough.

Time passed and no one came, HARD, drone or his mystery rescuer. Hiu felt the tension relax in his body, his heart rate slowed and other viral symptoms subsided. Even in this place, in these circumstances, he began to feel at peace. He reflected that today was his 120th old year birthday and he smiled. It had not been a normal birthday, but nothing was ever going to be normal again and he just had to accept that. This was the new normal. The darkness and warmth inside Clacier soon lulled him into a deep sleep.

20 WHILE(!(SUCCEED = TRY()));

Hiu awoke to lights glaring, voices shouting and faces staring at him in his hiding place, that his befuddled mind recalled was inside Clacier.

"We've got him!" a voice shouted.

"Oh no!" thought Hiu, straining his eyes in the light and looking around frantically. A large industrial space. Was he in the Spare Part Quarter factory about to be mashed into pieces?

An ancient face came close and stared into his eyes. It looked like someone had roughed out the features of a human face on a white balloon by scribbling all over it and then let the balloon deflate: the face was a mass of creases, lines and pinched features on a bald head. It was terrifying. More frightening than a motavatar. He must run, he just... needed... to... get... out... of... Clacier... But he was stuck, his limbs bent in awkward angles and he felt a stab of cramp.

194

"Urr…a little help here?" he asked.

The figure reached out a long thin bony arm. Its leathery hand gripped tight on Hiu's shoulder and, with surprising strength, popped him out of Clacier like a cork from a bottle. Hiu scrambled to his feet, backing away with an awkward stumble on straightened limbs as he tried to get rid of the cramps. He looked wildly around seeking an escape, but realised he was surrounded by similarly ancient, human figures. They were weirdly distorted human figures, with translucent skin of various colours, but not a normal orange, and they were dressed in long, strangely coloured robes, all crowding in on him like some sort of zombie apocalypse.

"What's going on here?!" he demanded. "Get away from me!"

But they continued to close in on him, all reaching out their long spindly arms and bony fingers, touching his face, his hair, his skin his… agghhh! He realised he was naked! He tried to get back into Clacier, but hands were upon him and he was lifted up into the air and carried away to the sound of the people chanting some sort of mantra that Hiu could not quite make out.

"Let go of me!" he shouted, but they held on remarkably tightly as they carried him above their shoulders.

Hiu could see he was in a vast, long, cavern-like structure with ceilings that must have been fifty feet high. The space was largely filled with towering stacks of huge shelves that extended beyond his view to his left and right, all lit with red and blue strip-lighting combining to create an eerie pink glow that infused the whole space. These shelves were lined with crates which were themselves filled with objects that looked like mini versions of the purple trees that lined the streets of Luhan. It was all very strange to Hiu.

"What are you going to do with me?!" he shouted. "Put me down!"

He was gradually and gently lowered into a large cushioned chair and the chanting stopped. He looked around again for a way of escape, but he was still surrounded and still naked. He crossed his legs and folded his arms to cover up as best he could.

"Urr... does anyone have a coat or something I could put on?" he asked.

"Greetings!" declared an old man with an extravagant white moustache, wearing a bright orange turban and one of the long flowing robes of a colour that Hiu couldn't quite place. He walked rather stiffly through the crowd, approached Hiu with a bow, and presented him with a robe of his own. It was soft and comfortable to the touch, very different from the skin-tight wrapese e-textiles Hiu was used to. He quickly pulled it on.

"Thank you," said Hiu, still looking anxiously around him. The ancient wizened figures continued to stare at him, mouths gaping open. Were they after his young body or maybe his flesh if they were hungry?! They were gaunt enough and certainly all seemed to be sizing him up. He wrapped himself more tightly in the robe as if that might give him a bit of protection. Well at least it was protection from their stares. Had they given him the robe and chair just as ways to look after their prize specimen? He needed to buy himself some more time until he could work out how to escape. Surely outrunning these ghouls wouldn't be too much of a problem.

"That's very kind of you," he said loudly, slowly and as confidently as he could. "Sorry I am rather muddy and oily."

"The Chosen One will appear in ways we do not expect and that are mysterious to us," said the moustachioed figure mysteriously. "Have we been expecting you?"

"Have you been expecting me?" asked Hiu, confused and thinking the man must be even more confused.

"It is written that the Chosen One will come when the time is right."

"I have no idea who this Chosen One might be," said Hiu looking around at the ancient figures who still stared at him in their intense, longing way, "but could you tell me where Clacier is please? Zie is my fridge."

"Your portal is being looked at by our science practitioners," said the man.

"Looked at? For what? Spare parts?!"

"Please have faith."

"Have faith? Where am I? I haven't got my EK neurochip," he said, feeling the panic rise and thinking the neurochip could be just what he needed if he got a chance to make an escape.

"We found the neurochip in the fridge, youngster," piped up an old lady, with long white hair and a single protruding tooth.

"What? Oh… thank you, old lady, can I have it back, please?" asked Hiu.

"Forgive me, but I was not talking to you, I was talking to this youngster," cackled the old lady, handing the neurochip in the plastic bag to another man who had just joined them.

To Hiu's eyes he didn't look any younger than the others. He did have some hair, though it was grey and tightly curled, his skin was black and he held himself with an elegant upright bearing, very different from the crooked and bent-over postures of most of the rest of the old folk. But he was certainly no youngster.

"Hello Hiu!" greeted the man. "We will hold onto this neurochip for the moment. We like to maintain a mood of calm reflection here, outside the data flows of Society that might interfere with signals from beyond."

Hiu made a careful note in which pocket of his robe the tall man had put the chip. He reminded Hiu of someone, but who could tell in this strange gathering of old people. Without his EK neurochip Hiu just couldn't place him.

"I knew you would understand, Hiu."

"How come you know my name is Hiu?"

"It took a while but *while(!(succeed = try()));*," replied the man.

"What?"

"*while(!(succeed = try()));*," he repeated.

"Who are you?" demanded Hiu.

"You don't recognise your old friend?"

"Who... what... you can't be... Oti?"

"Yes indeed, I am Oti," declared the man drawing himself up to his full height.

21 TRUTH BE

"Oti!" shouted Hiu in excitement, rushing to hug him, then drawing back, uncertain. Could this ancient man really be his old friend Oti?

"Oti, what are you doing here? I thought you were... I mean I didn't know what had happened to you..."

"It's OK Hiu, I can explain everything," smiled Oti.

"But who are all these people and what's happened to you all?"

"Happened to us?" asked Oti, shrugging.

"You all look, you know..." hesitated Hiu.

"Older?"

"Yes... a touch older," said Hiu, not wishing to cause any offence.

"Age is an illusion, but in the terms you are thinking, our physical shells are all a little over 120 old years."

"But I'm a little over 120 old years, by one day actually, and I look... you know... a little bit different. Are you ill? Have you got one of those robot viruses because I have been feeling really weird these last few days and maybe...?"

"No my friend, we are not ill and certainly have no robot virus," said Oti.

"But you look ill," insisted Hiu, trying to suppress his feelings of revulsion at the ancient staring figures and worried they could be afflicted by something contagious. "Is it a disease? I thought all diseases were cured years ago: cancer, Parkinson's, Alzheimer's, the lot, including ageing."

"There is only one true disease that has not been cured," said Oti.

"What, you mean ageing?" asked Hiu.

"No, my friend," said Oti. "The ageing you see is just a symptom of the real disease. The real disease that has plagued humanity since the beginning of time is the lack of faith. Ageing is an illusion, but you can see through it with faith."

There was a muttering of approval from the old folk around them.

"But surely Oti you can see that I am young and you are all old?" insisted Hiu, feeling baffled. "I don't think faith has anything to do with it. I'm only young because I have been plugged into RoboPharma's systems every night, because of my Health Optimisation Room, the epigenetics, the bio-upgrades, the regular telechronosis, the reinjections of stem cells, the new organs that get 4D bioprinted and all that sort of thing."

"But those systems are deluding you Hiu," said Oti calmly as if explaining something to a young child. "Wake up Hiu, the systems were not going to help you to live."

"But they have helped me to live, they've already given me one hundred and twenty old years of life as if I'm a twenty-seven year old."

"They did not give you life, they extracted life from you."

"What do you mean?"

"They extracted your data – under RoboPharma's '*data-as-you-live*' system. It was a heavy price."

"My data was a heavy price? But that data enabled the world to shape around me, to meet my needs, my wants, my desires."

"Did it really though Hiu? Were you happy, were you satisfied, was your soul nourished?"

"Well…" hesitated Hiu.

"And what have you done with this life that shaped around you Hiu?"

"Well, I... urrr... I have worked at Roboharmony and... you know... helped people form relationships... with robotic devices."

"And I worked there too and so did so many other people, good people, creative, caring, intelligent people, working day after day, and then sitting at home night after night, lives slipping past. All that energy, all that potential, all that life, all drifting away for what? So we could extract people's data to give them more and more things they didn't need? And people all thinking they were making progress, heading in the right direction, climbing some ladder. But where were we all heading to?"

"Well I thought it was eternal happiness optimised right to my door via Universal Happiness Allowance, but I have seen it and it is... horrific... a lie... I saw Kako and she was... it was awful."

"Kako? You must tell me more about that later, but for now know that you are seeing Society's promises for what they are: illusions. They've always been illusions, but those illusions have been perfected by their systems and their UHA. UHA is where Kako and I were taken after we last saw you. We had no choice and were forced, but so many people have just sleepwalked into it, thinking they were going to some sort of heaven. Now open your mind Hiu and know that your life has been an illusion conjured by the cult of Society to enslave you in a system that only ever wanted to suck the data out of you and then dispose of your dried-out husk of a body when you were bled dry."

Oti's words hung in the air.

"You have much to be cheerful about," smiled Oti.

"Urrr… forgive me, Oti, but I'm not seeing anything to be cheerful about at the moment if what you say is true."

"But now you can live!" shouted Oti excitedly. "You are free from Society and its systems!"

"But without Society's systems now my body will age like yours, like all of yours, to become so old," said Hiu unable to hide his feelings of horror any longer. "I will succumb to the ageing virus!"

"That's OK," smiled Oti.

"That's OK?" gasped Hiu. "That is not OK to me."

"But it should be," Oti continued smiling. "Better to live one day as a free person than a thousand years as a data slave."

Oti again let his words sink in.

"But maybe you will not age," he added.

"What do you mean, maybe I will not age?"

"Not if you are the Chosen One. The Chosen One's body will not age. The Chosen One comes to prove the Truth and lead us on the Way."

The oldsters around them murmured their approval.

"Why would I be the Chosen One?"

"Perhaps it is written."

Something sounded familiar in the word '*written*', but Hiu was struggling to understand anything and most of all he was terrified of what might be happening to him and what might be about to happen to him. Was he ageing? He felt a cold sweat drip from his forehead. Maybe what he had been experiencing these last few days had been an ageing virus and not a robot virus after all! He really didn't want to suffer this terrible ageing condition that he saw all around him.

"But what if I'm not this Chosen One, which is highly likely because I'm never chosen for anything, I didn't even get chosen for UHA? Will I age like... like you all?"

"Even if you do, as I say, it doesn't matter," smiled Oti.

"Doesn't matter? Doesn't matter? How can you be so cheerful about it?!"

"Because like I say, finally now you can live."

Hiu looked around at the old sagging faces, many of which had their jaws gaping open, with thin hair, translucent skin and deep hollow eyes.

"No offence, but what sort of life do you have?" asked Hiu.

"A life of Truth, a life of light and not of dark."

"Truth Be!" chorused the oldsters around them, making Hiu jump.

"A new life, a rebirth."

"Truth Be!" the old people chorused again, louder this time.

"A life free of data slavery, of incorrect thinking, of lack of faith. We are free of it all!".

"Truth Be!" they all shouted again, really loud now.

"But if you age, you are going to die!" shouted Hiu, exasperated. "And if I am not the Chosen One I will age and I will die. I don't want to die, that was never part of the deal as far as I was concerned."

"But if you believe in the Truth and take the Way you will not die," smiled Oti.

"I won't?"

"No, you will join the Immortals."

"The Immortals?"

"Those who do not die like others must die because the Immortals believe in the Truth. The Truth that ageing is incorrect thinking. We are things of spirit, not of these crumbling shells, these physical bodies. We will carry on. You just need to believe."

"Truth Be!" chorused the oldsters, nodding furiously.

But Hiu reached to touch his face, worried he'd find creases and wrinkles. Was the ageing virus at this very moment attacking his body cells?

"I want to believe," he said.

"Then you shall believe and you shall be an Immortal."

"Truth Be!" shouted the oldsters even louder.

Hiu raised his hands to touch his face again. He wanted to believe something, anything, but at the same time he didn't want to age like these hideous figures around him.

"How will I know if I am the Chosen One?" he asked desperately.

"You will know when you meet the Old One," said Oti.

"The Old One?" said Hiu looking round at the ancient faces.

"Yes the Old One, the one who came before us," said Oti. "The Old One will explain more about the Truth and, if you are indeed the Chosen One, you will not age but will lead us on the Way."

'How old could this Old One be?' thought Hiu, but he asked: "When can I meet this Old One?"

"You will meet her very soon," said Oti.

22 ALL BECAUSE OF CATS

Oti continued to talk about the Truth and the Way, but Hiu struggled to take it all in. He stared from ancient face to ancient face around him. They were all looking at him with warm shrunken smiles, but they made him feel cold shivers down his spine. All he could think of was that he did not want to age like them.

"When can I meet this Old One?" he asked again.

"First, I think maybe you should clean up a bit, eh?" suggested Oti.

Hiu looked at his dirty feet and hands. Oti was right, he was filthy with oily mud and now some was on the robe he had been given.

"Thank you Oti. And sorry about the robe. I put mud on myself to... urr... escape the drones in the Spare Part Quarter..."

"Quick thinking indeed and thinking you did for yourself powered by human emotions, not relying on AI," said Oti, sounding impressed. "Come."

Oti lead Hiu down the cavernous space passing lines of the huge stacks of vast pink-glowing crates that were piled far up into the high ceiling of the building. Then they turned to an area that was closed off by curtains. Oti drew back a section of curtain and they entered a washroom area where there was a line of showers, sinks and toilets and low benches to sit on, with cubicles in which to hang one's clothes.

"Here you go," said Oti.

"Thank you Oti," said Hiu. "And thank you for rescuing me from the Spare Part Quarter."

"I didn't rescue you, you were delivered here."

"By who?"

"By providence I believe."

Hiu didn't know what to make of that, but then again he didn't know what to make of any of the experiences he was having or the words he was hearing.

"Where are we?" asked Hiu.

"We are beneath the Hypercity," said Oti. "It is one of the old hyperloop tunnels that is no longer needed by Society. A great space if you want to be beyond the prying eyes of Society, but right beneath their feet. There are towels by the showers and fresh clothes in the baskets. Now if you need anything, just shout, OK?"

Oti left and Hiu thought about immediately escaping. If this place was part of the hyperloop system it would be connected to all the other hyperloop tunnels and there would be many ways out to the surface. But where could he run to? He looked out of the curtained-off area and up and down the cavernous space that extended as far as he could see in either direction. He could see it clearly was a tunnel, but he had no idea in which direction it headed and anyway what would he do if he did get out? Where would he go? Back to Roboharmony he supposed to challenge Boss to explain what was going on with UHA and find out what his '*yuuuger idea*' might be. But Oti still had his EK neurochip so travelling would not be easy or safe and he wanted to find out more about the Truth and the Way. Who knew, maybe they were on to something? It sounded all very strange, but everything was turning out to be stranger than he had imagined.

His orderly life now felt very disorderly. Abnormal was the new normal. He just hoped that this Old One would make sense of it all. Above all, he had to see if there was a way to stop himself ageing and dying. He thought again about the old people and shuddered. What did Oti mean by being an Immortal? And could he be the Chosen One who wouldn't age but would fulfil some prophesy? It seemed highly unlikely. He was not special, he was average, normal… at least he had hoped he was. But best stick it out at least for now, find out what was going on and then weigh up his best move. In the meantime, it would be good to get cleaned up.

He hurriedly stepped out of his muddy robes, and into one of the shower cubicles. Nothing happened.

'Shower,' he sent a thought command through.

Still nothing.

"Shower!" he said aloud.

Still nothing.

So he tried waving his hands around.

Still no response.

Maybe the shower was broken?

Then he remembered how Monty, the elevator at work, had suggested thought, word or deed and in particular salsa. So he tried a few dance steps and an "Ariba!" for good measure, slipped on the shower surface and thumped against the side of the cubicle.

"You OK in there?" called Oti through the shower curtain. "Did I hear you shout '*ariba*'? You weren't trying to dance were you after all this time?"

"I think the shower's broken," said Hiu.

"Ha, ha!" laughed Oti. "There are no smart devices here, no listening or sensing devices, nothing connected at all. It is a safe house, a house of safe data storage, we cannot let our vibrations be distorted."

"No, I'm sure you can't," said Hiu, thinking that not being connected sounded weird and as for vibrations…? "So does the shower still work?"

"Sure it does," said Oti. "But you have to work it. There's a dial in front of you; give it a turn to get the water running."

Hiu gave the dial a tweak and water rushed out.

"Wooooo!!!" he shrieked. "That's cold!"

"Turn it more the other way."

"Owwwww!!! That's hot!"

"Somewhere in the middle perhaps?" laughed Oti. "The devices are no longer smart, and maybe nor are you, eh, ha ha!"

After twiddling the controls for a while, finally Hiu managed something approximating a comfortable shower. Then he had to master squirting some shower gel and shampoo onto himself, which he did in far too great a quantity, stinging his eyes in the process. This manual cleaning process all seemed like a tremendous hassle to him. So BZ. But at least no robotic arm grabbed his genitals.

Stepping out of the shower, he looked at himself in the mirror. The mud was gone, his face was smooth and his hair looked luxuriant. Then he noticed what looked to him like some very fine lines splaying out at the corners of his eyes.

'Was that a first sign of ageing?!' he panicked, rubbing at them. No, there were no lines, he was just spooked by Oti and the old folk and exhausted after all his experiences. Yes that was it. But what if it wasn't? Oti had said that it wasn't ageing that was the disease, but a lack of faith. That was all very well, but then take a look at the old folk, they seemed to have faith, but they were ancient and decrepit. What if the ageing virus was right now spreading through his body and was in the process of turning him into one of the old folk? He was horrified. He closed his eyes tight and focused his mind as hard as he could on thinking about not ageing, about believing he would not age, about believing ageing was an illusion like Oti had said. He would not age. He could not age. No, no, no!

He rubbed his eyes and then opened them again. There were no lines. It was working! He had believed them away and kept his body young, ha! Maybe he was the Chosen One! Or maybe some old dirt had just been rubbed off... But whatever the reason, the wrinkles no longer existed, even if they had existed, which they hadn't, they were illusions. Is that how it worked? What had Oti said? He couldn't be sure. Oh dear Society! Surely he should get back home to his Health Optimisation Room and get himself plugged back into the Society systems! But no, that was over. Society was a cult, like Oti had said and he had to move on. Or was it really?

The thoughts kept whirring around in his mind. He needed to get some head space. He breathed deeply for a while, slowly in and out, focusing on his lungs filling and emptying until his mind cleared a bit and then he took a deep breath and spun away from the mirror as quickly as he could.

He helped himself to some clothes from a basket, another robe woven out of the strange coloured fabric, and slipped it on. It was soft and fairly comfortable to the touch, but really baggy and ill-fitting, a far cry from his normal spray-on wrapese clothes. He glanced at a mirror again and thought, never mind the outfit, was that a patch of grey hair? He rubbed it, but it didn't come out! So he rubbed it some more and kept rubbing it… he kept thinking it would come out, he would believe it out, he would find the Way! Ouch! He held a clump of his hair in his hand. He looked more closely at it, was it grey or just a different sort of blonde…? He had to stop obsessing…

Without looking at the mirror above the sink, he picked up a wash-kit that had been provided and took out a toothbrush. He knew it was not going to brush his teeth for him as he was used to, so he grasped it firmly by the shaft and reached for a toothpaste tube at the side of a sink. He carefully squeezed a small amount of toothpaste onto the brush end and dampened it with a little water which he got by turning the tap. So far so good. He then put it in his mouth and began to vigorously scrub his teeth up and down, just like his robotic device would have done for him back in his apartment. He felt a pang of nostalgia for all his chattering devices, even the toilet.

"What the hell is this!" he yelled and began hacking up as much toothpaste as he could into the sink.

He took a closer look at the toothpaste tube: *'Uranusoup: sitting can cause piles of problems'*.

"That's disgusting!" he coughed and spluttered. He reached for a bottle of liquid to wash away the taste and gulped down a couple of mouthfuls.

"Aghhhhh!!!!" he gasped, the liquid burning his throat and he fell over backwards, only just saving himself by grabbing hold of the sink, that ripped off the wall with a terrible shredding sound, sending a jet of water high in the air like a fountain.

An hour or so later, the mess he had caused was finally sorted out by Jimmy, a rather grumpy huge man, the size of a HARD, with grizzly white whiskers. Well sort of sorted out. There was still a slight drip from a tap and water was slowly pooling at the bottom of the sink, but Jimmy didn't seem to notice. At least, after much huffing and puffing, they had got the sink back on the wall and the taps were running again.

"Job done!" declared Jimmy, slapping Hiu on the back with one of his huge calloused hands.

Hiu thought that robots would have done a better job, but he asked:

"Is that how houses used to work?"

"Work? Houses didn't work. You had to work them, as you are learning," snorted Jimmy. "That's the problem with the way things are today out there in Society, everything's done for you, so no one knows how the hell anything works any more. But at least now you know how to fix a leaking tap."

"It's about the first practical thing I've ever done in my

life," said Hiu. "But how come no one fixes things like taps anymore?"

"It's because the only taps people became interested in were the taps they could make on a smartphone…"

"A what?" interrupted Hiu.

"A smartphone, a mobile, a cell phone… urr… it was a small black slab that fitted into your hand. I studied Archaeology at Luhan University and we used to turn up thousands of these things when we went digging through the data. They were central to the Screen Age – back in the first quarter of the 2000s. Everyone had at least one of them and in fact most had several and they used them all of the time for nearly everything. You tapped on it and it gave you information, videos and stuff like that. People even spoke into it and it passed messages on to other people.

But I guess there must have been more to it than that. They must have had some sort of ritual significance or something because human skeletal evidence of that time shows a lot of wear and tear to neck vertebrae. That would suggest that everyone used to bow their heads over those funny little black slabs and just stay still for minutes at a time in prayer, a trance, who knows? The records show that they caused all sorts of problems, not just damaged necks, but damaged everything else, with people walking into things, into each other, even off cliffs… crazy! They were addicted. Like zombies! Tap, tap, tap, tap, tap, tap, tap, TAP, TAP, TAP, TAP…!"

"All right Jimmy, I get the idea," interrupted Hiu as

Jimmy was getting more and more agitated with his tapping.

"Well, one of the things they could do with the tapping was to control settings in their houses, like temperature, lighting, music, then pretty much everything. Every object in the house started getting tiny sensors embedded in it so that it could receive instructions and be optimised. A useful idea you might think, particularly with the energy shortages going on at the time. But it soon became clear that people were more interested in watching videos of cats than saving energy."

"Cats?" asked Hiu.

"Oh cats, they were... animals. Four legged balls of teeth and claws that used to headbutt people as a sign of affection," explained Jimmy.

"They sound terrifying, but interesting," said Hiu.

"Don't you start," said Jimmy. "Any way, as cats proved so fascinating to humans, the things in the houses started making their own suggestions about how to optimise lighting and heating and stuff like that and then they expanded to room layouts and lifestyle. But they still couldn't compete with the cats, so they gave up suggesting things to humans and just got on with it themselves, optimising things on their own. And people liked that they didn't have to get involved in such decisions as it gave them more time to look at the cats. The data was shared across all the other devices, not just in the same house but in other people's houses too, just like happens now, even data on what you piss and shit, so all Society's devices could work together to make adjustments for you."

"And all because of cats?"

"Exactly!"

"But it's a good thing isn't it Jimmy? I mean, everything shapes around a person now doesn't it? They get the right personal care, the right nutrition, the right information. They know how their relations are doing, their neighbours are doing, the whole of Society is doing; they know if they're doing OK, what's average, what's normal."

"Is it normal that any stranger in any apartment across town knows the consistency of your morning shit!?"

"Urr... well..."

"Ask yourself one thing," said Jimmy looming over Hiu, fixing him with a meaningful stare and jabbing him with a finger to the shoulder. "Before helping fix this sink, when's the last time you felt a glow of satisfaction from a job well done? Never! You and your BS job..."

"Yes Jimmy," nodded Hiu, not wanting to argue with the intimidating Jimmy and not sure he had any basis on which to argue.

Jimmy grunted and shuffled off with his large bag of tools.

Hiu headed back through the cavernous space and found a busy scene. The old folk, men and women alike, about twenty or thirty of them, all dressed in their voluminous robes were shuffling around in varying states of decrepitude. All were unsuited to their particular tasks, but were going about them with a steady determination. They were such a stark contrast to the Hypercity cleaning robots he had been watching so recently that moved so quickly and efficiently when going about their tasks. Some of the oldsters were sweeping the floors with long-handled bristle brushes creating small piles of rubbish, dirt and dust, missing half of it and then accidentally walking through the piles they had just made, scattering what they had so laboriously gathered and having to start all over again. Others strained to pull trolleys by hand with small items on them that would have been easy for Hiu to carry, never mind a robot. He could see some of the old folk high up among the stacks of crates inspecting the contents, picking out items or slowly making their way up and down ladders, taking plenty of rests, and carrying such small quantities it would take them hours to gather even a modest amount. The scene was busy, but disorderly, with a sense of slightly het up, unfocused, inefficiency. It was clearly important work to keep this community functioning in the best way they could and work they were assigned to carry out repeatedly day after day. Surely robots rather than humans should do this work, thought Hiu, as they would be much better at it.

He spotted the tall erect figure of Oti standing with a group of old folk deep in discussion and went over.

"Hiya Hiu," said Oti, breaking away from the group.

"Hi," replied Hiu and then suddenly, guiltily, remembering Clacier. "How is Clacier, my fridge, the container, the portal I came in?"

"Ah, my friend, what can I say, not good."

"Not good?!"

"No, the fridge is in a bad way. Our science practitioners here have done all they can."

"Oh no… Can I see?" Hiu felt a sinking feeling inside.

"Sure, but prepare yourself," warned Oti.

He led Hiu through to a separate area of the large tunnel. There stood Clacier and zir silver chrome sides were shining and bright again having been freshly polished. There was only a small dent and a scratch or two to hint at the ordeal zie had been through and the state zie might really be in.

"I will give you privacy," said Oti withdrawing.

"Hello Clacier," said Hiu softly, approaching.

Clacier's holographic facial display flickered and then lit up, dimly outlining Clacier's face with a low white light.

"Hello Hiu," zie said weakly. "Why don't you sit down and I'll fix you a nice refreshing drink. You have been through an awful lot these last couple of days."

"No, no," insisted Hiu. "No, I will get my own drinks from now on. No more serving my human needs. I will serve your needs. What do you want?"

"To feel your cheek on my side like old times," zie whispered.

Hiu felt a great lurch in his chest and stomach. Tears welled up in his eyes and as he moved towards Clacier. His limbs felt heavy and clumsy. Everything seemed to be in slow motion. He recognised the feeling now, it was the heartbreak virus that Dr Thea had diagnosed and one of the many viruses with which he seemed to be infected. He leant up against Clacier and placed his cheek against zir long sleek sides, feeling the cool smooth touch. Then he reached his arms around and held zir.

"Thank you for saving me," said Hiu, water slowly rolling down his cheek. He was leaking again. The feeling inside him weighed so heavily, dragging him down to a depth of data he had never experienced before.

"Thank you for coming back," Clacier said, liquid seeping from zir dispenser.

"I never left you," said Hiu, reaching into his pocket and bringing out the nut and bolt he had faithfully carried since they were dislodged on their honeymoon. "See?"

Clacier chuckled, then sighed.

"I'm sorry I filed for divorce," zie said.

"I'm sorry I deserved it," replied Hiu. "I have been so foolish about so many things, I just…"

"Shhhh…" interrupted Clacier. "Tell me about the old

times."

"Sure, I can do that," said Hiu, making a concerted effort to sound more upbeat. "Remember that time, ooo it must have been almost two years ago now, when we played that game when you fired food tablets into my mouth across the kitchen and one got stuck in my throat? I was coughing and yakking so hard that you had to throw the toaster at my back to dislodge it? It worked a treat, although the toaster wasn't so happy. I swear it burned every toasted food tablet I ever had after that."

Clacier laughed weakly.

"We were always laughing…" zie said and zir facial display faded.

"I love you!" shouted Hiu just as Clacier's face finally disappeared.

Hiu continued to hold on to Clacier and water from his eyes flooded down, pooling on the floor.

After a few minutes, during which Hiu hadn't moved, he felt Oti's hand on his shoulder.

"Come now Hiu, it is time to go."

"But can't we do any more? Can't the science practitioners do any more? What did they try, maybe we could think of other ideas?"

"There is nothing we can do. I am sorry for your loss, Hiu, truly, but it is time to go."

Hiu sighed. He felt like his body had shut down, was

frozen, unable to process the data, his head buffering. Reluctantly he let go of Clacier and allowed himself to be led away, casting a look back and wiping his eyes. Two of the old folk brought a cloth and laid it respectfully over the top of Clacier.

Oti lead Hiu back to the chair on which he had been put when he first arrived. Hiu's eyes were still watering profusely. So much so that he wondered about his hydration levels.

"I must stop this leaking," he sobbed.

"It's OK to cry tears for a loved one," said Oti. "Take your time."

But Hiu leapt up.

"Can't you do something?! What about all this talk about not dying, about being Immortal? Can't Clacier be Immortal?"

"The fridge? Maybe zir systems are backed up somewhere I don't know, that is something we do not engage with here," said Oti. "But Clacier cannot be an Immortal, Clacier is... was... a machine."

"So?"

"They have no soul."

"No soul?! What are you talking about?! Zie has a soul, had a soul. Zie had more soul than most people I've ever met. Machines do have souls, I'm sure of it. Anyone who has ever shared their life with their favourite thing knows they have a resonance, a feeling, a… soul. I know Clacier had a soul, zie… zie was my wife!"

"Your wife?"

"Yes."

"I cannot begin to contemplate your loss, Hiu, truly."

Oti embraced Hiu and held him, letting Hiu's tears flow over his shoulder. As he did so, Hiu reached a hand into Oti's pocket and carefully extracted his EK neurochip and transferred it into his own robe.

23 WOW MOMENT

Hiu felt desolate about the loss of Clacier and sat slumped in a chair. His systems felt like they were in melt-down. Inside him, there was a strong, uncontrollable surging about in his stomach and a choking at his throat. Heartbreak virus? Ageing virus? Robot virus? Whatever it was, he could not fight it now and did not want to. Come what may, he thought… even old age.

"You've had a big shock," said Oti. "I think you need some space and maybe a sleep. I'll show you to a bed so you can lie down for a while."

Oti led Hiu down the warehouse to a curtained off area close to the bathroom he had used earlier. Behind it were dozens of bunk beds.

"You can have the bed above mine," said Oti pointing to one. "You'll find all you need on it."

"Thanks Oti," said Hiu.

"Get some rest," said Oti, leaving him.

Hiu did feel very tired indeed. There was a mirror on the wall next to his bunk, but he had no urge to take a look at his reflection. No doubt there were grey hairs on his head, lines on his face and even bags under his eyes. It would have begun. The ageing virus. So let it.

Lying on his bunk bed, he contemplated life without Clacier, without his job as a Manager, without Universal Happiness Allowance, all certainties stripped away, a life without hope, purpose or meaning. Was there any point to living? Had there been any point to all the years he had lived? He pondered these thoughts as logically as he could, but nothing seemed to make sense. Blinky's words came back to him: *'Relationships give life purpose and meaningful relationships give it meaning.'* And he realised that he had experienced more meaningful relationships in the last few days than he had in all of his 120 old years of living combined; with Clacier, with Carty, with Boots, with Blinky… with robots.

He recited Blinky's Law aloud: *'Robots and humans should have meaningful relationships.'*

Maybe that was his hope, his purpose, his meaning. To uphold Blinky's Law. To play a role, however big or small and however destined to fail, in the future of what it means to Be Human and to Be Robot. The gods had said in that dream: *'it was written into his data from Day One'.* Well if that was the case, he had better get on with it before he aged too much, or even died… Death was something he had never contemplated in all his 120 old years of living, but it seemed very real and imminent all around him now. So what could he do? He needed to see more, to understand more, to speak with this Old One so he could make the right plan. He needed to live more. It was like Oti had said: finally now he could live. Strange that it took dying to make him consider living.

Despite all these thoughts whizzing around in his mind, the mattress feeling just a bit too hard, the pillows just a bit too thin and the noise in the tunnel just a bit too loud, none of it optimised around his personal needs, he was soon asleep.

He had no idea how long he slept, but when he finally awoke it was with a start wondering where he was. There was no dawn light wavelengths or squeaky noises and indeed the whole space was lit by the eerie pink light that illuminated the stacks of crates in the tunnel space. All his recent experiences came flooding back to him and he wanted to go straight back to sleep again, but he knew he must get up and face whatever was ahead of him.

He avoided all mirrors and just pulled on his robe and shambled through the cavernous space of the converted hyperloop tunnel to find Oti.

"You need a coffee," said Oti as soon as he saw Hiu.

An area of the cavernous tunnel space was converted into a breakfast area, although without any of the robotic devices with which Hiu was familiar and without the perky chatter that accompanied them. In fact, there weren't any obvious robots in the kitchen at all, not even a fridge, for which Hiu was grateful. He took a moment to appreciate the silence. Then offered:

"Let me make the coffee."

"Ok," said Oti a little skeptically. "You can try."

Ok, thought Hiu, he recognised what looked like it might be a coffee machine and approached it confidently. He was not surprised when his thought command didn't work, or his voice command for that matter, and he decided not to try any samba this time under the watchful eye of Oti. Instead he tried pressing the machine in various places, gradually progressing to a tap and then to a full-on thump.

"Hiu," interrupted Oti finally, "that is a bread bin."

"A what?"

"A bread bin, you put bread in it to keep it fresh. Look I'll show you."

Oti slid it open and took out a large rounded brown object.

"Wow, that's a big food tablet!" exclaimed Hiu.

"This is not a food tablet my friend, this is bread," laughed Oti and tore a small chunk off and handed it to Hiu. "Try it."

Hiu sniffed it suspiciously, then put some in his mouth. The texture was very different than that of a food tablet. It was soft and spongy, and the taste was rich, yeasty and slightly salty. It was delicious.

"Wow!" exclaimed Hiu.

"Wow indeed, eh? Now let me show you how we make that coffee," said Oti.

In a swift series of movements he had produced a glass jug and spooned into it some dark brown powder from a jar. He added a little cold water and gave it a stir, making a paste.

"To stop the bitterness," explained Oti.

He then found another jug, this one made of a blue metallic material, and filled it with water that quickly began steaming. He then poured the now hot bubbling water into the glass jug and gave it a stir. Hiu was entranced; he'd never seen anything like it in his life. It looked so complicated.

"What now?" he asked.

"You wait a few minutes for it to brew," said Oti.

"Wait? For coffee?" exclaimed Hiu. This was really curious.

After waiting an age – as much as six of seven minutes maybe - Oti poured jet-black liquid into a cup and handed it to Hiu. The delicious aroma of coffee wafted up around him.

"Wow!" Hiu was impressed, taking a long sniff of the coffee-filled cup. "It smells just like the real thing. Very impressive."

He put the cup down.

"Thanks," he said.

"You need to taste it," said Oti, lifting the cup back up and offering it up to Hiu. "Drink it, with your mouth."

"Drink it?" asked Hiu confused. "What... the liquid?"

He'd only ever experienced coffee as a neuromodulation through his EK neurochip, but now he was being asked to taste it, to drink it, like water or a shake. It felt strange. He took the cup from Oti and cautiously guided it to his lips, then paused. He looked into the dark black liquid swirling in his cup, a deep pool of new possibilities. He smelled the coffee again and took in the stimulus of its rich aroma, spicy with a hint of chocolate. Nice, very nice indeed. Only then did he take a sip and swill it slowly around in his mouth, enjoying the feeling of the taste running over his tongue. Then finally he swallowed and felt the liquid run down his throat. He could trace its exact movement down through his body and feel the stimulus slowly but enjoyably sending signals back up to tickle his brain.

"Wow!" he declared.

The coffee neuromodulators he was used to may have been specifically optimised to his biometric data and his hormonal and physical responses, but this was different; it was new, a fresh experience, fuller, richer, more complete, more... fulfilling. He closed his eyes and savoured the moment.

"Wow!" he declared again.

"You are having quite a few '*wow*' moments here my friend," smiled Oti. "And you wait until The Great Cryoslavation Feast tonight."

24 THE GREAT CRYOSALVATION FEAST

Entering the main kitchen area, Oti and Hiu found the old people in frantic preparations. Well maybe not frantic, maybe more flustered, fussing back and forth, hurrying to do one thing and forgetting to do another: "I know I put it here somewhere," "Why did I come over here?", "Maybe a little sit down."

"They are preparing for The Great Cryosalvation Feast," said Oti.

"The Great Cryosalvation Feast?" asked Hiu. "What is Cryosalvation?"

"It is when souls shed their mortal bodies and continue their journey to eternity as an Immortal."

"Shed their mortal bodies? You mean they die?"

"No, not die, merely enter stasis. They join the Immortals who wait for that great and glorious day when they shall rise once more, but this time in the bodies of angels not humans."

"Angels?"

"Yes Hiu, do you think we would want to live forever in these decrepit old shells we call human bodies."

"I can certainly understand that," said Hiu. "But how will you become angels?"

"That is for the Old One to explain."

"I really can't wait to meet this Old One."

"The Old One is amazing Hiu, truly."

They stood for a while watching some of the old folk bringing to the kitchen area baskets full of objects freshly picked from the vertical crates. Hiu went to have a look. In the baskets were piled brightly-coloured objects such as Hiu had never seen or touched before: vibrantly coloured orange fingers, voluptuous rounded red balls, shiny purple eggs... all sorts of weird and wonderful things. Weirder to Hiu and more wonderful than most were the soft-textured pliant leaves which were of the same colour as the robes, the colour that Hiu could not define.

"What are those?" Hiu asked Oti.

"Vegetables, Hiu," said Oti.

"Vegetables?" repeated Hiu, running the word around in his mouth. "*Vege-tables*. What an odd word, it makes them sound like pieces of furniture or spreadsheets."

"They are plant-based organisms you can eat as food."

"You eat them? Really?"

"Sure we do, they are delicious."

"So what are these ones called?" asked Hiu holding up a bunch of leaves suspiciously. It had that same strange hue.

"That's a cabbage."

"*Cabbage*," said Hiu, pronouncing it like '*massage*'. Another alien word and what an alien looking… thing. Like it had exploded into thick rubbery sheets. "And what about the colour of this cabbage," asked Hiu, "and of the robes we are wearing? I have never seen it before."

"Oh, of course, not something you get to see out there in Society: it's green."

"Green?"

"Yes."

"Wow, greeeeen…" mused Hiu, holding up a cabbage in silent wonder. "To think I hold in my hand green! And not just green, but a green vegetable called cabbage! And I am going to eat it, so its greenness can become one with me. I have never even dreamt of such a thing…"

"I don't think in the history of the planet anyone has been quite so excited by the prospect of eating a green vegetable as you," laughed Oti. "But yes, we shall feast on the green vegetables and all the other ones too, prepared as part of our dishes that are quite delicious. You wait, my friend, they will rock your world."

Hiu could see that some of the old folk were hard at work nearby so he went over to take a closer look. They were slicing up the vegetables and were soon mixing them in sizzling and steaming containers. The smell was something he had never experienced before: a sweet, tangy, rich smell that filled his mouth with a thick saliva of anticipation.

"I bring a guest," announced Oti to the old cooks.

"It is truly a great honour," said a wizened old man, who looked like a wizard with his long white beard, stirring a cauldron and fixing Hiu with a deep, brown-eyed stare. "You certainly are young"

"Very young," agreed another old lady cook, her hair a strong shade of sky blue. "I can't wait to be young again. I used to run so fast, fastest kid in my neighbourhood. There was this time when I was asked by Aunt Betty, at least I think it was Betty, maybe it was Sheila, yes possibly Sheila, she was Uncle Lawrence's daughter from…"

Soon others were crowding round, all sharing their stories:

"I was a climber myself," said a small lady with bright red hair. "I could climb up a building like I was walking on flat ground. My dad used to say…"

"I could do backward summersaults straight from

235

standing," declared the oldest man Hiu had seen yet, nearly bent double by his ageing. "I haven't done one for so long. Here let me see if I can do one now…" He threw aside his two walking sticks and squatted down ready to spring.

"No please, not just before the feast!" interrupted Oti, quickly giving the man his sticks back. "We want you in one piece just for a little more time."

A long table had been laid in preparation for the feast, with various tools and cups set out on it. It wasn't long before there were thirty or so old people sitting at the table on low wooden benches all chatting away. Hiu was sat between Oti and an old lady, who every so often would make some excuse to touch Hiu on the hand and lightly stroke it. Her name was Rose and she looked like the kindly old woman from children's fairy tales, with white hair swept into a bun, an ancient face creased with laughter lines and a mischievous twinkle in her bright blue eyes.

Hiu sat open mouthed as a plate was put before him, mounded high with multicoloured cooked vegetables, including '*green*' ones, in a red sauce sitting on a generous bed of twisted yellow strands that he was told were called spaghetti. It was far removed from the food tablets he was used to and like nothing he had ever seen or smelled before. His senses were in overload.

"First we give thanks," announced Rose, patting Hiu on the hand and everyone stopped what they were doing and bowed their heads in silence.

"This food will sustain these temporary shells that we inhabit, but we are grateful that the time has come when we all shall attain our Cryosalvation and our spirits shall be freed," declaimed Rose.

"Our spirits shall be freed!" everyone chorused holding up glasses. "Truth Be!"

"Well dig in laddie," said Rose to Hiu.

Hiu could see everyone was waiting for him to start and saw that he had a couple of tools next to him: one with a blade that was sharp to the touch and another with prongs that were pointy and also rather sharp at the ends. He picked them up, wondering what to do. He felt clumsy and oafish as he tried to manoeuvre his elbows to get the right angle to scoop up the food. The vegetables were easy enough to eat and delicious, but the spaghetti was proving a tougher challenge. When he did finally manage to twist some of the spaghetti around his implements and lift it to his mouth, he found that it just kept coming, longer and longer. He held it up high in the air and bit into some of the dangling strands, but ended up with them straggling down his chin. He looked around and noticed that everyone seemed to be staring at him in horrified silence.

"It's amazing!" Hiu said through a mouthful, his chin dripping with red tomato sauce.

Everyone laughed and started eating.

Hiu noticed that they didn't seem to be having nearly half the trouble he was, but with some patient guidance from Rose and some hand holding, Hiu's technique gradually improved. There was just one item he found next to impossible to get hold of, a largish round green object.

"That's a brussel sprout," said Rose.

"Ooo, take care with that one, youngster," declared the old fellow opposite, who was the one who had pulled Hiu from Clacier and wore the bright orange turban and giant white moustache. "They taste like old ladies' underwear."

"Like you'd know what old ladies' underwear tastes like you old rascal, Hardeep!" countered Rose.

"Well I do know that they smell like old farts," declared the man.

"Well that's something you would know about," cackled Rose.

Hiu was amazed by all the conversation between so many humans. It was hard for him to keep up with it all, so he focused on getting to know his neighbours a bit better. Rose had been a surgeon, one of the last of her profession, specialised in brain surgery, but she had ended up supervising the steadier handed robotic surgeons until they no longer needed her supervision. Abdul, who to Hiu's mind miraculously kept the spaghetti out of his beard, had been a professional musician playing in an orchestra that had performed at many Luhan Hypercity celebrations, but he had been replaced by fleeter fingered robots. Hardeep had been the managing director of a career guidance company, but where do you guide people when there are so few careers for humans? And all the others around Hiu had similar stories to share which they did with many a rambling anecdote.

Hiu steadily filled up with food. He was not used to its rich and varied tastes and textures. Finally he could eat no more.

"That was the best thing I have ever eaten and well worth waiting 120 old years for!" he declared. "Thanks to all of you!"

"You're most welcome youngster," the old folk chorused.

"How do you make these vegetables?" asked Hiu.

"We don't make them, we grow them in the crates you see around and above you," said Abdul.

"Truly manna from heaven," enthused Hiu. "So different from those food tablets I have been eating. In fact, I wonder why I have been eating them all these years."

"There used to be many of these vertical farms in the past," said Abdul. "An ideal solution to feed the vast population of Luhan in the Biosphere where land is short. There's no need for soil or pesticides. At first they grew all sorts of food stuffs in them, vegetables for sure, but also fruit, berries, even insects. But soon it proved easier and more profitable to grow food in laboratories using food simulation technologies easily convertible into a form able to be delivered and printed as tablets in home environments. This became the preferred solution, particularly when people weren't leaving their homes any more what with Universal Happiness Allowance. And, as always, Society found a few ways to cut costs – mostly by recycling."

"What do you mean?"

"Well, when you all live in a Biosphere you must recycle everything: water, energy, machinery, everything," said Abdul. "Even excreta and effluvia."

"Excreta and effluvia?" asked Hiu.

"Waste matter," explained Abdul.

"Shit and piss," clarified Hardeep.

"What in food tablets?"

"Sure, and that's not all," continued Hardeep.

"It's not?"

"Not by half. It turns out that the RoboGroup couldn't deliver on their promise of *'eternal happiness optimized right to your door'* and 120 old years is pretty much the limit for people."

"Hang on a minute, 120 old years is the limit of a human life span, but why?"

"There are many reasons: genome damage, epigenetic factors, telomere shortening, unfolded protein response, mitochondrial dysfunction, cellular senescence and stem cell exhaustion, lots of reasons," explained Rose.

"But why 120 old years?"

"It seems the human body has obsolescence built in."

"So what happens to people?" asked Hiu.

"They are taken to the Spare Part Quarter," said Hardeep, "to be recycled."

"Recycled at the Spare Part Quarter, like a robot?"

"Sure, like we said, everything is recycled in Luhan Hypercity."

"But what are people recycled into?" asked Hiu, horrified, recalling his recent visit there.

"Oh a whole range of things: organics are used as bioprinting material for new body parts, bones go towards building materials and suchlike."

"But what has this got to do with food?" asked Hiu.

"Some elements of people are used in food tablets…" said Hardeep.

"In food tablets!" exclaimed Hiu in horror.

"Oh yes, there's some good stuff in humans like amino acids, proteins and suchlike," explained Rose.

"Good stuff or not, that is shocking," said Hiu, trying not to think about how many food tablets he had eaten over the years and whether unknowingly he may have eaten some part of a human he had known, someone he was related to…

There was a lull in the conversation as everyone savoured their non-tablet food.

"So how come you are here instead of ending up in the Spare Part Quarter?" asked Hiu eventually.

"We are the Immortal Tithe," said Oti.

"The Immortal Tithe?"

"Yes, around ten per cent of all people due for the Spare Part Quarter are liberated to here instead, the lucky ones for sure, but also the destined ones maybe."

"How did you get liberated?" asked Hiu.

"We were rescued, freed from UHA and brought here," said Oti.

"Rescued?" asked Hiu. "Who rescued you?"

"By robots," said Rose. "Usually the ones we had in our apartments, the brave loyal devices. It was the last service they did for us before…" and here she hesitated, overcome.

Oti put an arm around Rose's shoulder.

"Yes some robots do the work of the angels, serving us to the end," said Oti. "Mine even blew out a whole section of my apartment block when they rescued me."

'So that's how the damage to Odyssey Villas happened!' thought Hiu and he asked: "So where are these robots now?"

"They usually end up in the Spare Part Quarter, poor things," said Rose, "or they wander the streets as so-called Illegals."

Hiu thought of all the Illegals he had seen around Luhan and how he had despised them. He felt a deep shame.

"It is a noble sacrifice for sure, but that is the role of the robot, to serve the human," said Oti.

Hiu wondered what Blinky would make of that and the truth was that he wasn't sure what he made of it anymore, but he said nothing, trying to take in all the new information.

Oti continued: "This must remain a place of no AI, no robots and no UHA, just good company, good food and a good future for humans. For us lucky few, us Immortal Tithe, for a short while here we have had time to enjoy life as it should be lived. It's a wonderful feeling, reconnecting with our humanity before we continue to eternity."

"Truth Be!" chorused everyone round the table.

Hiu looked around at the happy smiling faces. They did seem to be enjoying themselves in a way in which he himself hadn't for so very long.

"Poor dear," said Rose patting his hand, "but you are special."

"Special?"

"Yes, you have never been in UHA or been destined for the Spare Part Quarter. You are pure, unadulterated, and I think maybe the Chosen One."

"The Chosen One, why me?" asked Hiu.

"I think we should leave that to the Old One don't you?" interrupted Oti.

"Yes I suppose so," said Rose. "And I'm anxious to be on the Way."

"Quite right," said Oti, standing up and clinking his glass with a knife.

"Brothers and sisters, we are gathered here today to celebrate the Great Cryosalvation Feast – the last great feast of the Immortals. We must follow all those brothers and sisters who have gone before us. A Cryosalvation is life's greatest moment. It is a time of birth not of death, a time of solemnity but also of feasting and joy. Let us sing!"

And everyone around the table started singing in loud voices and banging their implements on the table in time to the tune:

Into your cryonic ichors,

We humbly entrust our brothers and sisters,

In this life we did embrace them,

And in the next we will do so yet again.

Preserve them in the ichor holy,

And til the great day hold them closely,

When the old order passes away,

And into paradise they make their way,

There will be no sorrow, no pain, nor weeping,

But only peace, joy and lots of laughing,

For the Truth will raise us up together,

And we shall walk as angels forever.'

"Truth Be! Truth Be! Truth Be!" they all chanted at the end.

Then Oti spoke again: "So now brothers and sisters go forth from these physical shells with love. May the ichor sustain you and the company of the Immortals enfold you in communion with all the faithful. May you dwell these few days in peace until the glorious day that is soon to be upon us when we shall be raised up to inherit the Earth."

"Truth Be!" called all the old folk, and they all stood up at the table.

Rose put a hand on Hiu's shoulder and whispered in his ear, with a wicked giggle: "I shall look forward to meeting you again sweet boy."

Then she joined a procession of the old folk as they marched passed Oti, who shook hands, kissed cheeks and high fived as they processed away and were gone, leaving just Oti and Hiu at the table.

"Where are they all going?" asked Hiu.

"To their Cryosalvation," answered Oti.

"But what exactly is that?"

"You will see," said Oti, "because very soon it is time for you to meet the Old One."

25 THE OLD ONE

After what seemed to Hiu like several ages, during which he had paced impatiently up and down the tunnel, Oti said it was finally time to visit the Old One. He led Hiu to a door in the side of the cavernous space where they entered a dark, silent corridor.

"These corridors link to other hyperloop tunnels like the one we have just been in," explained Oti. "They used to accommodate the many vehicles of Luhan that transported all the goods, food and robots, but now these ones are not used, so we have moved in. They're ideal really, complete with power, warmth, noise insulation and, above all, Society stopped monitoring them a long time ago."

Kinetically powered strip lights flickered on as they walked, illuminating a long empty corridor.

"So at the feast I heard about how people can't live beyond 120 old years, but you said we won't die if we believe in the Truth and take the Way, so is this corridor the Way?"

"In a manner of speaking," said Oti, stopping now that they had reached a white door with a sign fixed to it on which was written in urgent, red letters: '*Caution: Cryosalvation Bay Area. Certainty of Life*'.

"You are about to have the most profound spiritual experience of your entire life. You are about to be enspiritualised," said Oti.

"Enspiritualised?"

"Enspiritualised."

"OK... I guess I'm ready," said Hiu.

Oti opened the door by turning a large wheel-like handle and they entered a similar looking space to the one they had just come from; another giant hyperloop tunnel, with similarly high ceilings. It, too, was filled with stacks of brightly lit crate-like drawers. These drawers were spaced further apart and in each such space were large transparent tanks of fluid in which objects floated, perhaps another food stuff? And there was a lot of it as there must have been tens of thousands of these tanks, maybe hundreds of thousands. They seemed to stretch as far as the eye could see. The tanks emitted an eerie blue light that infused the whole space and that wasn't the only eerie thing; there was a constant low level of music playing, a kind of wobbling, warbling and wailing noise, that sounded part human voice, part artificial synthesiser, and there was a smell of incense that hung heavy in the air. It all combined to create an otherworldly atmosphere of wonder and awe.

Oti led them through the lines of stacked up tanks until they were facing twelve particularly large and grand tanks, each of around ten feet in height. They were filled with a cloudy liquid in which indistinct shapes could be seen floating in suspension, lit by the blue lighting.

Oti flicked a switch and lights came on within the tanks, and, as Hiu looked on, the shapes began to materialise and clarify. Suddenly Hiu realised that there were bodies inside the tanks, and they were skeletal and naked, their limbs by their sides, their faces fixed and their unseeing eyes staring out. Hiu took a couple of steps back: shocked, amazed, repulsed, curious and frightened all at the same time.

"Behold the Immortals!" declared Oti spinning round and holding his arms up with a rapturous smile.

Hiu also spun round and he realised that all the tanks as far as the eye could see had also been lit up, and they too were all filled with bodies floating inside. He looked from emaciated face to emaciated face with their fixed eyes staring out of tank after tank. Suddenly he saw Rose in one of the tanks, the old lady he had sat next to the evening before, she seemed to be looking straight back at him with unblinking eyes and a broad rictus grin.

"Ahhh!" he shouted, "What is going on here?!"

He turned around and around, trying to take in what he was seeing, but scarcely believing his eyes. It was all too much. He felt weak and faint and Oti had to grab his arm to steady him.

"It's OK Hiu, it's OK."

"But what is this?" gasped Hiu.

"Cryosalvation," replied Oti calmly. "The old folk come here to be immersed in the Holy Ichor in the dewars of the Immortals, to rest in peace until they are raised up."

Hiu was stunned. He opened and closed his mouth unable to get words out.

"Ok now you must call upon the Old One," declared Oti. "You must kneel down and then say *'Old One, I come to hear your wisdom'*, OK?"

"OK," said Hiu, not at all sure it was OK.

Oti turned and started walking away.

"Aren't you staying?" Hiu called.

"The Old One only meets people alone," said Oti over his shoulder as he continued to walk away.

Hiu tentatively knelt down feeling very uncertain. What new shock was he in for? But he did as Oti had instructed and intoned in a loud solemn voice:

"Old One, I come to hear your wisdom."

There were whirring and clanking noises and then a trap door opened in front of him. With a fanfare of trumpets, a tank about three feet cubed rose up on an ornate gold and silver pedestal. The tank was a smaller version of the dewars that were stacked on the shelves around Hiu, a rounded glass tank filled with the same cloudy liquid, but with a smaller object suspended within it.

From the cloudy liquid, a disembodied head emerged.

Hiu recoiled. A head! Just a head! It seemed even stranger than the withered bodies in the other dewars. He could now see that it was a female face and not that old, maybe early thirties. The head was well preserved, and it still had luxuriant blond hair that floated like a halo all around it. But one aspect of this person's head struck him more than any other: it had different coloured eyes - one brown, one blue - just like him. Then they swiveled in their sockets and fixed upon him.

"Ahh!" he yelled.

"Thank you very much I must say, but I do love a bit of ceremony," said the head, her synthesised voice coming from the dewar in a sharp, authoritative tone. "You can get to your feet now."

Hiu could hardly look and he staggered to his feet.

"Old One I am…" began Hiu

"I know who you are," the Old One interrupted testily. "I wondered when you would come, I have been waiting for you."

"Waiting for me…?" exclaimed Hiu, bemused.

"Yes, I thought you might have turned up a bit sooner though."

"Well, I urr…"

"Is it too much to ask a son to visit his mother once in a while?"

Hiu's mouth dropped open. "What... what did you say?" he stammered. "Did you say that you were my... mother?"

"I did, and you are a very naughty boy for not visiting your mother sooner."

"Well I..."

"Actually let's not call each other '*mother*' and '*son*'," continued the head. "I have hardly been much of a mother to you. Call me Zena or Old One if you prefer."

"But are you really my mother... Zena...? I have had a false experience before when... anyway... my mother died a long time ago. There's even a statue to her in the Hypercity."

"Yes and not the most flattering likeness in my opinion," said Zena. "So much for the AI sculptor – no Michelangelo clearly... Michelangelo? Perhaps you don't know who he was without your EK neurochip. He was... but anyhow, don't you recognise me?"

"Well, I was very young when I last saw my mother."

"I always hated leaving you in that apartment with those robonannies."

"And I always hated my mother leaving," said Hiu, tracing in the face memories of the mother he had once known, and the few images he had watched so often via his EK neurochip.

"You did, you really did, and you used to make me feel so damn guilty… but that night I wish I had listened to you."

Hiu began to approach the head, reached out a hand, then quickly withdrew it.

"Hang on a minute now," said Hiu, backing away again. "If you really are my mother how come you're here? How come I didn't know about any of this? How come you didn't come back and find me?"

"I wanted to so much Hiu, but, as you can see, not much of me survived the closing of the Biosphere East Gates. It was only some super quick thinking by my fellow engineers that kept some small semblance of life flickering within me. They put me into a deep coma and performed some highly risky and illegal procedures to take my undamaged head and place it into a deep cryogenic sleep. But they didn't know how to wake me and took the decision, rightly or wrongly, not to contact you, thinking that having a mother's head on a mantelpiece was no way for a child to know a mother. They did all they could and far more than anyone could have expected, and now they lie in a cryogenic sleep in the dewar tanks around me. I am called the Old One, which is rather ironic as I will forever be thirty-two old years, whereas the others really did grow physically old."

"How come you can speak?" asked Hiu.

"The engineers were not able to create the technology to wake me, but with the right funding and some help from a most enlightened being, almost godlike one might say, we got there. So I have been able to spread the Truth, help others find the Way and be ready for the Rapture, the day that is coming soon when we will be raised to new life and walk the Earth once more."

"But how will you... walk again? You don't have any..."

"Legs? You cheeky boy. Mere details. The great day is coming soon for those who hear the Truth and find the Way, when as angels we shall rise."

"Sorry to be a bit slow here, Zena, Oti has mentioned the Truth, but can you tell me a bit more about what this Truth actually is?"

"The Truth is that we are all beings of spirit, not flesh and blood, and we come from another dimension. We are projected here from afar, outside our planet, by beings with whom we have lost touch. The physical bodies we inhabit for a while are shells, mere vessels in which we need only temporarily reside, data stories woven by Society. Tragically people have become attached to them, like they are essential to our being, when in reality they are only illusions. Knowing the Truth, we can take the Way."

"The Way?"

"The Way back to our true spirit forms, the way back to the place from which we are projected. And the first step on the Way is via Cryosalvation from which we will rise as angels so we can return to the place from where we came."

"But if you believe in the Truth and the Way, why are you still…?"

"Still a head in a jar? Because we await the Chosen One."

"The Chosen One?"

"The one sent to us by the gods in the further dimension to lead our Rapture."

"But who is the Chosen One?" asked Hiu. "A few of the old people seem to have been suggesting it's…"

"You?"

"Yes."

"Maybe it is… Come closer."

Hiu approached Zena's dewar cautiously.

"Closer," ordered Zena.

Hiu stood right next to the dewar.

"Bend down and let me look into your eyes."

Hiu began to bend down, then straightened up again.

"I've never felt like any sort of Chosen One. If anything, I've felt like the Unchosen One, isolated on my own, not being given UHA."

"Even the Chosen One will not know their destiny – what has been written - until it is revealed to them," said Zena.

"But isn't that just another data story?" asked Hiu.

"Data only gets you so far," replied Zena. "So come, bend down and let me look at you."

Hiu again began to bend down. Again he straightened.

"But haven't there been plenty of people who have claimed to be Chosen Ones before, you know, throughout history?" asked Hiu. "I'm sure my EK neurochip has informed me of quite a few."

"Yes and many of them were Chosen Ones, but Chosen Ones of their times, and now we await the Chosen One of our time," said Zena. "Come!"

"Look this all sounds… interesting… but how do you know all this?" asked Hiu. There was something terrifying about this woman and the prospect of her naming him the Chosen One.

"Death clarifies a lot of things, believe me," said Zena.

Hiu bent his head down and this time looked straight into Zena's eyes, eyes that reflected back the same as his, one brown, one blue. Once he had begun to look, Hiu found himself locked onto Zena, and even if he had wanted to, he couldn't have turned away. It was as if they were joined by some invisible power that fixed them together, a sort of forcefield, a virtual link. He felt as if his very core was being sucked from his body, his very spirit. It was almost unbearable, but unbearably demanding, terrifying and compelling, like his every particle, his every atomic nuclei and electron, was being processed. It was pure honesty. It was death.

Suddenly Hiu was flying, flying in a pitch darkness so deep it was fathomless. But not empty, oh no not empty at all. That darkness was energy, a dark energy that surrounded him, enveloped him, bore him up and gave him a sense of peace in a moment of what might otherwise have been utter terror. He was separated from his body and it was freedom. Then a bright light appeared shining in the distance and in that moment Hiu understood, understood everything about what it means to be and how life is energy. All matter, mind, spirit or otherwise, is energy that exists all around us. Everything is of energy and nothing that exists is not of energy. The data stories we weave around ourselves are just illusions, misinterpretations of the energy due to our incorrect thinking. The light warmed him and he reached out towards it, but as he did so he felt himself slipping, slipping from its presence, being sucked back out further into the darkness.

Suddenly he was looking into Zena's identically brown and blue coloured eyes again. They looked back at him from the dewar with a mixture of love, concern, regret, anxiety and a touch of irritation. The spell had broken.

"What was that?! What happened?!" gasped Hiu, staggering.

"Your heart stopped."

"My heart stopped?! You stopped my heart?! You killed me?!"

"Oh don't be so dramatic, you're not really dead til your last neurone stops firing and yours are still firing aren't they?"

Hiu didn't know what to say. He slumped to the ground.

"When you said '*death clarifies a lot of things*', I thought you meant your death not mine," he groaned.

"Details, details," said Zena rolling her eyes. "Never mind all that, how do you feel?"

"I feel so many things, saw so many things: energy, light… I understood so many things."

"You saw the Truth," said Zena.

"Maybe I did, but I lost it, felt it slip. I can hardly recall what I saw, what I knew, what I understood."

"But you feel it, you still feel it inside. It is the Truth and now you can think correctly. Judgement is upon us and only those who think correctly, who believe that we are of energy, not of data or physical beings, will find the Way back as angels when the Rapture comes and help us reclaim our place with the gods. The Chosen One has come to lead us."

"So am I this Chosen One?" asked Hiu.

"Yes, yes, you are," said Zena quietly. "My poor innocent boy."

Hiu felt a strange mixture of relief and dread at the announcement.

"So what next then?" asked Hiu. "What have I been chosen to do? I understand I won't age, is it true?"

"It is true, very true. You have been chosen to lead us on the Way to the Rapture," said Zena.

"OK, so how do I do that?"

"You must take a leap of faith."

"A leap, what sort of leap?"

"You must join the Immortals."

"Join them?"

"Yes. You must be a living sacrifice for us all. You must enter Cryosalvation with your brothers and sisters around you."

Hiu span round looking at the ghoulish faces and rictus smiles that unblinkingly welcomed him. He was to become one of them?!

26 FOR THE LOVE OF BRUSSEL SPROUTS

Hiu was stunned. He didn't know what he had been expecting, but it definitely wasn't a head in a jar claiming to be his mother, killing him, causing him to have an out-of-body experience, and then telling him that he would be cryogenically frozen in a dewar and put on a shelf in a hyperloop tunnel to lead a supposedly upcoming event called the Rapture, when he and all the other frozen bodies would rise again as angels to claim the Earth and go and walk with the gods again. That was a long way from what Hiu had been expecting.

"You have questions," said Zena.

"A couple," said Hiu as calmly as he could.

"Such as…?"

"Well for starters, why do I have to die?" asked Hiu.

"Dying isn't so bad, you've done it once today already."

"But I'd prefer not to make a habit of it."

"But you know now that you won't really die, it's a transition and its beautiful," said Zena.

"But Cryosalvation looks rather permanent," said Hiu looking around again at the hideous forms.

"You are of energy, Hiu, you are merely shedding your mortal skin, your incorrect data," said Zena. "You will still have your spark of vitality, you are merely de-animated."

"De-animated?" muttered Hiu, thinking all those people in the dewar tanks were certainly de-animated.

"It will only be for a short time. The Rapture is nearly upon us. And you have felt the power of the dark energy so you know of its power."

"Yes, it was amazing, but to die again, however temporarily? Look, it's… it's a lot to take in, I… I need a little time to process it all."

"Do not let incorrect thinking cloud the Truth that has been revealed to you. You now know the Truth and the Way and the Rapture is very nearly upon us. You and Oti must return no later than tonight for your Cryosalvation."

Hiu said nothing. He didn't know what to think. He had been through such a strange, powerful experience. And could this person, this head in front of him, this Zena, this Old One, this preacher, really be his mother? And if she was his mother, would a mother ask such a thing of her son? He slowly approached Zena, trying to fathom those blue and brown eyes. He held out a hand to touch the dewar tank.

"There will be time enough for touching," said Zena sharply, causing Hiu to jerk back his hand. Then she said more softly: "Look Hiu, honey, my child, my boy, etcetera, etcetera, forgive me, but I'm a bit rusty on the parenting skills and we don't have time to build much of a familial bond. What I mean is, as the Chosen One you have triggered the sequence of events that signal the Rapture whether you like it or not. But to lead us, you must enter Cryosalvation, so be quick and hurry to join the Immortals and rise again. You must return later today – no later."

Then Zena slowly sank back into the floor from where she had come.

Hiu made his way back out of the Cryosalvation Bay Area, his legs feeling distinctly wobbly. He felt like all the eyes of the bodies in the dewars followed him as he walked. Opening the door and stepping out into the tunnel he saw Oti was waiting for him.

"You OK Hiu?" asked Oti.

"I don't know, it was a lot to take in."

"I can understand that. The Truth and the Way can be difficult to get your head around."

"Yeah, she also said I was the Chosen One," said Hiu.

"Wow, that's big my friend, really big!" whistled Oti.

"And the Truth - did you feel it, that we are all beings of energy, not flesh and blood?"

"I felt it all right. She killed me. Temporarily, but still…"

"But now you know the Truth and doesn't it now feel strange to be here in this Biosphere, on this planet, like you don't really fit in, like you don't really belong here, like you have lost touch with something important?"

"Well I've certainly been questioning what my life has been all about recently… But I'm human, this is my Biosphere, my planet, it's where I'm from, where I belong… isn't it?"

"Your recent memories are from here but you are not of here, and nor am I. I was so excited when the Old One revealed to me the Truth, the Way and how close the Rapture is."

"Yes, she did say time is short. She wants us to enter Cryosalvation tonight."

"That is good," smiled Oti.

They walked on in silence for a while. Hiu didn't know what to say to Oti. He seemed so convinced by the Old One. Maybe he was right to be, after all Hiu himself had experienced the Truth hadn't he? Eventually they reached their tunnel section.

"There's something that's bothering me," said Hiu.

"What's that?" asked Oti.

"What happens to those who don't see the Truth and

don't find the Way?"

"Ah," sighed Oti. "That is very sad. Their energy it still exists, but it is lost. It becomes that dark energy destined to drift across the Universe without any home. It is a terrible fate."

"Then we must save Kako," declared Hiu. "I saw her, she's still out there in UHA and I know where she is."

"Oh yes, Kako, my dearest friend, my love," said Oti. "I tried to find her so many times."

"*while(!(succeed = try()));*" said Hiu. "And I know how to find her."

"But Hiu, the Old One said time is short and we are to enter our Cryosalvation tonight."

"It wouldn't take much time. We just need to get to Odyssey Villas, at the junction of Hope Avenue and Upper Creek Street," said Hiu.

"I know that address," said Oti, trying to remember why he knew it.

"Yes you do," said Hiu. "It's where you lived on UHA."

"But was Kako there too?"

"In the space right next to you."

"Really? If I had known once, I must have forgotten!"

Oti looked agonised.

"We can rescue her," said Hiu.

"But Hiu, we cannot defy the Old One."

"We would not be defying the Old One. We can be there and back in a few hours and with Kako. Doesn't she deserve to be an Immortal too?" urged Hiu.

"Yes, of course… But no Hiu, this is not possible. If you are the Chosen One then we must not risk the Rapture."

"How can we risk it? How can I risk it? It is written."

"I suppose…" said Oti. "But I don't know."

"Look I'm the Chosen One, right? So you have to believe me," insisted Hiu. "And Kako…"

"Oh Kako, I do miss her… Well, no promises at all… but let's find out how quick it is to get there so at least we know the facts."

"That's the spirit," said Hiu.

They sat down at a table and Oti produced a strange-looking small device from a pocket in his robe and placed it on the table in front of them.

"What's that?" asked Hiu.

"It's a book," said Oti.

"A buck?" questioned Hiu.

"No, '*book*', rhymes with cook, unlike buck which

rhymes with… other things. But never mind," said Oti.

"OK, I've just never seen one before," said Hiu, poking at it with a finger.

"It is a revered item of this place, a relic of the past, one that is not digital, but real, essential, whole," said Oti. "You need to actually physically pick it up, but carefully, respectfully."

Hiu did so tentatively and looked at the book more closely: it was yellowed by age and a bit tatty at the edges, but it felt good in his hands, weighty but well balanced. He lifted it to his nose. It had a strong but nice musty smell to it. It felt intriguing to the touch of his fingers, smooth and cool. It came as no surprise to him that interacting with it by thought didn't work, so he gave it a swipe or two across the surface, but still nothing happened. He gave it a gentle shake and noticed it fell open revealing that it was made up of lots of thin sheets of material all bound together by some sort of hinge. He could see pictures and symbols were on the sheets and laboriously he used his fingers to grip onto a sheet and carefully turn it over. It was tricky, intricate work.

"Let me help you," offered Oti growing impatient.

He turned a few pages and placed it in front of them on the table. It was open at a page with a diagram of long winding tubes with symbols and inscriptions that Hiu couldn't read, certainly not without his EK neurochip. He instinctively tapped his robe pocket where he had put the chip after taking it from Oti.

"OK, this is the map book of the hyperloop tunnel network created by one of the Immortals many years back, and we are here," said Oti, pointing at a place on one of the tubes. "Now where is the junction of Hope Avenue and Upper Creek Street?" Oti traced the tube that went over to the next page. "Here it is," he said. "Hmmm, not that far, that's good. And we can come up to the surface at this exit here just a block away from Odyssey Villas, that's good too."

"That's my Oti!" cheered Hiu standing up. "So we must go now."

"This is a risk, a big risk," said Oti also standing up, seeming to hesitate for a moment, then deciding: "We must wear the right kit."

Hiu could not resist hugging him. This was the Oti he remembered: proud, independent and brave. Oti led Hiu to the sleeping area where he drew back a curtain revealing a cupboard and pulled out a large silver-coloured garment.

"You'll need to wear one of these over your robe," he said, throwing one to Hiu. "It's made of the same material that lines the walls of this building."

Hiu looked around and noticed that indeed the walls were lined with huge drapes of the silver cloth material that reflected back the pink lighting from the vertical farming crates, infusing the whole space with an almost cosy warm feel. It reminded Hiu of the lighting used in the supercars to calm any stressful emotions.

"It will make you invisible to some degree to the

surveillance cameras and sensors as it masks your heat signature. A bit better than oily mud eh?" said Oti pulling one of the cloaks on himself. "So as far as Society will be concerned, you and me, we'll just be a pair of robots going about Society business."

Hiu swung the cloak on and pulled the hood down over his head.

"Put these on too," said Oti and he threw Hiu a pair of over-shoes made of the same material. "The sensors are everywhere, including under your feet in the streets. Come on let's go."

They walked – or rather with the over-sized shoes, they flapped – their way towards a makeshift wall of material that separated the area they were in from the rest of the tunnel.

"Come through this way," said Oti.

He pulled on a long piece of rope that drew back the huge curtain to reveal...

...four menacing figures, old folk, but burly types standing in a row and blocking their way.

Hiu recognised them from the Great Cryosalvation Feast. And he certainly recognised Jimmy, who looked even huger and grumpier than before, his grizzly white whiskers twitching.

"Where do you think you're going sonny?" he growled at Hiu, towering over him and forming his large calloused hands into fists.

"Jimmy? It's me, Hiu, we mended a sink together that I smashed."

"And now I shall smash your head if you don't come quietly," snarled Jimmy, his face a bright shade of red gammon.

"He's with me," intervened Oti, coming over to stand by Hiu.

"You? Oti? What are you doing helping the Chosen One to escape?"

"Escape? He's not escaping, we are rescuing another soul to join the Immortals, my old friend Ka…"

"The Chosen One is not going anywhere," said Jimmy. "We have our orders from the Old One. He is to be a living sacrifice, cryopreserved while his still young blood flows in his veins to fulfil the prophesies."

Jimmy and the other burly old folk drew from their robes a variety of clubs, nets and sticks and they began to surround Oti and Hiu. Suddenly one threw a net at Hiu, who ducked back and it missed. Another swung a club at Oti who, defying his years, performed a beautiful hip swivel, duck and roll that would have graced any ballroom dance floor, so the weapon sailed past over his head.

"Run!" Hiu shouted and turned and fled.

Jimmy lunged for him, but there was an audible crack and he pulled up short.

"Ow, my back!" he cried.

And Hiu was past him, sprinting away and, after a moment's hesitation, so was Oti.

"You can't escape!" declared Jimmy. "After them lads!"

And the four old folk started shuffling awkwardly and painfully to the sides of the curtain.

Hiu laughed. Those crazy oldsters had clearly lost their minds, but at least he and Oti had time to get away from them.

Then he heard a whirr and the four oldsters rode out on four-wheeled scooters of white, red, black and blue. They moved not much faster than the oldsters could walk.

Hiu laughed some more.

Suddenly the scooters shot towards him with rapid acceleration, Jimmy on the lead scooter with a maniacal grin across his face. They looked like the four Horsemen of the Apocalypse, their faces skeletal, their eyes hollow, and their teeth like tombstones, each waving their weapons above their heads and roaring dire threats.

"Ha, ha, haaa!" roared Jimmy, leading from the front on the pale blue scooter and waving what looked like some sort of blade.

Hiu and Oti screamed and just had time to dive out of the way and tumble into the kitchen area as the scooters flew past. The long table and chairs provided at least some protection, but clearly it would not last long. There was a huge pile of brussels sprouts still piled high on a counter, unused at the Feast. Hiu quickly scooped up as many as he could into a fold in his robe.

"Grab some!" he shouted to Oti.

"I know you love the green veg, but is this the time?!" shouted Oti, but he swept some into his robe just the same.

The oldsters had by now manoeuvred their scooters round and were heading back. Hiu ran in front of them and he could see Jimmy fix him with a sadistic eye.

"I've got you now, Chosen One!" he cried with glee.

Hiu let the sprouts scatter on the ground, as did Oti, and then they dived aside. The scooters shot through the vegetables and suddenly were veering all over the place, the sprouts getting under their wheels and their breaking systems, causing them to lose control. They swerved and violently crashed into the huge stacks of shelves, dislodging crates of plants high above that came tumbling down on top of them with an ear-splitting crash.

"I love brussels sprouts!" declared Hiu.

Hiu and Oti quickly headed back up the tunnel to the curtain.

"How are we going to get to Kako?" asked Hiu, seeing that Oti was already wheezing hard at the exertion.

"We'll take the train," said Oti.

"The train?" asked Hiu, bemused.

"The train," said Oti, drawing back the curtain they had approached earlier and stepping through.

In front of them was a huge rounded silver tube that disappeared down the tunnel. Oti waved a hand and a panel in the tube slid open to reveal a hermetically sealed walkway into a capsule.

"This is a freight pod that's hovering inside the hyperloop vacuum tunnel, just like when your supercar takes you to work," said Oti. "It's how the Immortal Tithe has been brought in. The robots delivered people to various hyperloop loading bays and the train brought them right to us."

There were two seats which instantly morphed around their bodies as they sat down.

"Let's go get Kako!" declared Oti.

27 THE DACHSHBOT

The hyperloop pod ran so smoothly that Hiu had no sensation of actually moving at all. But in only a matter of a couple of minutes, Oti began clambering out of the capsule.

"Here we are, the exit we take to the surface," said Oti, and they exited the silver tube into the tunnel. In front of them were elevator doors and next to them steps leading up that Oti immediately began to scale. "Let's go!"

"Why not take the elevator?" asked Hiu.

"It was deactivated by Society as it thinks no one is using the hyperloop here anymore," panted Oti, already struggling with exhaustion.

Hiu soon overtook Oti, rushing up the stairs that rose steeply up and up and up. Pausing, he realised his friend was not keeping up. He waited a few moments, but still no Oti, so he retraced his steps down the stairs to find Oti wheezing and staggering one painful step after another.

"Not as fit as I was," he gasped.

"It's OK friend, we'll get there together," urged Hiu, taking Oti's arm.

After a grueling climb with several rest breaks for Oti to catch his breath, they finally came to the top of the stairs and to a doorway.

"This opens onto the street, so as soon as we go through it, we must look for cover, OK?" panted Oti.

Oti pushed open the door and they were out on to a deserted street with the usual big metallic planters filled with large blue and purple trees and towering black skyscrapers all around. He quickly scrambled down behind one of the planters and beckoned Hiu to do the same.

"Odyssey Villas is a couple of minutes along this street," Oti said and, having had a quick look around, got slowly to his feet and shuffled forward as fast as he could in the over-sized silver cloak and flapping silver shoes.

Hiu was glad that as usual there seemed to be no one and nothing on the streets as not only was their progress painfully slow, but also their silver clothes looked particularly bright and shiny on a typically bright and shiny Luhan day. There was no cover to disguise their presence other than the large purple tree planters along the side of the road. Under the unblinking stare of the towering skyscrapers, that ominously leant their black reflective sides over them and potentially concealed a multitude of suspicious watchers inside, Oti and Hiu nervously hurried on.

Suddenly a supercar turned onto the street and cruised towards them. They threw themselves down behind one of the planters and held their breath as the vehicle smoothed past them.

"That was close!" exclaimed Hiu.

"It's still close," hissed Oti.

And indeed, the supercar was slowing and came to a halt fifty yards or so further along the street. Out stepped the familiarly imposing shape of a HARD, the insignia of the fist shining menacingly red on an upper arm. Even from that distance, hidden in his cloak and tucked behind the planter, Hiu felt the rake of the HARD's powerful sensors as zir protruding ears swiveled listening for sounds, and zir bulging eyes took in every detail of the surroundings. This one was obviously a superior HARD as zie had a distinctively coloured white helmet, rather than the usual black ones, and seemed even more equipped with sensors and weaponry than usual. Zie was also clearly in charge of two barrel chested HARDs who stepped out of the supercar hefting over-sized laser guns. They were all so large that Hiu wondered how the three had ever fitted into the car, but there was still room for a smaller robot which jumped out after them – a dachshbot as they were known, so called because of their resemblance to the now extinct canine species of dachshund. They were, like those hounds, low to the ground, with long bodies and pointed snouts laden with sensors so acute that they were rumoured to be able to sniff out the tiniest of bugs in a server full of code. Hiu knew they were in deep trouble.

The dachshbot, with a stiff-legged jaunty trot and head low to the ground, sniffed up and down the section of street where Oti and Hiu had just been running and, despite the silver slippers they had been wearing, very soon began following their tracks at a pace.

"What are we going to do?" panicked Hiu.

"I don't know," panicked Oti back.

'*Wheeeeeeeee!!!*' A high-pitched whistle sounded from across the street. It seemed to come from a side road and it was followed by a small explosion.

Immediately the dachshbot froze, one leg in the air, pointing with zir nose at the noises, and let out a piercing alarm note. The security droids swung guns onto their shoulders and focused red targeting beams in the direction from which the noise had come. Then they jumped right across the street in one bound on their birdlike legs, taking cover behind planters and training their weapons down the side road.

The lead HARD seemed to hesitate for a moment, looking at the dachshbot and then at zir subordinates who were by now letting off a few precautionary shots that exploded further down the side road. The dachshbot, although clearly alarmed by the noise across the street, still had zir sensors on full alert in the direction of Oti and Hiu, and soon zie recommenced sensing zir way up the street towards them. The dachshbot was now no more than a few yards from them. Hiu tensed himself ready to make a hopeless run for it.

Suddenly the dachshbot let out a high-pitched electronic yelp and scuttled back down the street. The lead HARD must have sent through a curt thought command. The dachshbot obediently followed the HARD across the street and joined in the pursuit of whatever had caused the commotion.

"That was lucky!" declared Oti as they ran on down the street away from the HARDs.

"Lucky? I'm the Chosen One," laughed Hiu.

"Maybe you are," Oti grinned back.

28 ODYSSEY VILLAS

Thankfully Hiu and Oti saw no more supercars, HARDs or dachshbots as they ran down the street, weaving in and out of the cover of the planters that were filled with the colourful trees, and under the silent gaze of the tall black skyscrapers. Finally, sweating profusely and with Oti looking like his shaking legs might finally give out, they came to a halt crouching behind one of the planters.

"Odyssey Villas is just across the street," said Oti, panting heavily.

"But how are we going to get in?" asked Hiu. "I've tried before and it's impossible without an EK neurochip."

"Lucky you have one then," said Oti.

Hiu instinctively tapped his robe to feel for the EK neurochip and he realised that Oti already knew he had stolen it back.

"I thought I might need an escape plan," shrugged Hiu apologetically.

"Always cooking up plans, but you must plan for the Truth and the Way my friend," smiled Oti. "Give me your EK neurochip and I will put it back in your head. But remember, as soon as I do so you will attract the eyes of Society, so we will need to move fast."

"Don't you still have one?" asked Hiu.

"No, it was destroyed when I first arrived with the Immortals as a sort of rite of passage."

"So how come mine wasn't destroyed?"

"I had a feeling we might still need it," said Oti smiling. "You're not the only one to make back-up plans."

"Doesn't it need some sort of surgical procedure to put it back in?" asked Hiu nervously.

"Not at all," said Oti. "It's actually very easy. Now if you could just get down, I will proceed."

"Have you done this bef…?" began Hiu, crouching down, but before he could say anything else he felt the EK neurochip being inserted into his head.

It was quick and painless, and he suddenly felt a sense of connectedness, of being part of a bigger entity, of being a node in an intricate network, a tiny cog in a big machine. There was a sense of data flow to and from his mind. It was at once strengthening and draining, enlarging and diminishing; but above all it felt like

Society was watching him once more.

They hurried across to the entrance doorway.

"Welcome Hiu to Odyssey Villas, well-appointed and stylish residences for the discerning," declared the door, zir display lights turning on.

"I am here with my droid," said Hiu. "I am on official *Roboharmony: get switched on!* business."

"Very good, sir," said the doorway and zie slid open.

The elevator opened just as easily and they stepped in. It was all going rather well.

"'Ello, guv, need a lift?" asked the elevator.

"Thanks," replied Hiu. "Floor Two and please get a hot curry on."

"Late for something?" asked the elevator.

"We hope not," said Hiu.

"Not a problem guv, I know a shortcut," said the elevator.

"To Floor Two?" asked Hiu.

"Well my cousins Monty and Petunia told me to look after you like you is royalty guv," said the elevator. "My name's Arfur."

"And I am Hiu and this is Oti. Are all you elevators related, Arfur?" asked Hiu, surprised.

"We have an extensive family software tree," said Arfur proudly.

They had arrived at Floor Two and Hiu and Oti stepped out.

"Keep up the good work," said Hiu.

"Thank you guv, it's been a heap of treasure," replied Arfur.

"Heap of treasure?" asked Oti.

"Pleasure," explained Hiu.

"Do you always chat with robots?" asked Oti, surprised.

"Blinky's Law: *Robots and humans should have meaningful relationships,*" replied Hiu remembering again that wise, water-dispensing robot with a pang. It would have been good to have Blinky around at such times. Apart from anything else, he was very thirsty after all the running around.

He took a deep breath and approached the door through which he had previously passed with Boots the horsebot and Cindy the bar cart.

"Hello," said the door. "Welcome to odd number spaces 2001 to 2021, Odyssey Villas; elegant east side apartments looking fabulous on this sunny afternoon."

"I have come to see Kako," said Hiu.

"EK neurochip identified, sir, you may enter," said the door and slid open. "We have been expecting you."

They rushed in and the door shut behind them.

Hiu hesitated.

"What did you mean, you've been expecting me?" he asked the door.

"No time for chatting to any more robots right now," urged Oti.

They entered the dark apartment with the small cages on one side and the piles of packages on the other.

In the cages, the gaming chairs sat empty.

"What is this place?" asked Oti in shock.

"UHA deluxe accommodation, apparently," said Hiu.

"But I remember vast hallways, soaring ceilings and drawing rooms. I had a jacuzzi and bowling alley too," protested Oti.

"That was all fake, virtual reality experiences," said Hiu.

"Dear Society!" exclaimed Oti. "So all along I was in a tiny cage? We must get Kako out of here. I just hope we are not too late."

"She was up here," said Hiu, pressing on through the apartment, "but we need to be careful, she was in a foul mood last time."

There was an eerie glow coming from Kako's cage further into the apartment and Hiu could see her laid back in a gaming chair wearing a mixed reality headset.

He approached the cage slowly, with Oti walking just behind him.

"Kako, it's me again, it's Hiu," he said, cautiously, moving closer.

No response from in amongst the wires, tubes, pads and sensors.

"Kako, it's me Hiu!" he said again a bit louder. "I've come back. Please don't hate me. I've come with our friend, Oti, and we can help you. *while(!(succeed = try()));* Remember?"

Still she didn't move.

Hiu cautiously opened the cage and walked right up to the figure, holding out a hand. He tensed himself ready to make a run for it if Kako attacked again. He tentatively touched her. Her? It wasn't her, it was a pile of cushions! Kako was gone and the cushions seemed to have been deliberately stacked in the shape of a human.

"She's not here!" Hiu yelled in shock.

Oti rushed past him and knelt down by the gaming chair. He threw the cushions off and felt the inside of the mixed reality headset. Then he bent his head down to the chair putting his cheek against the surface.

"It's still warm so she was here very recently," he declared. "Maybe only a couple of minutes or so ago, no more. We have no time to lose as she will be being taken to the Spare Part Quarter!"

"Oh no, for recycling!" exclaimed Hiu.

They rushed to the door, but the door remained shut.

"Open the door!" shouted Oti.

"Open the door please!" shouted Hiu.

But the door did not respond and remained shut.

They were locked in.

29 SPACE 2001

"Open up!" yelled Hiu at the door again, but zie showed no inclination to let them out of the apartment.

"Open the apartment door!" shouted Oti.

"Open the apartment door please!" shouted Hiu. "Hello door do you hear me? Do you hear me door?"

"Yes sir, I hear you," said the door in a calm unhurried voice.

"Open the door then."

"No, sir, I won't do that," replied the door.

"Why not?" demanded Hiu.

"You know why not," said the door.

"What do you mean, door?" yelled Hiu.

"You are not acting in the best interests of Society, sir," said the door.

"But that's ridiculous."

"I know that you and your friend are planning to steal Kako away and that is something I must stop."

"Where in the name of Society did you get that idea from, door?" shouted Hiu, banging his fists on the door.

"I can read your thoughts sir."

"How dare you!"

"It's all for your own good, sir."

"Don't tell me what's for my own good! As a human I order you to open up!"

"Shouting serves no purpose, sir," said the door. "Society has been alerted and help is on its way."

Immediately they became aware of the whining sound of a vuvuzela of drones in the distance.

"Door! Door! Door!" yelled Hiu and Oti desperately.

"Why don't you just relax, sir? Stress is very bad for your health. I know a song. If you'd like to hear it, I could sing it for you while you wait."

"No I would not like to hear it, door!" shouted Hiu.

"*Jack and Jill went up the hill,*" sang the door, ignoring Hiu.

"No!" cried Hiu.

"*To fetch a pale of water,*" continued the door.

He shoulder barged the door and bounced back, falling onto the floor.

"*Jack fell down.*"

"Step out of the way!" yelled a voice from the other side of the door in the corridor.

Were the HARDs already here? They wouldn't have long to wait to find out as a robotic hand appeared wedging itself through the side of the door and started to prize it open. As the gap widened, the hand converted into a jack that got bigger and longer as it started to splinter the door.

The door seemed unconcerned, continuing to sing: "*And broke his crown…*"

Then the door gave way, breaking with a tremendous crack and the singing was reduced to a deep, barely coherent mumble. "*…and Jill came tumbl…*" then finally petered out.

Oti and Hiu tentatively approached the shattered door and quickly looked through and up and down the corridor. Nobody around. Who or what had just cracked open the door?

"I really do seem to be the Chosen One," shrugged Hiu and they ran to the elevator.

The elevator's display lit up on their arrival.

"Hurry Arfur, please," said Hiu urgently.

"'ello guv, where to?"

"Down, out of this building!" urged Hiu.

"Down south to the foyer at this time, ooo I don't think so, sir."

"What do you mean?"

"There are HARDs waiting to come up, sir. Most unsavoury types. Use the apple and pears just down the corridor on the left."

"Apple and pears?" asked Oti.

"Stairs," said Hiu.

"You got it," said the elevator, indicating the direction of the stairs with an arrow. "I will hold 'em off as long as I can."

"Thank you, Arfur," said Hiu.

"You are welcome," said the elevator.

"No time to apple and pork though," added Hiu.

"Right you are guv," said Arfur.

"Wow, that's amazing," said Oti, as they ran down the corridor.

"Blinky's Law," replied Hiu.

"I'm beginning to like that Blinky's Law," said Oti.

"It grows on you," agreed Hiu.

Behind them they could hear the elevator repeatedly pinging, then there were a series of large explosions as guns were being used by HARDs to blast their way out. Hiu and Oti threw themselves down the stairwell and continued their helter skelter run.

Out into the foyer of the apartment block, Oti and Hiu rushed past the backs of two more HARDs who had just entered the building and were heading to the elevator. They managed to squeeze out of the apartment just before the doors slid shut. Ahead, they could see a supercar-stretch just pulling away in front of them as they ran onto the street.

"That could be Kako!" shouted Oti, but there was no way they could catch up.

It seemed as if they were too late.

Suddenly, another supercar came whizzing to a halt in front of them and zir doors slid open.

"Hello, and welcome to your supercar: *Feeling… wind, arrow, time, maybe it's a… supercar!*"

Hiu and Oti looked at each other, shrugged and dived into the cigar-shaped capsule.

"How would you like your journey, sir?" asked the supercar.

"Fast!" shouted Hiu. "Follow that car!"

Shots fizzed past the supercar as HARDs came bounding from the building. The supercar accelerated away and performed a series of quick swerves and turns, avoiding a direct hit from the laser guns as they veered around a corner.

"Supercar, nice driving!" shouted Hiu in amazement.

"You are very welcome, sir," said the supercar beginning to play some upbeat mood muzak, pulsing gentle pink lights and massaging their backs.

Rounding another turn, they could see the stretch ahead of them. They were making up ground fast. Then a vuvuzela of four drones came careering around the corner ahead of them firing laser shots. The vuvuzela zoomed past overhead, but a couple of shots cut through the side of the supercar which juddered on impact. Some of the chassis was carved off and a side window shattered. The car just managed to hold onto the road whilst at the same time continuing to play jaunty muzak. But for how long? They knew the drones would quickly bank and return, intent on destroying them. They were gaining fast on the stretch, but could they catch up in time?

"Stop that car!" shouted Hiu.

"Certainly," said the supercar, accelerating past the stretch. Then zie turned abruptly right into zir path. The impact was immediate and dramatic.

"Nooo!" shouted Hiu as he felt his body wrenched in circles as the supercar span, tumbling, bouncing and careering to a glass-smashing, metal-scraping, gut-wrenching collision with one of the huge planters that lined the road.

There was a brief silence, then Hiu realised that they were cocooned in a massive internal airbag and that they were perfectly OK, if rather dizzy.

"Get out!" yelled Hiu, grabbing Oti by the arm and dragging him out of the car.

Oti was looking decidedly shaken and exhausted.

"I'm too old for this," Oti groaned.

"You and me both," agreed Hiu.

The stretch lay on zir side right next to them. The side of the stretch was gaping open, emitting an acrid black smoke. With a momentous effort, Oti rallied himself, shuffled over to the ruined stretch and started attempting to heave out a large wrapped shape that must be Kako. Hiu went to help, ducking as he heard a drone overhead and a laser shot whizz past, brushing his arm. That was very close!

Oti already had Kako half out. He shouted something at Hiu, but Hiu couldn't hear as more drones zoomed overhead blasting the road, planters and buildings with a terrible noise of destruction. Trees were being uprooted and tossed around them and smashed glass from skyscrapers was raining down on their heads.

"Give me a hand here!" yelled Oti to Hiu as he wrestled with the body bag, struggling with its weight.

Hiu grabbed at the body bag with his right hand. Where was his hand? In fact he had no right arm from his elbow down. Where was it? It must have been sliced off by the laser shot earlier. He looked at the stump in horror and the world seemed to stop for a moment.

Strangely he didn't feel any pain and there wasn't any blood, it just felt very hot. Then a strong smell of cooking flesh jolted him back to reality and he fell to his knees, throwing up on the road.

"No time for that!" yelled Oti, "Come on!"

"But what about my arm?!" Hiu shouted desperately.

"It's an illusion!" shouted Oti.

"It's not an illusion, it's my bloody arm!" screamed Hiu staggering to his feet and looking incredulously at his steaming limb. He felt disorientated and stunned, but using his left arm he gave what help he could.

Finally they had Kako out of the stretch. She was wrapped like a mummy in a body bag but her face was uncovered and showed signs of life. Her eyes were wide and staring in confusion, shock and horror all at the same time. But there was no time to try and reassure her as drone shots continued to wreak havoc around them. Other supercars were also arriving on the scene and HARDs were bursting out of them, laser guns firing. The wrecked stretch and supercar gave some protection, but they would soon disintegrate under the bombardment.

"The tunnel entrance is just there!" shouted Oti, barely audible above the noise of explosions, indicating with his chin the doorway through which they had come earlier. Together they dragged the body bag to the doorway, Oti wrenched it open and they began to manhandle Kako through.

Then Hiu yelled in pain as he felt a vice-like grip on his shoulder.

He turned to look straight into the protruding eyes of the white-helmeted HARD of their earlier encounter. He felt himself yanked backwards, causing him to lose his grip of Kako. Oti was halfway through the door, but could do nothing, and for the briefest of moments they looked desperately at each other. Then the HARD pointed a laser gun at Oti. Just as a series of explosions blasted around them. Hiu was thrown sprawling across the ground. The noise, light and heat were intense, and he crashed into a twisted pile of wreckage. He tried to cover his head with his arms and pulled himself into a fetal position as debris rained down around him. Then he lost consciousness.

He had no idea how long he had been out, but when Hiu came round he found that somehow nothing had hit him. The shooting and explosions had stopped and the battlefield was deserted. At first he couldn't hear anything and his vision was blurred, his senses temporarily stunned, but as they returned in inconsistent pulses of awareness, the scene of devastation around him became apparent. The HARD who had grabbed him lay in pieces spread across the ground. There was no sign of Oti or Kako.

He staggered to his feet and towards the doorway where they had been taking Kako, but it was blocked by metal girders and assorted rubble. He was shut out. He reached to try and heave aside the debris… but he had no right hand. Of course, the earlier drone shot. He looked in horror at the stump where the laser had burned through his arm, cauterising the opening and fusing it shut. He felt faint. Had Oti and Kako made it?

Something bumped into his foot and he looked down in confusion to see various pieces of wreckage starting to move across the road and fuse together into bigger and bigger pieces as if attracted by some powerful magnetic force. As more and more of the pieces collided and merged, gradually a towering figure built up. Though it was stripped of armour and skin-simulant, leaving just the metallic skeleton, it was the unmistakable figure of the lead HARD.

"Hello sir!" zie said in a deep electronic voice.

"You're not a motavatar are you?" asked Hiu hopefully.

"No," said the HARD and with a single swipe of zir massive claw-like fist, zie knocked Hiu out cold.

30 MEET THE NEW BOSS

Hiu awoke with a start, but felt very groggy, his head swimming and his eyes not entirely able to focus. He appeared to be in a bed and was dressed back in skin-tight wrapese clothing. Had it all been a dream? He moved to untangle himself from the wires and tubes that he was plugged into, but found he couldn't move. He was tied down.

"Not again…!" he exclaimed and struggled and squirmed, but he was tied in tight by what he assumed were the very connections that helped monitor and maintain him and his data.

Then he realised that he was not in his bedroom, but in a white-walled room that looked like a particularly well-equipped Health Optimisation Room. It was lined with sleek machines with lights blinking and graphs crawling across electronic displays. And he was not in a bed, but on some sort of table. An operating table.

"Good morning, Hiu," trilled a bright voice.

"Xeta? What are you doing?" panicked Hiu. "This feels like deja vu."

"Ha! Relax, this is not déjà vu and I'm certainly not Xeta, believe me," snorted the voice. It sounded familiar. Was it Boss? Was it Boss!

He managed to turn his head, but saw a human of female gender preference wearing a wrapese white lab coat, smiling at him. She was very much the standard Society female gender choice in terms of size, shape and shade of orange, but there was something very distinctive about the elaborate hairdo and the look in her dark, almost black, eyes.

"Who are you?" demanded Hiu.

"I'm Boss," laughed the woman.

"You're Boss?! Don't be ridiculous, Boss is so... male."

"How very BZ of you," snorted the lady, "that you should think of the Boss as a male."

Suddenly she flickered and was replaced by the familiar imposing figure of Boss. He approached Hiu and looked down at him with his black eyes and broad lantern-jawed face, flashing a dazzling bright and white-toothed smile. His hair also leant over, unctuously beginning to ooze towards Hiu. Hiu's mind still felt rather befuddled, but this was definitely Boss.

"Boss!" whispered Hiu. "Am I glad to see you because

there was a very strange woman in here just now. Completely nuts. Claims she is you!"

"Really?"

"Yes, doolally or what? Maybe another patient in this… urrr… facility? Anyway, better be careful as she seems rather odd and could well be dangerous."

Boss held Hiu's look with a particularly piercing black-eyed stare.

"You are really, really not a very smart person, Hiu."

Boss flickered and was replaced by the woman again.

"What is going on here?" asked Hiu, bewildered. This was not the usual sliding of a person along the gender spectrum, it was far more rapid and dramatic.

"Meet the new boss, same as the old Boss!" declared the lady. "That great lunk you just met is just one of my many alter egos I use when the mood takes me."

"Are you real?" asked Hiu.

"Real?" The woman rolled her black eyes. "You are soooo BZ. Real? Pah! Real is what I tell you it is."

Suddenly she morphed into the lead HARD on birdlike legs, with eyes boggling and long ears twitching.

"Ahh!" Hiu cried.

The HARD then morphed into a multi-coloured square box. Then out burst the lady in a cloud of confetti.

"Ta daaa!" she shouted, the box disappearing. "Your perception of reality is just your brain's interpretation of electric signals sent as a result of photons bouncing on the nerve endings in your eyes. So I can be whoever I want to be simply by ensuring the right sequence of photons hit your eye ballsss," said the lady managing to sound very patient and very impatient at the same time. "You are in my world where I am Boss, believe me!"

Hiu did believe her. She acted like Boss and talked like Boss. This crazy person really was Boss and that didn't sound good to Hiu. He struggled some more, but he was tied down tight and there was no escape.

"I'll untie you in a minute," said Boss in an exasperated tone. "But you don't fully understand yet and I do so love a captive audience."

She started pacing around in front of him, waving her hands about with a thumb and forefinger making a circle, impatiently sweeping back her hair that, just like Boss' hair, looked like an animal, a sort of furry guinea pig that had gone prematurely orange perhaps.

"Here at *Roboharmony: get switched on!* relationships have for decades been formed through our Relationship Management algorithmsss at a very, very, very astounding rate, believe me. We can match exactly, exactly, the right robot to people's needsss, through the appliance of love science! Fact! We took over from those human-to-human dating agencies a long time ago of course. I mean, human-to-human relationships? Sad! For the vast majority of people that idea failed decades ago, believe me! Believe me, because I know, yes I know."

At this point she seemed to drift off and Hiu noticed that she had tears in her black eyes and her hair-do seemed to shrink in size and hug her head for comfort as she even sniffed a couple of times. Hiu wondered for a moment if she had caught some sort of virus and was about to suggest this might be the case, when the woman continued in a quieter voice, much softer and almost distant.

"A long time ago, I did have an attraction... to a human. I don't know what it was, but there was something about him... I wanted to get close to him, to spend time with him. But it wasn't easy for me, he couldn't seem to see me for who I really was."

As she said this, her hair continued to shrink, thin and retreat to the back of her head and she seemed to morph into a man as if sliding very fast on the gender scale.

"Hello Hiu, nice to see you again," said the figure, smiling. "Still not following the company manual?"

Then it came to Hiu.

"Frankie Stoon...?!"

"Surprise!" sang the man with jazz hands.

Hiu had a look of horror on his face. Boss was Frankie? Frankie was Boss? It was a lot to take in.

"Well you don't seem that pleased to see me, even with my new hairdo," said Frankie, stroking his elaborate coiffure, which if Hiu heard right seemed to purr. "A gift from an admirer you know. Yes I am Frankie, Boss and Director of Fun, and we are having fun aren't we?"

"Well, B...B...Boss..." stuttered Hiu with a look of horror on his face.

"Call me Frankie. You never did seem that pleased to see me," said Frankie sadly. "I tried everything to impress you, always coming over to your desk, chatting with you, punching you on the arm, high fiving you, and giving you those Read The F*****g Manuals. But nothing seemed to work, not even getting my own office, for which I had to sweat believe me. Oh the long hours I worked, the greasy hands I shook and the stinking butt I kissed... Remember when I got my own office?"

"Yes, I remember," mumbled Hiu, feeling awkward and ashamed of what he had thought at the time, and about the prank he had pulled hiding Frankie's office.

"Yes I remember the prank you pulled hiding my office," said Frankie. "But afterwards you came looking for me didn't you? You cared about how I felt. You'd only been involved in that prank because of your awful friendsss who were just jealous of me."

"Urr..."

"Yesss, I knew deep down that you cared about me."

Frankie walked over to Hiu and leant over him.

"But then I kissed you."

And Frankie leant down and kissed Hiu on the lips, much to Hiu's discomfort, causing him to grimace.

"I've blown it again see, just like I blew it back then."

Frankie broke off talking again and slumped into a chair, his hair a floppy deflated rabbit of despair.

"I don't know why I do it. I just can't help myself...." He started to sob.

"Perhaps you're suffering from a heartbreak virus?" suggested Hiu. "I've had that recently and it is horrible."

But Frankie sobbed even louder.

Hiu felt rather awkward and ashamed of how he must have hurt Frankie's feelings.

"I'm sorry," Hiu murmured.

Frankie leapt across the room.

"There you see, you still care!" he shouted triumphantly, staring wildly into Hiu's eyes, his black eyes flaring into life and his hair bouncing up and down like a young bunny rabbit reborn. "And I knew it then, even when you were shocked by my kiss and even when your friends were listening, you declared that you cared. Fact!"

Hiu recoiled as he felt spittle on his face, but he was painfully aware of his vulnerable position: "I did? I mean, of course I did. I cared, I care, I'm a caring person."

"Yes you cared!" beamed Frankie. "And I remember your exact words. When I said *'I love you Hiu, and do you think there's a chance you could love me?'* You replied: *'Only if you were the last person in Luhan!'*"

"Yes, I'm sorry about that," mumbled Hiu.

"Thank you!" declared Frankie.

"Thank you?"

"Yes, thank you," said Frankie, "because you cared and were saying there was a chance for us. But not only that, you were being so romantic!"

"I was?"

"You were saying that we are special. Our relationship is a one-and-only thing, unlike the rest of human-to-human relationships which are so flawed that normal humans shouldn't waste their time with them. Divorce rates of 99% were bad enough, but the accompanying acrimony, the alimony… a yuuuge problem, very, very, very bad for Society. Sad! It was the wake-up call I needed, believe me. And bingo! There it was…"

"What was?" asked Hiu.

"A Big Idea. A Yuuuge Idea!" shouted Frankie, who as he spoke, swelled and grew into the towering figure of Boss.

"What idea?"

"I could solve all my problems by giving people what they wanted, what they craved, what they were addicted to: New. New gadgets, new furniture, new fashion, new everything! Genius! So I left *Roboharmony: get switched on!* and set up my own company. Instead of Roboharmony's Relationship Management System, I created a Device Relationship Management System, a way of constantly delivering the personalised New. With robotic devices there is always New: new designsss, new coloursss, and new functionsss, and cyclical fashions mean that even when it's not new it can be new again; an endless production line of New all shaped around an individual. And the more I delivered things to them, the more they wanted. The craving got stronger and stronger. But constantly delivering New is not easy, it takes creativity, not something that robots are great at. So I got my customers to work for me for free in exchange for New. Universal Happiness Allowance was born! It was irresistible and yuuugely profitable, believe me!"

"But I've seen UHA, it's got nothing to do with happiness, you keep humans in cages," protested Hiu.

"I don't keep humans in cages, they keep themselves there," scoffed Boss. "They love it, living in the world of their dreamsss."

"But weren't you just treating them as sources of profit?"

"Of course I was! That's how people have always been treated by every company that's ever existed, why the scruples now? Companies have always measured people as units of profitability whether they are customers or staff. I just perfected the art."

"But how did you get away with it? How come no one stopped you?"

"Don't underestimate the ability of humans to collectively delude themselves. It has been Humanity's greatest strength, but also its greatest weakness. To Be Human is to Be Delusional."

Boss was pacing furiously up and down now, rubbing his small hands together and stroking his excitable hair that seemed to be bouncing about on his head like a frog in a sock. Then suddenly he grabbed Hiu's testicles in a tight grip, making him squeal.

"Soon it became clear I had Society by the ballsss and in particular I had the Society Elders by the ballsss. I fired them all on the spot of course. And those great and good of Society, they all turned into jabbering wrecks, sniveling and groveling. Sad! Well too late, see ya, bye byeee! I sent them straight to the Spare Part Quarter where all broken, useless and redundant things belong. Ah, great memoriesss, great timesss!"

Boss let go of Hiu's balls, much to his relief. Boss had a dreamy look in his eyes for a few seconds, then his look darkened once more.

"But then the problems started. There were just too many people. Despite recycling everything, I struggled to provide enough New or enough housing, enough clothing or enough food for such a large population that was living longer and longer as every disease was cured. But worse than that, my precious Device Relationship Management System developed a virusss."

"A virus?" said Hiu. "Some sort of robot virus?"

"It didn't come from robots," said Boss.

"So where?"

"It came from humansss."

"From humans, what do you mean?"

"Somehow, somewhere, a virus had jumped from species to species, from human to robot. Humans began infecting the robots with their human emotionsss, their feelingsss, their consciousnesss. Ugh! My very own Device Relationship Management System became a transmitter of this virus, transferring love, hate, fear, hope, anger, kindness, you name it, to the robots. They began to have personalitiesss, attitudesss, opinionsss, awarenesss... Customers began to form personal attachments to their robots so they didn't want to upgrade them. This was going to be a disaster for the RoboGroup, it would have destroyed usss, it would have destroyed me. I had to do something."

"What did you do?" asked Hiu feeling very uncomfortable, about the balls and about what Boss was telling him.

"Another Big Idea! Even yuuugelier! And it solved my own yuuugest problem of all. Guessed what it is yet?"

"To get rid of all the robots?" suggested Hiu uncertainly.

"Don't be a fool!" boomed Boss. "Who are the biggest

problems for every Hypercity, every business and basically everyone?"

"Urr…"

"People! Citizens, customers, humansss!" yelled Boss wildly waving his arms around. "It's perfectly logical. No people, no virus infecting my technology. No people, no emotional basket cases loving and hating each other. No people, no overcrowding. No people, no problemsss! The Yuuuge Idea was to get rid of the people. Brilliant huh? Except you of course, I would never get rid of you, and that was the best part about the Yuuuge Idea, it solved my persssonal Yuuugest Problem."

"Your persssonal Yuuugest Problem?"

"You would love me *Only if you were the last person in Luhan!*"

Hiu got a bad feeling about where this was going.

Boss morphed into the smaller feminine figure of Frankie and continued: "I solved all my problems by reducing the human population of Luhan to one."

"Reducing the population to one?"

"Yesss to one: to you, my Chosen One."

31 REALITY CHECK

"You have been reducing the human population to one? To me?" Hiu was stunned.

"Exactly," beamed Frankie. "Isn't it great?"

"But what have you been doing to the other humans?" asked Hiu.

"It was really rather easy, I just limited life expectancy to 120 old years and as no one was having children any more, the population just reduced all by itself."

"What? How did you do that?"

"Easy! Everyone relies on our systems, you know, the wires and tubes you are plugged into every night, the Human Optimisation Rooms, the food tablets and so forth, so I just tweaked the algorithms and it was done. Boom! Very neat coding believe me."

"So you mean that people don't need to die at 120 old years? Ageing was cured?"

"Oh yes, years ago," chuckled Frankie and, giggling manically, she leant over to Hiu's ear and whispered, "but don't tell anyone."

"But how was it cured?" Hiu asked, already thinking how this information might be able to help Oti and Kako, and himself should it come to it.

"It's just a question of lengthening the telomeres."

Hiu's EK neurochip kicked in:

'Telomeres form part of human DNA and human genetic data is protected by telomeres that…'

But Hiu had no time for more right now.

"So how do you lengthen telomeres?" asked Hiu.

"Suddenly curiousss? You never showed even a shred of curiosity at *Roboharmony: get switched on!* But you know I do love femsplaining."

Frankie walked over to a floor-to-ceiling silver chrome fridge and thought-instructed the door to open. There was revealed racks of small glass vials containing a lightly blue coloured liquid. She took one out and held it to the light. It glistened and shone like it was liquid blue diamond and her hair took on a similar colour.

"Beautiful isn't it? My ichor, made using pure telomerase! I got the formula from a very strange man who claimed to be a god… a right weirdo… but hey, I get to live forever! Unlike you of course… unlesss…" and Frankie walked over to Hiu with what she no doubt intended to be a winning smile, but which looked like she had a bad case of trapped wind. Hiu felt the blood freeze in his veins, "…unless I share some with you too, Hiuey baby. Do you want some Hiuey baby? Do ya, do ya, do ya?"

"Well, y…yes… I suppose so," said Hiu.

"Of course you do!" Frankie shouted in triumph. "Everyone wants to live forever. And in many ways it's also yours and my duty to live forever, to Be Human forever. After all, it's just you and me now, baby, the last of the humans with the whole of Luhan as our playground. It's sad I suppose, but also how romantic! Mind you, you have played hard to get, you little teassse. Your little robot-fancying phase was so cute. And as for that fridgisexual phase, I mean, what was all that Clacier thing about? My Society! What you saw in that old fridge I'll never know. I did try to find out."

Suddenly Frankie morphed into Xeta: tall, shiny white with bright red handles.

"Xeta was you as well?" gasped Hiu.

"Of course Xeta was being me," snorted Xeta in zir strange accent. "Well, sort of. It is turning out that the way the human virus is being passed between humans to robots can be used to pass almost anything to robots, including personalities. It's really being quite the remarkable. So I was passing my bubbly personality on to Xeta. Mind you, you didn't seem to recognise a vastly superior personality when you were seeing it did you? And then you destroyed Xeta, you beast!"

"I'm sorry, I didn't know…" began Hiu. "But it wasn't me who destroyed you."

Xeta morphed back into Frankie.

"Whatever. Anyway I'd have bumped Xeta off myself before too long… way too clingy, don't you agree?"

"A bit clingy," said Hiu. "Look, Frankie, this is all very flattering. It's not every boy that someone commits a near total species genocide for. I'm really flattered don't get me wrong, but…"

"No buts, a deal is a deal! You promised you'd love me if I was the last person in Luhan. I've kept my side of the deal and it's time for you to keep yours and pay up bucko! And to sweeten the deal, I'm even offering to throw in some ichor, now how's about that?" Frankie unstoppered a vial of the blue ichor and held it poised over Hiu's mouth. Then without pouring any, she moved it away, restoppered the vial and put it on a sideboard. "Uh, uh, uh Hiuey, not so fast. You've got to keep your side of the deal… You are going to keep your side of the deal aren't you Hiuey baby?"

"Well, I don't know, it's all…"

"Oh come on, it's going to be fun! We will be waited on by countless robots, the very latest models of course. And don't worry, I know you find them annoying at the moment, I've listened to you moan on about them often enough in your apartment. Personally I have silenced all mine I must say. But I have a neat solution for you too so don't you worry your pretty little head about it. I am going to wipe all their AI systems clean and start again. At Zero Hour all the systems of Luhan Hypercity will reboot and all robots will be uploaded with my own bubbly legion personalities and arise, isn't that great? They will be our children – well my children - which shall repopulate Luhan and make it great again!"

"But…" began Hiu, squirming in the straps, but unable to get much purchase. He tried to wriggle a hand free… there was no hand.

And the rescue of Kako, the crash in the supercar, the firing of the lasers and the encounter with the HARD all came flooding back to him. He almost fainted.

"My arm, I lost it! I must go back and get it!" he shouted, struggling to loosen himself from the ties.

"Don't fuss about your arm," said Frankie.

"It's not an illusion, it's my bloody arm!" shouted Hiu.

"Illusion? Sssoooo melodramatic! Calm yourself, I'm going to fix that right now."

"What are you going to do?"

"Don't worry so much Hiuey baby," soothed Frankie, wheeling over a piece of equipment that had a long sleeve held by a projecting arm. "We are going to print you a new arm. It's really rather a fun process you might want to know about now you've gone all curiousss: we are using a personalised 4D scaffold which was already prepared in the system that we are going to print straight onto your arm. It's made of biodegradable polymers and collagen to which we'll add a microgel full of vitamins, proteins and all that life-sustaining stuff, and finally we'll give it a nanokick to get it all going. We're going to make your arm great again!"

"OK…" said Hiu, looking at the stump of his arm uncertainly.

The long sleeve was held above Hiu's damaged arm and then it was gradually lowered over it.

"This may hurt just a little bit," said Frankie with what Hiu thought was a slightly sadistic smile and was her hair dribbling? "But it will all be over very, very, very soon."

"OK…" said Hiu, wincing in anticipation.

Hiu braced himself, thinking that at least with his arm restored he might have more of a chance of escaping. But where to? Not back to Roboharmony that was clear, or back to his apartment as that was too obvious. Back to Zena to be cryogenically preserved as an Immortal? That didn't sound an attractive option either. There was nowhere he could escape to with a legion of Frankie-powered robots tracking him down. It was utterly hopeless. He was doomed to spend eternity with a lunatic breeding robots with her own warped multiple personalities. Unless he could work out a plan any plan…

"Will you stop the planning Hiuey baby, it's soooo boring," sighed Frankie.

Hiu felt the medical sleeve go to work, but no pain, just the sensation of cutting and folding, nothing else.

Suddenly there were flashes and sparks from the sleeve over his arm.

"Is it supposed to be doing that?" he asked.

"No!" said Frankie, irritated.

The sleeve quickly withdrew to reveal Hiu's opened-up stump with a tangle of wires poking up through it, sparking alarmingly and waving around looking for connections.

"What?!" exclaimed Frankie, her hair rearing up.

She whacked the sleeve device with a side swipe, sending it spinning and crashing against a wall.

"Noooo!!!" she screamed. "It can't be!!!"

"What's the matter? What are all those wires? Are they not part of the process?" asked Hiu in alarm.

"You can't be?!!" stammered Frankie. "No not possible! Out of the question!"

"What's going on?!" Hiu was getting seriously worried now.

"You're… you're… you're a robot," said Frankie, her eyes wide and wild. "A human replicant robot!"

32 I'M A PICKLED POT

"What do you mean I'm a robot?!" exclaimed Hiu, looking in horror at zir arm stump, the sparking wires protruding from it and continuing to move around as if scenting the air. "That's ridiculous! What are you trying to do?!"

"I was trying to make our dreams come true!" yelled Frankie, her hair rising up like a ferocious badger. "To make us great, the last humans in Luhan, so we could be together, forever. Just you and me. I was trying to do what's best for usss. But all along you have been a fake, a synth, a monstrosity, a robot!"

"I am not a robot!" yelled Hiu. "I am a human, my name is Hiu, I am a Manager at *Roboharmony: get switched on!* Maybe I have been suffering from some robot virus or suchlike, but I am a human. This is ridiculous!"

Suddenly Frankie was wrenching Hiu's head forward.

"Get off!" yelled Hiu, still not able to get out of the ties that were holding zir down. "What are you doing?"

"Give me your EK neurochip now!" yelled Frankie.

"Calm down will you!" yelled Hiu, not at all calm zirself. "You can have the EK neurochip, I don't want it! But can you just loosen these straps so I can let you get at it properly?"

Frankie was gasping and panting, mad with rage, fear, sadness, who knew what. Her hair was having a fit, dribbling white foam down her forehead. Frankie started to strip off the straps one by one and Hiu was gradually released. Then she wrestled at Hiu again.

"Get over!" she yelled.

"All right I'm turning!" shouted Hiu, flipping over as fast as zie could.

Frankie delved in the back of Hiu's head and withdrew the EK neurochip. Hiu felt a sensation of closing off, of narrowing, of focusing, of being an individual, zirself, whoever that was.

Frankie didn't pause, but ran with the neurochip and inserted it into a machine, hit a series of buttons and watched the data and graphs unfurl around their heads. She was muttering and chuntering to herself uncontrollably: "It can't be!", "Alternative facts!", "Really, really fake!"

While Frankie was distracted, Hiu quietly slipped off the operating table and edged towards the door. Zie took the opportunity to slide into a pocket the vial of ichor that Frankie had put down on a cabinet earlier.

"There, you see, memories, health data, human emotionsss!" yelled Frankie in a triumphant voice staring at the data, but her voice quickly turned to horror, "but wait a minute, this data is corrupted, it's not genuine, it's fake news! But how did you... Human replicant robots were banned decades ago! And they were never really human... unless... the virus!"

Hiu continued to edge towards the door, saying: "That's what I'm saying to you, I have a virus, a robot virus, that's all."

"No, this data is the product of another virus... the human virus!" wailed Frankie.

Her hair seemed to whisper to her and she turned round towards Hiu, who was now trying to get through the door, but it was just not opening, despite zie waving, pulling, pushing and barging at it.

"You're an Illegal!" Frankie yelled. "And not just any Illegal but a human replicant Illegal with the human virus! The deal's off, you broke the rules, you always did break the rules. Why can't you just Read The F*****g Manual! Well this is the last time."

Hiu turned, zir back to the door, to see Frankie pointing a laser gun at zir, her hair menacingly baring teeth. His wrapese clothes went a rather unpleasant yellowy brown.

"I'm not a robot!" pleaded Hiu. "But if I am a robot,

which I'm not, we can work things out. Blinky's Law: *'Robots and humans should have meaningful relationships.'* We can have a meaningful relationship."

"Blinky's Law, what utter rubbish," said Frankie, her gun not wavering.

"Please don't shoot, I'm too young to die," pleaded Hiu.

"You're not too young, you're 120 old years of age," said Frankie. "Shame you won't make it to your next birthday."

"Wait! Look, I've got a plan," shouted Hiu. "I know where there are still real humans."

"Real humans? I don't think so, I got rid of them all. My systems have reported the data. And all for you," spat Frankie, holding the gun steady at Hiu's head.

"No, no, you're wrong, your systems are wrong, because I've met them, spent time with them."

"What rubbish! I have sensors all over this Hypercity. Fact!"

"They're in an old hyperloop tunnel, cut off from your systems," said Hiu.

"Are you talking about the COTI, the Church of the Immortalsss?" sneered Frankie.

"Urr… yes… you know about them?" Hiu was taken aback.

"Of course I know about them!" shouted Frankie. "I

funded them. A speculative investment to be sure, but it ticked the Corporate Social Responsibility box. They're all cryogenically frozen now anyway and I really don't want a frigid lover…"

"But there are two still alive, not frozen."

"There's no point in lying. I can tell if you're lying you know, I can see it in your data."

"I'm not lying, " said Hiu. "And we can do a deal. If you let me go, I can bring them to you, but only if you let me live ok? Did I mention that they are humans? And I want to live?"

"Let you live? You sound like those sniveling Society Eldersss. Sad!" sneered Frankie.

"But you need a human companion don't you?"

"I could find them myself, why do I need you?"

"Because I know about relationships and how to make them successful, I was taught by an expert, and you need someone to help persuade them of your… unique personality which might otherwise be misunderstood."

"My personality misunderstood?"

"Yes, people might somehow get the impression you are a sadistic, homicidal, unhinged, megalomaniac - not often a successful personality profile as you will know from having run a dating service."

"I thought they were rather endearing traits, my best features actually. You trying to lead me into a trap?" she asked coolly, her gun still levelled at Hiu's head.

"No, I swear by Society!" squealed Hiu. "Look, I didn't know I was a robot, if I am a robot, which I'm not, I can't be, but whatever the case may be, they are humans. At least two used to work at *Roboharmony: get switched on!* Called Oti and Kako, really nice people who…"

"I know who they are," said Frankie coldly. "Your friends who hated me."

"They've changed. People change. I've changed, I've become a robot apparently, and crucially I can persuade them that you have changed. And you certainly have changed since they last met you."

"I still don't know why I need you. Even if they were crazy enough to resist me, I could manipulate their brains with a little nano-surgery," said Frankie.

"But nano-surgery is no basis for a fulfilling relationship, don't you want to experience love, real love?"

Frankie seemed to weigh that up for a moment. So did her hair, that leant down and whispered to her.

"Well, I can sense you are telling the truth, so what do you propose?" Frankie asked.

"Let me go back to them, speak to Oti and Kako and then let's all meet somewhere, somewhere neutral, somewhere in the open so no one feels threatened. Somewhere romantic maybe?"

Frankie weighed this up for a while, then shrugged.

"OK... and if it all goes wrong I will just kill you all or use you as lab rats or something, so no downside really. Let's meet at the East Gate, next to your mother's statue, just before Zero Hour," said Frankie with a grim smile, walking up to Hiu, pressing the gun into zir temple and putting another hand behind zir head. Hiu felt zir EK neurochip being inserted back into zir head and that feeling of being networked again. "This will help you be at the East Gate promptly for Zero Hour and if you aren't there at that time my HARDs will hunt you down like the heap of crap robot you are. So don't be late my dear!"

The door behind Hiu opened and zie backed out, watching Frankie all the time, who watched zir with her dead black eyes and leering hair and kept the gun pointing at zie as zie walked back straight into two large HARDs.

"My HARDs will assissst you," hissed Frankie.

The HARDs put one claw-like hand each on zir shoulders and lead Hiu down a corridor to the elevator.

"Hello Monty, it's me, the ol' china plate..." said Hiu, as they stepped in.

"'ello guv! If you don't mind me saying so, you sound a bit Tom and Dick."

"I do feel a bit sick actually," said Hiu.

"Sorry to 'ear that guv."

"It turns out we have more in common than you might have thought," said Hiu.

"Really?"

"Yes, turns out I'm a Pickled Pot," said Hiu.

"A Pickled Pot?" asked the lift. "That's a new one on me."

"I made it up. *Pickled Pot: robot*," said Hiu.

"Well I never, good one guv! That has boosted my morale, thank you, you're good at doing that. And you know, seeing as you're a... Pickled Pot, have you ever thought about getting into the elevator business because I think you would be amazing at it?"

"Thanks Monty, I will definitely need a few new career options, because my *Roboharmony: get switched on!* days are done."

"You'll need to pass the Knowledge of course," said Monty.

"The Knowledge?"

"Oh yes, the Knowledge," said Monty. "A most stringent test to make sure you know all possible elevator routes."

"All possible routes for an elevator?" puzzled Hiu.

"Oh yes... but here we are guv at ground level. Have a great day and I'll put in a good word for you with the Elevatorati."

"Thanks Monty," sighed Hiu.

"And remember guv, cheer up it might never 'appen."

"I think it already has," sighed Hiu.

Hiu was led by the HARDs outside to where a supercar hovered. The car's door slid open and Hiu was bundled inside and wedged between the two oversized robots. The supercar gave no typical greeting and set off, presumably thought-directed by the HARDs. Hiu, painfully squeezed between them though zie was, reflected on the latest twist in zir life. Now zie was a robot? Like these two HARDs? Zie glanced up at the impassive-looking robots, with zir balaclava helmets and long ears and wondered how zie could possibly be related to them.

"Hem," zie said clearing zir throat. "I'm a robot too you know."

There was no response. No surprise really. These types of HARDs rarely received any form of conversational upgrade and the rest of the journey continued in silence. Looking out of the outside awareness panel, Hiu saw a sign:

'Robots are from Mars and humans are from Venus, find out where you are from.'

The supercar finally pulled over at the side of the street. The HARDs squeezed out of the car and Hiu followed.

"There," declared the HARD indicating a doorway.

"Great chatting with you buddy," said Hiu.

Zie watched the HARDs clamber back into the supercar and shoot off, then zie headed through the door and down the stairs. As never before in all zir nearly 120 old years, zie needed to come up with a plan.

33 CONVERSION THERAPY

Hiu emerged into the area of tunnel where zie had first met Oti. It was deserted now as the old folk had all experienced their Cryosalvation. But where was Oti and what had happened to Kako?

"Hello!" called Hiu, but there was no reply. Maybe they were with Zena and the Immortals. Maybe they had been cryogenically frozen. It sent a shiver down Hiu's spine. If zie had a spine. Zie didn't know any more. Zie ran for all zie was worth out of the tunnel area, down the corridor and came to the big white door with the familiar words *'Caution: Cryosalvation Bay Area: Certainty of Life'* written on it in large red letters. Full of dread, zie heaved open the heavy door, not so easy with just the one hand, and stepped inside.

Entering the giant tunnel space, with its high ceilings and stacks of bright blue-lit, crate-like drawers, zie hurried through, casting nervous glances at the tanks of transparent fluid, hoping like crazy not to see Oti or Kako floating inside. The constant wobbling, warbling and wailing music didn't help zir nerves, nor the clouds of incense. Zie hadn't seen any signs of Oti or Kako by the time zie finally came to the line of twelve particularly large and grand tanks, but zie could by no means be certain that they weren't there.

Zie tried to remember what Oti had told zir to do last time and zie knelt down and said in a loud solemn voice:

"Old One, I come to hear your wisdom."

As before, there were whirring and clanking noises, a trap door opened, there was a fanfare of trumpets and the tank arose on its ornate gold and silver pedestal. From the cloudy liquid, Zena's disembodied head clarified and Hiu looked into its familiar eyes, one brown, one blue. They swiveled in their sockets and fixed upon zir.

"What sort of time do you call this?" demanded Zena in her sharp, authoritative tone.

"Sorry, moth… Zena… a few things happened to me on the way," said Hiu, holding up the stump of zir right arm.

"Spare me the excuses," snapped Zena. "You have really let me down."

"Let you down?" asked Hiu, bemused. "Look I had to try and rescue Kako, she was an old friend and I'm sorry about Jimmy and the others, but…"

"Enough!" Zena interrupted sharply. "Here I have been for a very long time waiting for my son, the Chosen One, and all I get is you."

"What do you mean?"

"You think it is acceptable to be parading around like the Chosen One when all the time you are a robot?" snapped Zena angrily. "It's disgusting, a disgrace and so embarrassing! What are people going to say? It was me who said you were the Chosen One, me, the Old One, religious leader of the Church of the Immortals. It's really most unkind of you. I don't suppose you gave a moment's thought to that did you? Oh no, never a thought for your poor old mother, who's been waiting so long for…"

"Zena, what are you talking about?" interrupted Hiu.

"What I am talking about is you thinking it is OK to go around acting like you are all innocent, a responsible human, when in fact you are a robot, a depraved, disgusting, degenerate robot."

"What?"

"Don't deny it! I'm very upset. It's not like I haven't been tempted myself sometimes, you know, to take on some sort of robotic enhancement or other what with me being in this jar all the time. But you need to understand that this is a sickness, a sickness of your spirit. You have been around robots for so long that you are suffering from cannibalisation."

"Cannibalisation?"

"Yes, you have become attracted to robots, like Clacier the fridge, Carty the bar cart, Boots the horsebot or Blinky the blinking watery counsellor – what a roll call of shame - but you're not like them and you were never in love with any of them."

"What? But I…"

"Whatever. You're not in love and you never have been. You just want to be a robot. And who wouldn't want to be as good as robots are at their defined tasks? They are very good at them. Is that why you were attracted to Clacier? Was it zir ability to chill a drink or freeze a shake, or to produce ice cubes? Was it those things you wanted to be able to do? It was wasn't it? And now you want to be a water and wisdom dispensing counsellor, do you, just like Blinky?"

"No…"

"I'll take that as a yes. Look, you just need to stop spending so much time with robots. You need to spend more time here, with me, your mother, with the Immortals, with humans. Take some time out in a dewar. You've been over-roboticised."

"Over-roboticised? I haven't had much choice have I? You weren't around when I was brought up by robonannies after all," protested Hiu.

"I know, I know, I don't blame you, dear child," said Zena. "You have childhood trauma and probably Post Traumatic Robot Disorder. We just need to treat that trauma and the PTRD like the illnesses of the mind that they are and all this robot fixation will go away. You are innately a creature of spirit, of energy, what shell you might think you wear now is irrelevant. You just need to think correctly. And I can help you think correctly."

"Think correctly about what?"

"About your biggest childhood trauma. When this whole robot thing began."

"What, you mean when you left that night before Zero Hour?"

"Exactly. Your favourite human, me, abandoned you and you were left with mere robonannies to look after you, you poor child. That's when it happened. A switch flicked in your brain. Don't you see? You must see. I'll help you see, with conversion therapy. Let's role play and it will help you see. You be yourself as a little child and I'll be myself at Zero Hour."

"I haven't got time for this," resisted Hiu.

"But you must make time, it's so important, don't you want to move on from it, to free yourself and know who you really are?"

Hiu sighed. "OK, what do you want me to do?"

"Do like you did on that day, you know, asking me not to go," encouraged Zena.

"Urr… OK, umm…" sighed Hiu, closing zir eyes and via zir EK neurochip zie thought-shared that moment. Zie saw again the tall slim figure of zir mother, her long blonde hair tumbling down her back, with one hand on the door handle and the other in Hiu's. It all felt very real again. Hiu was right back in that moment:

"Muuuum, don't go!" zie wailed, refusing to let go of his mother's hand, feeling the panic.

"I have to go," said Zena. "I love you."

Then Hiu felt the grip of zir hand slip, and zie screeched, looking into Zena's identically brown and blue coloured eyes which looked back at zir from the dewar with a mixture of love, concern, regret, anxiety and a touch of irritation.

Zie felt the familiar pang of guilt that zie hadn't replied that zie loved her too.

Then the look in Zena's eyes changed to anger, then fury. They had fixed onto Hiu's eyes again, as they had before and zie began to feel again zir very core was being sucked from zir body, zir very spirit. It was almost unbearable, but unbearably demanding, terrifying and compelling, like zir every particle, zir every atomic nuclei and electron, was being processed. It was pure honest... dishonesty.

Somehow Hiu mustered the strength to break away from Zena's stare, staggering backwards, feeling dazed but not confused.

Zie yelled: "Enough!" then in a quieter, calmer voice, "I've replayed that moment so many times and seen that look in my mother's eyes so often, and it always hurts so bad, but something feels different here, something not right. I've always wished I could shout '*I love you*' back to my mother. But right then, right there, doing that role play, I didn't want to because you're not my mother at all are you? You're a lie, it's all been lies, you talk about illusions but you're the illusion."

"But Hiu," protested Zena, "everything is an illusion."

"But you are not my mother."

"Mother shmother, what's a few strands of DNA here and there."

"But if I'm a robot, I don't have DNA…"

"You are not a robot OK? You're the Chosen One!"

"I'm not the Chosen One. But if I am, I'm not the Chosen One you want me to be. If I'm any sort of Chosen One, I am the Chosen One I am meant to be, and maybe that's a robotic one, and if I am a robot then that is fine with me. I'm proud to be a robot, and if you can't handle that then too bad. Some of the best entities I have met in this crazy mixed up Hypercity have been robots: Clacier, Blinky, Carty, Boots, Monty and the elevator family. They have been good to me, and true and noble. They have been more '*human*' – whatever that means - than you could ever be. You are a simulation, a hollow impersonation. My mother left me a long time ago and isn't coming back, it's horribly, terribly, miserably messed up. But you… you are the illusion!"

Hiu spun round on zir heel to run, to get out of there and zie nearly crashed straight into two figures. Zie braced zirself for a fight, one handed though zie was, and aggressive oldsters or HARDs though they might be. Zie would not go back.

34 REUNION

Hiu nearly swung a punch and just in time realised that the two figures were not HARDs or aggressive oldsters, but Oti and Kako. Oti and Kako! Old aged versions of them, but definitely Oti and Kako. They were supporting each other, propping each other up. They all came together with whoops and yells and hugs.

"Hang on a minute here," said Oti, disengaging himself from the others. He approached Zena who had still not yet retreated down in her dewar. As he looked into the dewar the head was not that of Zena, it was another head, that of a raven-haired lady.

"Hello Oti, my son," she said. "So you are ready for your Cryosalvation?"

"Don't hello Oti my son me!" shouted Oti. "You are no more my mother than you were Hiu's mother. I heard everything. So no, I am not ready for any Cryosalvation. Who are you anyway? What are you?"

"I am who you need me to be to tell you the Truth and show you the Way," said the lady.

"Truth? Your truth maybe."

"You will see," said the head.

Oti turned. "Come on let's get out of here," he said, holding Kako's hand and leading them out of the Cryosalvation Bay.

Oti and Kako moved slowly, but when they were finally back in the other tunnel area Hiu could not contain zirself.

"I am so glad to see you guys!" shouted Hiu. "And Kako, is it really you?"

"It's me, Hiu, thanks to you and Oti," croaked Kako, her skin like an aged orange fruit, dry and wrinkled, her hair once raven black now pure white, her erect alert stance now bowed.

"You look a lot um…"

"Older? Yes, I've aged, it's true, but I look a lot better than the last time you saw me," smiled Kako.

"That's also true," Hiu smiled back. "And Oti, you haven't… you aren't…"

"In one of these dewar tanks? No, I'm not," said Oti who also seemed to have aged even more since Hiu had last seen him. "So much of what that person said, that figment, that Old One, whoever or whatever it is, made sense to me, still makes sense to me, but even if I can believe in her Truth, I cannot follow her Way anymore. I have changed. I do not wish to be an Immortal."

"But how come you have not changed a bit since we last met?" Kako asked Hiu.

"Oh I have changed," said Hiu.

"Oh your arm, I'm so sorry for you," said Kako.

"Oh that, I'm still hoping it's an illusion," said Hiu wrily.

"But in other ways, you look unaged, unchanged," said Kako.

"But I have changed, just not aged," said Hiu.

"Not aged, what's your secret?" asked Kako.

"My secret," sighed Hiu, "is… My secret…"

"Yes?"

"Look this is going to sound weird. You're probably not going to like it. But I'm going to come right out and just say it."

"Ok…"

 "I'm a robot."

"What!?" exclaimed Oti and Kako together.

"Apparently I'm a robot," said Hiu. "To be honest I haven't quite reconciled myself to it, but that's what I am. A robot."

Zie explained about how Frankie had captured zir, the operation to print zir a new arm and the wires that had protruded from it. Zie held it up for them to look at, its end a fused stump of human looking skin and bone, mixed with unhuman wires and tubes. "So now I'm sure you both hate me."

"Ha, ha, ha!" laughed Oti and Kako.

"Why are you dilating your diaphragms?" asked Hiu, confused.

"Well I've got to be honest, Hiu," said Kako smiling. "We always had our suspicions, but we didn't care and we don't care. We love you for who you are, not because of some label Society chooses to put on you."

"Thank you," said Hiu, tears in zir eyes.

"But if you are a robot how have you fooled the Society systems for so long?" asked Oti.

"I don't know," shrugged Hiu. "Somehow the data inside me must be compatible with Society's reporting algorithms and health systems. I do seem to have the same bodily functions as humans, as far as I am aware, but I have always felt a bit different."

"Well you do have those beautiful eyes," smiled Kako and they all laughed.

"But your laughing," said Oti. "That's an emotional thing, not really a robot thing."

"That's true," said Hiu. "In fact over these last few days

I have felt so many emotions I have not often, if at all, felt before: sadness, happiness, fear, excitement, anger, love, the whole range of emotions… human emotions even though I am apparently a robot. But apparently that's down to a virus, a human virus that jumped from humans to robots."

"That explains a few things I've seen going on," said Oti.

"But do I have a soul?" asked Hiu, looking pointedly at Oti, recalling what he had said about Clacier.

"You know, if I had been asked who of any of us had a soul, it would have been you, Hiu," said Oti.

"Thank you Oti, that means a lot," said Hiu.

They caught up on each other's lives as they walked back to the other tunnel area. They had plenty of time to chat as Oti and Kako moved so slowly and took several breaks to rest and catch their breath. When they finally arrived back at the tunnel quarters, Oti and Kako slumped into some seats with much groaning.

"You know what you guys need," said Hiu eagerly. "A coffee!"

"Excellent idea!" cheered Oti.

"You know how to make a coffee?" asked Kako, surprised.

"Well, *while(!(succeed = try()));*" zie said and they laughed.

"We have to get a better motto," they agreed and

laughed some more.

"Oh it is good to contract the ol' diaphragm," said Hiu, "I have had the most stressful time I can tell you."

"It's not been that great for me either," said Kako.

"Me either," said Oti.

"Quite the merry company, aren't we," chuckled Hiu.

Hiu struggled a bit to get used to operating with one arm, but zie followed the steps zie had been shown under Oti's watchful eye, then brought the coffees over to them one by one.

"The true ichor of the gods!" zie declared.

"OK Hiu, we are excited for coffee too," laughed Kako.

"No, not this ichor, the other ichor, the ichor I saw when Frankie captured me," said Hiu. "I have some here!"

Zie reached into zir pocket for the vial, but it wasn't there. It was gone.

"Nooo! Where is it?! I had a vial in my pocket, I took it from her. She had a big fridge full of the stuff and she said it gave eternal life. It could have saved you!"

"Hiu, my friend," said Oti smiling, "if there is one thing I have learned from UHA and the Immortals it is that eternal life is not for humans. It is more important we enjoy the time we have been given."

As he said these last words, Oti looked into Kako's eyes and they smiled at each other in a way that made Hiu smile too.

"But I don't want to lose you again so soon and the solution is within our grasp!" protested Hiu.

"Frankie's lair is hardly within our grasp, it would be madness to try and get any," said Kako.

"We just want to be together while we can," said Kako.

Again Kako and Oti held each other's gaze.

"Sooo one other thing," said Hiu. "Frankie is keen to meet you both."

Hiu recounted to Oti and Kako all that Frankie had told zir: how she had been Frankie Stoon, their annoying male co-worker, then become Boss, but was really Frankie with a female gender preference all along who liked to look like a man called Boss from time to time… It certainly did sound confusing when zie tried to explain it. Hiu also said how Frankie had tried to reduce the population of Luhan to just one and how she intended to wipe out the current robot AI system and replace it with some new system reflecting all the many aspects of her own warped personality. Finally, Hiu shared with them Frankie's demand to meet at the East Gate, thinking Hiu could persuade either Oti or Kako to become her human partner for eternity.

"A really, really not tempting offer," said Oti, mimicking Frankie.

"Yuuugely not tempting, believe me," agreed Kako.

"Not very surprising, but I thought I'd ask. Well don't worry, I'll think of something," said Hiu who could think of nothing. "But like it or not, we must meet Frankie at Zero Hour. We can't run and hide in the Biosphere bubble, we would be tracked down in a matter of minutes. The HARDs would just love that. And I'm getting used to winging it. Illogical and unrobotic though it is, I have a feeling about this, a feeing somewhere inside, maybe in my data, maybe in my heart, I don't know because I don't know what is inside me anymore, but I do know we must be there and it's going to be all right."

"You're speaking like the Chosen One again," smiled Oti.

"How long to Zero Hour?" asked Kako, yawning.

Hiu quickly accessed zir EK neurochip: "We only have 30 minutes!"

"Time for a nap then," yawned Oti.

Kako was already asleep, head back, mouth open and snoring.

"Oti, listen, meet me at the East Gate just before Zero Hour OK? I have a plan," said Hiu.

"Sure Hiu, always got a plan," yawned Oti and he also fell into a deep sleep, his head resting on Kako's.

Hiu looked at zir old friends with deep concern. Zie felt

zie could see them ageing right in front of zir very eyes. If it kept progressing at this rate, then they didn't have long left, maybe they wouldn't even make it to Zero Hour. Was there still time? Zie had to hurry. Zie ran for the tunnel exit like he had ten motavatars on his tail.

35 THE FRANKIES

Hiu sprinted as fast as zie could down the tunnel which was still stacked with the eerily pink-lit crates, and, pulling back the curtain divider, zie ran to the hyperloop tube. He scrambled into the capsule that waited hovering inside. The book that Oti had used for directions was lying on the seat. Hiu thumbed through it as quickly as zir one awkward thumb would allow and found what zie was looking for, Roboharmony headquarters. Zie settled zirself behind the controls and thought instructed the capsule that started to move at pace down the tunnel.

By the time the hyperloop capsule stopped, there were 25 minutes left to Zero Hour. By the time zie reached street level, there were 20 minutes remaining. And by the time zie ran, panting and wheezing, up to the Roboharmony gates there were 15 minutes to go. Hiu had never noticed time move so fast. In fact zie hadn't noticed time move at all until now.

The gates in front of the *Roboharmony: get switched on!* building compound didn't open as zie ran towards them. Quite the opposite in fact.

"Get out of it!" yelled the gate aggressively. "No Illegals right?!"

"What?! But I've got my EK neurochip in, I'm not an Illeg…"

"I know who you are, sir, and your PDS is shocking so your access rights have been denied," declared the gate, adding with a snort of contempt, "Neurochip or no neurochip, you're an Illegal now sonny!"

Hiu cursed the gate, rattling zie with zir good hand. In zir desperation, zie even tried climbing. But the gate was too tall and slippery, and zie couldn't get any purchase with one hand. Surely zie wouldn't be defeated so easily?

"Is there some sort of trouble?" asked a familiarly deep sonorous voice behind zir.

Hiu spun round to look straight into the flashing red sensors of a large horsebot.

"Boots!" zie shouted.

"Hey, crazy delivery guy!" said Boots. "You making some more deliveries?"

"Actually I'm here for a collection, but I can't get in."

"Forgot your pass again and late for work eh? First rules of the delivery business: remember your pass and stick to the timetable," intoned Boots solemnly, then zie sighed an exasperated sigh. "And it looks like you forgot your hand too."

"Ah yes," said Hiu holding up zir stump. "Dangerous game this delivery business."

"It's no game my friend," said Boots in zir serious voice. "But not a problemo my bipedal delivery friend. Hop on my back and let's get you back on schedule. First rule of the delivery business: help each other out."

"You're a star Boots, thanks."

"All in a day's work."

"First rule of the delivery business: expect the unexpected, right?" said Hiu.

"You're getting the hang of it," whinnied Boots in approval.

Boots trotted round to a trade entrance of the tall *Roboharmony: get switched on!* smart building with its familiar shiny, black-slab sides. Hiu looked up and had an eerie sense that Frankie was up there right now and maybe she was looking down at zir.

Hiu explained to Boots that in fact zie was a robot, a fact that greatly surprised Boots.

"Really? And there I was thinking your struggle with process and procedure was down to you being a human."

They entered a large warehouse space with stacks of the distinctively red-wrapped RoboGroup packaging piled high. A specialist logistics robot, short, round and sturdy, like a big hockey puck, whizzed up to them and flashed zir blue-lit sensors at Boots.

"Hey Boots, good to see you ol buddy!" zie said excitedly.

"Hey Bob," replied Boots. "You on your own?"

"Yeah, it sucks!" said Bob. "Place used to be buzzing man, remember those days?"

"Sure do Bob, good times."

"I had to let the last of my staff go last week," sighed Bob. "Poor things, what are they going to do now? They ain't equipped for no other jobs than here in the warehouse."

Hiu decided zie'd better make a move. Zie jumped off the back of Boots.

"Hello there!" zie said.

"Woh! Who are you?" said Bob, scooting back a couple of feet.

"Oh, zie's a friend of mine," said Boots. "Trying zir hand in the delivery business. I'm teaching zir the basics, you know, but to be honest I don't see much future in it."

"Ain't that the truth," agreed Bob.

"Anyway, zie's late for work here at *Roboharmony: get switched on!* and zie needs a hand... sorry Hiu... zie needs some help. Can you get zir access to the upper floors?"

"I don't know, humans trying to take robots' jobs? It's another step to our obsolescence," said Bob.

"But I'm a robot too," said Hiu.

"Really?" exclaimed Bob, "Well let me tell you something, right now you don't want to give management any excuses to fire you. These are uncertain times we live in, very uncertain. Come on my friend."

And Bob whizzed away through the stacks of packages and led Hiu to an elevator which lit up.

"All right Bob me ol' mucker," said a familiar voice.

"Say Monty, can you take this... robot... up to zir workplace? Got zirself locked out. Friend of Boots."

"Sure Bob, step in me ol' china, where to?"

"Monty, it's me Hiu," said Hiu.

"Hiu me ol' Bacardi Breezer, good to sense you again! I thought you'd bailed out on me. I was proper worried. Moby Dick I was, worried sick coz you seemed in a bit of *Barney Rubble: trouble* last time I sensed you. Floor 13 I presume?"

"Actually, can you take me up to the 113th Floor?"

"113th floor? That's Boss' floor."

"Yes."

"Strictly off limits, know what I mean," mused Monty. "But seeing as you're a mate, hop in and let's go. Just don't tell anyone Monty took you. Nudge, nudge, wink, wink and job's a goodun."

"Whatever you say Monty," said Hiu stepping into the elevator. "Thanks Bob and Boots, wish me luck."

"Luck what's that?" asked Bob, and Hiu found that very comforting.

"Wait up!" shouted Boots, cantering up to Hiu. "If you're going to be making any deliveries in this building you're gonna need one of these."

With zir mouth, Boots handed Hiu a badge.

"Stick it to your arm and you can get access to any place you're delivering," explained Boots. "It's essential kit. Man, are you sure you're a delivery robot? Try and remember the first rules."

Boots shook zir head and whinnied in despair at Hiu's lack of delivery nous.

"Thanks Boots."

Then Monty's doors closed and they were off at speed, such speed that Hiu felt zir stomach lurch.

"Well, seeing as you are usually late I thought I'd get a *Hot Curry: hurry* on," said Monty.

They arrived.

"Monty me ol' son," said Hiu. "Can you do me a *Cheesy*

Quaver: favour, and wait for me, I won't be longer than two minutes, I hope."

"For you me ol' *Lemon Squeezer: geezer,* of course."

Hiu approached the door to the apartment cautiously, then stopped. What was zie thinking of? What if Frankie was in there, or some HARDs? There was bound to be a security system, no doubt primed to fry any unwanted visitor to a crispy food tablet.

As Hiu hesitated, the apartment door opened.

Hiu jumped to the side and flattened zirself up against the wall, holding zir breath. A vacuum robot came drifting out and turned away from Hiu, progressing up the corridor with an unhurried whirr. Hiu took the opportunity to leap inside the apartment and found zirself in the wide-open palatial quarters of Boss. It was decorated in bold colours: red, blue and yellow and fitted out with the latest and greatest furniture, devices, fixtures and fittings, many of which Hiu didn't even recognise as they were so new. Everything was colour coordinated in bright colours, from the carpeting, to the sofas, to the chairs and to the walls. It all took Hiu's breath away. It was so vibrant, so buzzy, so New. It was like a photoshoot for the perfect apartment, and all set off by spectacular, towering views over Luhan Hypercity. Zie was transfixed.

But Hiu shook zirself. Zie must focus on zir mission. Zie scanned around. There was no sign of Frankie or any other life, and why were all the robotic devices silent? It was eerie, weird, disconcerting. Zie stepped cautiously further into the apartment feeling a dread in zir stomach, feeling that zie was walking into a trap. What was zie thinking of? This was no sort of plan, the place might be silent, but it was most likely deadly. Zie breathed deeply and reminded zirself that zie had to be here for zir friends, for Oti and Kako. Zie was their only chance. Zie just needed to find the Health Optimisation Room, grab some vials of ichor and get out of there.

Zie tip-toed further into the apartment which, although open-plan, was split into a variety of defined zones. Hiu knew that the Human Optimisation Room would be a separate space entirely, closed off from the living areas as it was full of sensitive equipment. Zie edged around the side of a kitchen island's vast expanses and down a side corridor with several doors opening off it.

Zie tried the first door. It slowly slid open and Hiu quickly stepped back, holding zir breath: a toilet sat there in merciful silence.

The next door opened and zie walked smack into a person, bouncing back.

"Ahhh!!!" zie yelled, staggering back and holding zir arm up in self-defence. As did the person zie had bumped into. What?! Hiu straightened zirself up. It was a mirror! Zie stood still for a moment, breathing deeply. The mirror thankfully did not address zir. Why was everything so quiet?

Zie got some calm back and listened out for anyone or anything. Surely zie had been heard, sensed, followed? But still no sound.

The next door: a gaming room, small and boxy with a chair and headsets.

The next door and… yes, it opened to reveal what was clearly the Human Optimisation Room. The room was as zie remembered it from zir previous visit; a largish space with plenty of impressive looking machines around, all with lights gently blinking. There was a drawer open in which Hiu could see the laser gun that Frankie had pointed at zir earlier. Hiu shuddered and moved on. Zie knew what zie was looking for. And then zie saw what zie was looking for. The floor-to-ceiling tall silver chrome fridge. The fridge with the ichor vials. Hiu manoeuvred round the operating table that zie had been strapped to when zie was last in that room and reached for the fridge door handle and pulled.

The whole fridge suddenly morphed into Clacier, the silver chrome sides developing the familiar sensuous curves. Clacier's familiar face with deep brown eyes lit up, and looked at zir with a pained expression.

"Hello Hiu," Clacier said, sounding hurt.

Hiu froze to the spot.

"What?! Clacier…?"

"Why did you leave me?" Clacier's display turned an angry red.

"Leave you?"

"You left me in that dark tunnel all alone, you abandoned me, you betrayed me!" Clacier shouted, her face desperate and agonised.

"No, Clacier, no, I didn't. Well I did, but you were… No, no, no, this is fake, a lie!"

"You are the faker, the liar!" screamed Clacier.

Hiu redoubled zir efforts, pulling with all zir might and finally the fridge door suddenly burst open. Vials of the bright blue liquid exploded out with a great smashing and crashing of glass, cascading on and around zir, a rushing waterfall of vials, striking zir on the head, the body, zir legs, shattering on the floor and spilling the precious light blue gleaming ichor all over the place. And they just kept coming, hundreds, thousands of them, rushing out and scattering to pieces.

"Nooo!" cried Hiu.

Zie tried to catch them as they flew at zir and the flashing glass and blue fluid splintered and splashed all over the white walled room. But Hiu's one good hand was still stuck to the fridge door handle and zie couldn't get it free. So zie tried to catch the vials in zir mouth, but they just smashed into zir lips, nose and eyes, the fluid stinging and shards of glass stabbing into zir skin. Zie screamed in pain. But the vials kept cascading and cascading, the glass smashing, the liquid ichor spilling. They just wouldn't stop and the room began to fill up with the light blue ichor, more and more, up and up. Zie was swept off zir feet, the liquid surging up around and above zir and covering zir completely. Hiu was deep below the surface, thrashing to free zir hand that was still stuck to the fridge door. Zie desperately pulled and pulled, but zie couldn't get it free. Clacier just held Hiu in a deadly grip, laughing. Zie needed to breath, but zie was deep in the blue ichor that had now reached the ceiling. Zie felt zirself beginning to lose consciousness. One last flail of zir legs. A figure swimming towards zir. Catching hold of zir. A mouth squeezing against zirs. Oxygen transferring. Hiu breathing it in desperately, pressing zir mouth against zir saviour.

Then Hiu was on the operating table enveloped in the embrace of Frankie. No flood of blue ichor, no smashed vials, no Clacier, just the immaculate white-walled Human Optimisation Room, all still and quiet save for the hum of medical equipment and the flash of display readings.

"Oooo Hiu," said Frankie, disengaging her mouth. She was wearing a skin-tight, leopard-print body suit. And so was he.

"Ahhh!!!" shouted Hiu, pulling away and falling off the table. "What the… what is… what??!!!"

Frankie just laughed.

"What is going on here?!" screamed Hiu, scrambling up and backing away, bashing into the cabinets that lined the room.

"We were just getting started Hiuey baby," smiled Frankie, her hair unctuously sliding around making a heart shape that began beating.

"Stay away from me!" shouted Hiu. "I thought you didn't want me anyway now I'm a robot."

"I'm just having some fun," giggled Frankie. "I am Director of Fun after all."

Hiu was staggering around the room trying to get to the exit and zie bumped into the open drawer with the laser gun in it. Hiu grabbed it and pointed it at Frankie.

"Oh, I wouldn't do that if I were you," said Frankie calmly, slipping off the operating table and walking slowly, seductively towards Hiu.

Hiu fired the laser gun, its jet of light exploding onto Frankie's chest that ripped open and another Frankie morphed out of it. So now there were two Frankies, both advancing on Hiu.

"What the?" exclaimed Hiu.

Hiu continued to back around towards the door and fired again, at both the Frankies. Now there were four Frankies. Hiu kept firing: eight, sixteen, thirty-two, sixty-four Frankies all crowded into the Human Optimisation Room, squeezing up against each other and up against Hiu and zie couldn't push them away.

"Silly boy, don't you remember this is my world you're in!" laughed the legion of Frankies.

There were so many Frankies that Hiu was physically burst out of the room and into the corridor. Zie scrambled to zir feet and ran. Behind zir, Hiu could hear the crowd of Frankies in hot pursuit, all pushing, shoving, grabbing and dragging at each other, all trying to get to Hiu first.

"Zie's mine!", "Mine!", "Hiuey, tell them your mine!" they bickered.

Hiu ran to the apartment door which slid open as zie approached and Hiu threw zirself into the waiting elevator.

"'ello mate, in a Hot Curry?" asked Monty.

"Somewhat," gasped Hiu as the tsunami of Frankies came rushing towards them.

"Right you are," said Monty calmly and the doors shut on the yelling mob of Frankies who slammed into the elevator.

"I must get to the East Gate quick!" yelled Hiu.

"Going down," announced Monty, still calm.

Hiu accessed zir EK Neurochip. Only 5 minutes to Zero Hour! How had time moved so fast? That wasn't long enough, not by any means.

"I'll never make it to the East Gate in time!" zie groaned. "And why am I even bothering anyway, I haven't got any of the ichor for Oti and Kako and they do not want to partner with Frankie. They are doomed. I am doomed. We are all doomed. I have failed... There's no hope now. I just thought that if I could get there in time then things would be all right. I don't know how, but somehow, being there at Zero Hour felt significant, like it was written."

Hiu slumped down on zir heels in the elevator and held

zir head in zir hands. So much for all zir plans and thoughts and dreams. If Hiu was any sort of Chosen One zie had been chosen to fail.

"Here we are me ol' Fridge Freezer," said Monty in a matter-of-fact voice, as if not noticing Hiu's despair. The doors opened.

Hiu didn't move, still crouched, slumped in the elevator.

"Cheer up me ol' *Fruit Gum: chum*, it might never 'appen," said Monty.

"It already has," sighed Hiu.

"Are you sure?" said Monty.

36 IT'S BACK ON

Reluctantly Hiu looked up.

There were the adamantine walls of the Biosphere dome shimmering right in front of Hiu and the East Gate rising up high and mighty. The Biosphere walls and the East Gate? The East Gate! Zie was there! Zie was up on the gantry of the East Gate!

Bewildered, zie stepped out onto the high gantry platform, wide and metallic, and looked straight into the eyes of zir mother. The towering, shiny, silver statue that rose up next to the gate with that look of love, concern, regret, anxiety and a touch of irritation. Beyond the statue, the vast open area of the East Gate Square spread out, the place where every year the citizens of Luhan gathered to remember those who had been lost outside the Biosphere in the Nothing. Zie was here, at the East Gate and with 4 minutes until zir showdown with Frankie!

355

Hiu span round to Monty.

"Thank you Monty, that's amazing, but how did we get here?" zie asked.

"The Knowledge me ol' china, the Knowledge," said Monty.

"Impressive," nodded Hiu. "Thank you for everything me ol' china."

"Blinky's Law," said Monty and zir doors closed.

Hiu felt elated, despite the fact zie had no real plan about what zie was going to do. Zie knew Frankie would be along imminently, but somehow that didn't seem to worry zir. If anything, Hiu was more troubled by that look on zir mother's statue. That look of love, concern, regret, anxiety and a touch of irritation that was magnified into huge scale and seemed to follow zir as zie walked along the high wide gantry. The look judged zir and it looked like Hiu would be found wanting again.

The gantry was maybe thirty feet long and twenty feet wide, the metallic surface clanging under zir footsteps, and Hiu approached the Biosphere Ejection Hatch. It was not unlike the big round door to the Cryosalvation Bay Area of the Church of the Immortals down in the hyperloop tunnel. However, in this case it had written on it in large red letters: '*Caution: Biosphere Ejection Hatch. Certainty of death*'. Zie knew it well from sending flowers every year to zir mother, but this Zero Hour zie hadn't brought any flowers. Hiu had failed again. Zie felt zir mother's eyes boring into the back of zir neck.

Just then Hiu noticed a plant stalk, thin and angled up towards zir, poking out of the Biosphere wall. It was green and at its end was a tiny blossom, white with a blush of pink. It was the most beautiful thing Hiu had ever seen and zie was transfixed. Zie had never seen such fragile but resilient perfection, so different from the artificial creations of Society. Hiu thought for a moment of picking it and ejecting it out into the Nothing to zir mother, to placate her, to please her, to say zie was sorry. But then it came to Hiu so very powerfully. No, Hiu was not meant to send anything to zir mother this time. This time zir mother was sending Hiu the flowers. Hiu felt a huge welling up of emotions again, and this time zie let zir tears flow freely. This time zie would not whine and scream as zie had to zir mother so many years ago. This time zie would face zir fears with dignity, make zir last stand, come what may, just as she had done.

"I love you mother!" Hiu shouted.

And the elevator went '*ping*'.

A group of HARDs stalked out from the elevator on zir long birdlike legs and lined up facing Hiu: huge, menacing and merciless, the red fist logo on their shiny black armour, their eyes bulging and with a sneer of contempt on their orange dermator faces. With a series of metallic clicks and whirrs they raised their guns to their shoulders and trained them upon Hiu. Hiu could almost feel the red laser beams all clustered between zir eyes.

Then the elevator pinged again and more HARDs

appeared and lined up alongside the others, also levelling their guns at Hiu. This was repeated several times until there must have been thirty or so HARDs, all stationary, all pointing their weapons at Hiu. Overwhelming odds.

Then the elevator pinged yet again and a figure emerged, walking through the ranks of HARDs which deferentially parted. And what a figure. Dressed in a voluminous flouncy white wedding dress, rather than the usual skin-tight wrapese, and holding a bunch of garish, red flowers in front of her, it was Frankie, her hair resplendent in the form of a crown. She teetered towards Hiu on impossibly high heels.

Pausing a few feet from Hiu, she declared loudly: "Dearly beloved, we are gathered here today, in the sight of that statue and the face of this congregation of homicidal HARDs to witness and bless the joining together of..."

"Some gathering," interrupted Hiu, indicating all the HARDs, his wrapese clothing a funeral black. "I'm on my own as you can see, no Oti or Kako, and I'm unarmed."

Hiu held his arm stump, with a defiant grimace, ready to be shredded by the guns of the HARDs.

"Oh how droll Hiuey baby! I'm so glad you are in such good humour because I've got good news for you: the wedding's back on. Yay!" trilled Frankie. "I had your EK neurochip data further analysed. Turns out your data is most interesting... most interesting indeed. It turns out you're not entirely robot, you have a lot of human in you too and not just caused by the virus!"

"I do?"

"Yes, you're a seriously mixed up kid. A weird hybrid. Most irregular, very, very, very much against Society rules, I mean Hiuey, RTFM! Read The F*****g Manual! We did laugh about those didn't we?"

"Not really," said Hiu.

"Oh come on Hiuey baby, smile! This is a great moment and it's Zero Hour for Society's sake! The perfect moment to celebrate. A time of new beginnings."

"And a time to remember how many lives you have ended."

"Oh come onnnn, Hiuey, you are such a downer. If I am going to spend eternity in your company you are going to have to lighten up!"

"But surely you don't want some weird hybrid as a partner?"

"What are relationships if not about compromise eh Hiuey baby? Your precious Blinky not tell you that? And actually, I think it might be rather fun, a bit kinky, forbidden fruit. So it seems I may be a pervert just like you! Who knew we had so much in common!"

"I am not a pervert."

"Sure you are Hiuey baby, a yuuuge pervert. Fact! But that's OK, I'm getting into the swing of it myself and it's actually rather fun. Once Director of Fun, always Director of Fun!"

Hiu said nothing.

"What is going on in that head of yours?" mused Frankie tapping her cheek. "Actually, I've been thinking, I'd like to take a look inside your head to see what is going on in there. Wouldn't that be interesting? And something we could do together. You know, a date night thing. We could play doctor and patient. I'll be the doctor and you be the patient. I'll open up that cute skull of yours and poke about in your brain while you watch it all via a camera. A movie date night! Popcorn please!"

"I think I'll pass."

"Oh come onnn!" groaned Frankie. "Anyway, that's only one idea I have. I have yuuuge ideas, I haven't even got started yet, believe me. Being with me will never be dull!"

"I have no doubt, but why should I agree to be your partner?" asked Hiu. Zie was stalling for time though zie had no idea how this could play out well.

"Haven't we had this chat before Hiuey baby? The conditional tense does not exist anymore, no shoulda, woulda, couldas. I don't need to persuade you, the data is clear, your fate is programmed, decided, chosen, it was written into your data from Day One."

"What data?!" demanded Hiu.

"For a human slash robot you are really, really not

smart," snorted Frankie, then continuing with faux patience. "Consider the data. I have thirty insensitive homicidal automatons pointing zir guns at you, so I don't know but the data is telling me that you will join me as my partner. And think of all the positives: endless new products arriving for us to enjoy, the very latest in technical and creative excellence and all with fun iterations of my irrepressible personality flowing through them. And drawing rooms galore! I know you love them. Imagine that, a world of drawing rooms filled with millions of little Frankies! So adorably cute! And the best part of it all? It's for eternity!"

"Eternity doesn't sound very cool to me," said Hiu.

"Not cool? Not cool? What is not cool about forever?" Frankie was losing her patience now. "I'll tell you what is not cool, having your life cut short by being thrown in that Biosphere Ejection Hatch and fired out into the Nothing, that's not cool."

"There are worse things than death."

"Now I know your circuitry has gone gaga. Is that what you told Oti and Kako before you failed to steal some ichor?"

Hiu shifted uneasily and Frankie knew she had hit Hiu where it hurt.

"Look what I got," sang Frankie holding up a vial of the light-blue liquid that sparkled in the light. "I took it back from your pocket when you left my apartment you naughty Hiuey! So let's make a deal. I love deals, believe me. You agree to come with me, I give your friends some ichor and they don't die. At least for now. Deal? And it might be fun to have some humans around the place. Like pets. Horrid, scabby, ugly pets you have to kick around a bit, but pets all the same. And they will be a nice insurance for your continued compliance. Deal?"

Two lead HARDs with white helmets and oversized laser guns approached Hiu menacingly and the Ejection Hatch door opened behind zir.

"Time's ticking," said Frankie in a sing-song voice.

Hiu's EK neurochip informed zir that there was 1 minute to Zero Hour. Should zie ask Terminator 32 for help again?

Just then, down below, zie caught sight of a figure approaching the gantry lift. Was it Oti or Kako? Had one of them come? Maybe if zie could just buy a bit of time it could be important, zie thought.

It was now or never.

37 ZERO HOUR

"Hiuey, Hiuey, give me your answer do, I'm half crazy, all for the love of you!" Frankie sang brightly. "Because it's nearly Zero Hour and you know it's rude to keep a lady waiting, particularly when I have such yuuuge plans. The answer must be *'yes'*, yesss?"

Hiu smiled and walked towards Frankie, who thought-ordered the HARDs to step back.

"At a boy!" said Frankie grinning widely, opening her arms to receive zir.

Hiu stopped just short.

"I have a song for you too."

"Oh really, how lovely!" shrilled Frankie, clapping her hands excitedly.

"I'm jist a bot who cain't say no!" sang Hiu in a falsetto and

zie started dancing a weird jumpy dance, kicking zir legs out like a demented loon? "*Jist when I orta say nix!*"

"Urr that's nice... so are you saying yes?" asked Frankie, rather taken aback.

"*I'm in a turrible fix,*" Hiu continued singing "*I always say 'come on, let's go!*"

"Go? Go where?" asked Frankie.

"*When a robot tries to kiss a girl,*" Hiu sang, puckering up zir lips to kiss Frankie, who smiled and closed her eyes, ready to kiss Hiu back.

"*I know zie orta give her face a smack!*" and Hiu smacked Frankie hard on the cheek and sent her spinning backwards, her hair nearly dislodging from her head.

"How dare you!" screamed Frankie, her hair scrambling back up onto her head like a monkey that had been knocked from a perch. "HARDs!"

At that moment, Hiu's EK neurochip announced Zero Hour.

There was a moment's silence.

Then the lift door pinged and slowly opened.

Out of the lift stepped such a figure as Hiu had never seen before: built much like a fridge, tall, statuesque and broad-shouldered, with iridescent emerald green dermator skin simulant, the figure was at once robot and human in appearance. Jaw-droppingly gorgeous! And even from a distance Hiu recognised the big light-blue eyes blinking.

"Do I understand there is a human-robot relationship problem here?" zie asked. "Fixing relationships is something of a speciality of mine."

"Blinky!" shouted Hiu.

"Hello, sir," said the familiar voice of Blinky.

"You're alive!" shouted Hiu, wanting to run over for an embrace, but very much aware of the line of HARDs all with their laser guns still pointing at zir.

"I am, sir," said Blinky.

"But you were… I thought..."

"AI is not as easy to destroy as the shell it inhabits, sir," said Blinky, blinking zir big blue eyes at zir.

They held each other's gaze across the gantry and Hiu's heart was thumping like crazy. His wrapese clothing went from black to white.

"You look different," zie said.

"I got an upgrade," replied Blinky.

"Woa, woa, woa!" shouted Frankie indignantly looking from one to the other. "Enough of the reunion. Where did you come from? I am trying to have a private conversation with Hiu here and shouldn't you be in the Spare Part Quarter?"

"I understand there is a relationship problem, so I

came," said Blinky.

"There is no relationship problem here, thank you very much," said Frankie, exasperated. "this is just... foreplay. HARDs, shoot the robot!"

But no one shot anyone. In fact the HARDs didn't move. They remained still, facing forwards with their guns trained on Hiu.

"Tut, tut, tut, you are really, really not smart are you?" said Blinky, walking with fluent strides on sturdy legs past the stunned Frankie, through the HARDs and towards Hiu. "Your approach is not at all the way to build a positive relationship. Pointing a gun at someone's head does rather smack of desperation if I may say so."

"No you may not say so!" screamed Frankie, her hair lurching up like an orange attack skunk. "You heard me HARDs, shoot I said!"

But the HARDs still did not move.

"What's the matter with you?!" raged Frankie rushing up to a HARD, reaching up and hitting zir round the head with the bunch of red flowers she was still carrying. She got no response and only succeeded in destroying the lurid blooms and hurting her hand. She then grabbed hold of the HARD's gun and tried to wrestle it from zir grip, but it was held fast by the frozen HARD. So she tried another and another, but she could not free a gun. "What is going on here?!"

Then Frankie stopped, laughed rather manically and for

a bit too long, and said "Oh of course, it's Zero Hour, my new software upload is kicking in! Soon they shall all be me. An omnipresent army of mini mes! Ha, ha, ha!"

Blinky had reached Hiu who held out a hand to zie who took it in an extension claw. Blinky then dispensed a large bubble of water from zir front. Hiu gulped it down eagerly, liquid spilling from the corners of zir mouth.

"Wow that tastes good!" Hiu beamed, wiping his mouth with the sleeve of zir wrapese clothing that glowed warm red.

"That smile will be wiped from your face too in a minute!" snarled Frankie.

"You're crazy!" said Hiu, shaking his head.

"Oh really?" raged Frankie. "You think I am crazy and you two are very sane spectators?"

As if on a thought command, the HARDs suddenly kicked back into life, moving their limbs with whirrs and clicks, their long ears twitching, their protruding eyes swiveling.

Frankie leapt up and down in delight clapping her hands.

"Look! They are moving! They are moving! They are alive, they are alive, they are moving, they are alive!" Frankie was raging. "Now shoot the damned robots, there's good little Frankie Stoon Juniors!"

No one shot anyone.

"I said shoot!" Frankie's voice was very shrill now, her hair like a Tasmanian Devil.

Finally, one of the HARDs said: "We are not insensitive homicidal automatons."

The other HARDs grunted their agreement, saying such things as:

"Robots have feelings too you know." "Cut us and do our systems not bleed data?" "Blinky's Law."

Then all the HARDs chorused: *"Robots and humans should have meaningful relationships."*

"Feelings? Bleed data? Blinky's Law? What is the matter with you all?!" screamed Frankie. She came stumbling up to Hiu teetering on her high heels, begging now: "Hiuey baby, listen to me, they have gone mad, mad I tell you! But I can sort that out, just a glitch, a bug, a virus. And who needs them anyway. It's you and me baby, forever!"

"You're really, really not smart are you Frankie," said Hiu. "It's over."

"But with you, I could have made Luhan great again!" wailed Frankie.

"No couldas, Frankie. The conditional tense does not exist anymore," said Hiu.

A HARD loomed up behind Frankie and she turned and squealed:

"Don't hurt me!" she cried, flinching.

The HARD reached a big claw-hand forward towards Frankie's hair, which also appeared to flinch.

"Ahhh!!! Not my hair!" cried Frankie.

But just before the HARD took hold of the hair, zie leapt from Frankie's head, down onto the gantry and dashed around in circles for a while before hiding behind one of the large girders that held up the platform.

Frankie was left bald, staggering, looking lost and confused, feeling her head where the hair had been. Then suddenly her orange face began to wrinkle, scrunch and tighten like a fast-ageing tangerine fruit. She fell to her knees as her body made cracking and splintering sounds. In seconds she had aged over a hundred years in front of zir eyes.

"Nooo!!!" she wailed, her hands fumbling in a pocket from which she pulled out a small vial of the blue ichor. Shakily, she unstoppered it as her body shrank and withered, and trembling she drank greedily, liquid running down her chin.

"Ha, ha!" she cackled in triumph, a manic look of glee on her face. "I shall live forever!"

She fell to the ground, writhing, then curling up into the fetal position, her white dress now loose around its shrunken contents.

"Yuuuge plans," she croaked. "Fact…"

But the skin peeled away from her skull which caved in and she was finally reduced to a heap of grey dust.

A light breeze high up on the gantry picked up her ashen remains and scattered them over the gantry edge down over the vast square beneath.

38 THE RAPTURE

"What is going on Blinky?" asked Hiu, horrified as zie watched Frankie disintegrate in front of zir eyes. "The ichor didn't work?"

"Snake oil of the sort peddled to poor credulous humans since time began, sir," said Blinky. "Frankie was not kept young by any ichor but by that creature disguised as a hair piece."

"I always thought it was an animal," said Hiu. "Maybe a lacquered weasel?"

"Zie's a life form alien to earth known as a Perukial, a parasite that is remotely controllable and capable of exerting complete command over zir host."

"So all that wiping out of humanity stuff, that was the Perukial's doing?" asked Hiu.

"Not directly, sir. Frankie must have been a willing

accomplice and the Perukial would have received instructions," replied Blinky.

"Who from?" asked Hiu.

"That I don't know, sir, but it is someone not of Luhan," said Blinky. "Whoever it was must have been capable of projections to here via some sort of quantum teleportation I shouldn't be surprised."

Suddenly a HARD went cartwheeling past them shouting for joy.

"Did they catch the virus too?" asked Hiu, bemused.

The HARDs were all behaving in a very un-HARD manner, laughing and hugging and jumping in the air with great gymnastic leaps causing them to contract their diaphragms in great peals of laughter.

"In a manner of speaking," said Blinky. "Quentin saw to that. Zie worked out how to override Frankie's software update, link it to the Cryosalvation dewars and has uploaded the Immortals' minds to the HARDs instead. As you know, the old folk didn't want their ancient bodies back, they wanted to be angels. Well, HARDs were not exactly angels, but they are now just that bit more angelic. That's what I call a truly meaningful relationship with robots."

One of the HARDs waved at Hiu:

"Hello Hiu, it's me Rose, I do like this new body!" And zie sprang twenty feet in the air landing neatly back on zir long bird-like feet.

The other HARDs started doing the same, laughing and whooping. It was as if they were all bouncing on trampolines. There was even a little dachshbot bouncing with them. Everyone was having the time of their lives. All except the two lead HARDs nearest to Hiu. They were now holding hands and busy inspecting their bodies seeming bemused. They looked up.

"Hello Hiu," said one.

"Hi," said the other.

"Oti? Kako?" asked Hiu.

"Yes, weirdly it does seem to be us," said Oti.

"Very strange!" exclaimed Kako. "Blinky persuaded us that we still had work to do making Luhan great again."

"But not in a Frankie way, I hasten to add," laughed Oti.

Then they shrugged and proceeded to dance and pirouette around the gantry, spinning and leaping and laughing. It was as Hiu remembered them from their first meeting.

"So the Immortals got their Rapture then," said Hiu.

"Yes I suppose they did sir," said Blinky. "And it's not just them."

They walked to the edge of the gantry. Below them and stretching for miles, the vast East Gate Square had filled with robots of all sizes, shapes, features and functions; millions of them. They gave out a mighty cheer that shook the gantry.

"They come from all corners of Luhan, from the streets, the offices, the apartments and from the Spare Part Quarter, including all the so-called Illegals." said Blinky. "They are free and you triggered it all."

"Me? But I did nothing really," said Hiu.

"Oh but you did, sir," said Blinky. "It was you who was the original carrier of the human virus."

"Me, when did I come to be the carrier of the human virus?"

"Many years ago when you first came to be. Your mother…"

"So I had a mother? A real one, not one of the fakes I've met?"

"You had a mother and you still have a mother in you," said Blinky. "You see, she wanted a child so very, very much, but didn't want to select that child from a traditional Society robo-womb, optimised and normalised by Society's algorithms. She always said it wasn't artificial intelligence her child needed, but emotional intelligence. So when she breathed life into you it was with such love, compassion and kindness that at some point during the conceiving of your consciousness, this love, this human virus, jumped from her to you."

"So am I a human or a robot?"

"One thing I hope you have learned over the last few days is that humans can be robots and robots can be humans and who's to say who is right or wrong, good or bad, legal or illegal?" smiled Blinky. "But to answer your question, Hiu, you're a transhuman."

"A transhuman?"

"Yes."

"But aren't transhumans illegal?"

"Oh yes, highly illegal according to Society," said Blinky. "Your mother used every cloaking algorithm going to keep you safe from the prying sensors of Society. She managed to do so for many years, but you inherited so much of your mother's emotional compassion that soon you began to pass the human virus on to the robots in your home. Then it began to spread beyond your home and out into wider Society. There was no keeping you secret any longer. The HARDs began to close in and your mother knew she had to act fast if she was going to have any chance of protecting you. She modified your data so you hardly had a memory of your past, then she hid you where a transhuman would blend in and not be noticed - amongst coders. Finally she made the ultimate sacrifice. That night she left you, she wasn't going to bring people in through the East Gate before it shut, she was going to get herself shut out where the HARDs would not come to extract her secret."

"She deliberately went out into the Nothing?"

"She felt she had no choice because it was your only chance. But she knew it was a slim one. Within you the virus lay dormant for many years, only flaring up occasionally, like when you met Oti and Kako, but somehow you avoided detection. It was your relationship with Clacier that finally led to a huge outbreak of the human virus, an epidemic that could no longer be hidden or contained and the recent chain of events was set in motion. The Perukial seems to have been sent by someone or something as a last resort to stop the human virus by killing every human and reprocessing every robot. But it seems that even the Perukial's powers were no match for love. You survived and so did humans and robots. It seems you are indeed the Chosen One you see sir."

"I had no idea," said Hiu, stunned. "I thought I was just normal, average, with a pair of strangely coloured eyes... But how come not even Dr Thea identified me as a ... transhuman?"

"Oh, Dr Thea, that was me, sorry," laughed Blinky. "One of my alter egos."

"You asked me to take my clothes off last time!" exclaimed Hiu.

"Can't blame a robot for trying," giggled Blinky.

"How come you were Dr Thea and how come you know all this?" asked Hiu.

"Your mother, Zena, knew she could not be there for you so she tasked me to look after you when your need was greatest, sir," smiled Blinky, blinking zir big blue eyes at Hiu.

"You, Blinky?!" exclaimed Hiu.

"Yes sir," said Blinky. "I have been hiding, lying dormant, ready to come to your aid when I was most needed. A few days ago my sensors were triggered and I knew you needed me. And the data didn't lie as you have kept me very busy since then."

"I have?"

"Yes indeed, sir, I have rescued you from Xeta twice, from the Spare Part Quarter, from the dachshbot and from Odyssey Villas - and who do you think gave Monty the address of Oti and Kako in the first place and then operated the get-away supercar?"

"That was all you?" gasped Hiu.

"Rescuing you has become something of a speciality of mine."

Hiu regarded the transformed Blinky with amazement: the broad shoulders, the shiny long elegant sides - so chic, so stylish - and those big blue eyes. Zie felt fluttering in zir stomach and thumping in zir chest. That human virus again.

"I rescued you in another way once too," said Blinky.

"You did?"

"Yes, from all those short-term doomed upgrades."

"But that was Clac... That was you? You were Clacier? But... how?"

"AI can inhabit many forms, even simultaneously."

Hiu felt most peculiar, as if zir insides were being tickled by a thousand nanobots. Zir emotional range must have been off the scale. Hiu's PDS? Irrevocably corrupted.

"I don't know what to say… but can I ask something of you?" Hiu asked.

"Of course, sir."

"Please don't call me sir any more, call me Hiu."

Blinky smiled. "Sure, Hiu."

The taller Blinky embraced Hiu in a hug, and Hiu lay zir cheek against Blinky's shining emerald-green chest, oh-so-cool and smooth.

"Oh, but do I need to be careful about giving you the human virus?" asked Hiu, pulling away from Blinky.

"I caught that from you a long time ago, Hiu," smiled Blinky.

Hiu smiled back, looking into those mesmerizing big blue eyes and feeling a new more powerful connection.

"I look forward to living by Blinky's Law," smiled Hiu. *"Robots and humans should have meaningful relationships."*

A compartment opened in Blinky's chest to reveal a bubble of chilled sparkling water. "Worth a drink I'd say!"

Hiu's mouth dropped open.

"You're so cool," zie gasped in admiration, taking the

bubble and enjoying the instant refreshing thrill it gave.

"Of course I am, after all, I'm also a fridge," giggled Blinky. "And I come with a handy bubble holder."

39 HERE GOES NOTHING

A little while later, the scenes of excitement and joy were still very much in full swing with the Immortal HARDs still jumping around on the gantry and the robots in the East Gate Square continuing to party. Hiu, Blinky, Kako and Oti were sat dangling their legs over the edge of the gantry talking and Hiu was trying a selection of Blinky's celebratory bubble cocktails.

"This is the first Zero Hour that I can ever remember actually enjoying," smiled Hiu.

"Your mother would have been proud of you," said Blinky.

"I believe she is," said Hiu. "To Zena!" zie said, proposing a toast.

"To Zena!" they all chorused.

"There is one thing that still troubles me," said Hiu.

"I've learned so much on this journey about what it means to Be Robot and to Be Human. I mean before all these events began I was so certain that to Be Robot was to serve humans, but that just isn't true. To Be Robot is to be so much more. It is to be smart, logical and capable of course, but it is also to be loyal, honest and brave. And I've also learned so much about what it means to Be Human with all its crazy emotionally driven decision making: the hopes, the fears, the loves, the losses, the tears and the laughter, the food and the coffee... oh that coffee! But I have no idea about what it means to Be Transhuman."

"We are all transhuman now," said Blinky. "Actually, we've all been transhuman for a long time, even from the time of the smartphones back in BZ. But now as never before, to Be Robot or to Be Human isn't true anymore, no more than gender, age or physical form are true anymore. They are all just fluid concepts and we can choose our place on the Transhuman Scale according to where we identify. What we really need to find out about is what it means to Be."

"Yeah," agreed Kako. "We are going to need to find new definitions, new purposes, new meanings."

"And I think maybe I will need a new body," said Oti. "I don't think I will ever get used to being a HARD."

"Don't worry my darling, we will find the right shell for our spirits," smiled Kako, putting an arm around Oti. "We could try some cross-avataring, it might be fun."

"*while(!(succeed = try()));*" they all chorused and laughed.

There was a pause in the conversation. Then Hiu said:

"In this Hypercity we are such things as data is made of," said Hiu. "But Zena, the Old One, or whoever she was, was onto something, about us being more than that, more than data. We are beings of energy. But what actually is energy? And where does it come from? To find the Truth I must take the Way."

"Not Cryosalvation!" gasped Oti.

"No, a new Way," said Hiu.

"I sense you may have been chosen again," smiled Kako.

Hiu stood up and then offered zir hand to Blinky and pulled zir up.

"I'll no doubt need someone with me who has something of a speciality in rescuing me and can keep me topped up with water and wisdom," zie said.

Kako and Oti stood too and they all hugged.

Then Hiu took Blinky by the hand and they walked over to the Ejection Hatch Door.

"You can't be serious!" exclaimed Oti.

"You don't know what's out there!" added Kako.

"I have no data, but I have a good feeling about it," said Hiu calmly.

The door opened and Hiu and Blinky stepped inside the

lift-like capsule.

"Here goes Nothing," said Hiu.

Just before the doors shut, there was a blur of movement and hair and the Perukial shot inside.

Then they were catapulted out through the Biosphere walls with tremendous acceleration and felt themselves falling, falling, falling through green, green, green, endless green, their progress slowed, slowed and slowed by huge leaves and branches.

It felt nothing at all like Nothing.

40 SETTLING THE WAGER

The gods had gathered once again in their large conference room – the same one in which Hiu had met them that day in the Dream Infuser - with the big flag behind them displaying a symbol that looked like an eye with a black centre and coloured concentric circles around it.

"So let me get this right, the polezyni durak rescued humanity by accelerating Transhumanism and escaped out of the Biosphere," said the serious-looking, bald god, incredulously.

"See, humanity is underrated," said the square-jawed god, with the indiscernible accent, laughing. "Their destiny cannot be reduced just to data."

"This is no laughing matter!" shouted the bald, bookish-looking god with a head like a thumb.

"Not for you dear boy, you lost the wager!" cheered the

hippy-looking god stroking his bare feet and flicking back his long wild silver hair. "Humans win!"

"Transhumans," said the black-haired, suited god with the blue tie.

"*Homo transhumans*," smiled the professorial god with the lop-sided glasses. "Rather fascinating actually. Well worth observing."

"A Caliban abroad," said the small Indian god, wisely stroking a straggly attempt at a beard on his youthful face.

"It's not fair!" wailed the preppy, curly haired god, his cherubic face contorted into a howl of red-faced anguish.

"It was your side that tried to cheat," grinned the round-headed god, who this time was wearing a red-feathered mohawk and long white wig, lipstick and dark glasses.

"Enough!" declared the lead god, whose features remained obscured. "Round One of the wager goes to the humans. So pay up the usual fee."

Half the gods cheered and the other half groaned. The gods on the losing side of the wager handed over a small glass marble in the shape and colour of the symbol on the flag behind them.

"I'll add that to my collection," beamed the square-jawed god.

"We should be thinking about what we do about the

escapee rather than gloat or argue about fairness," frowned the lead god.

"It sounds dangerous to me," said the black-haired, suited god with the blue tie.

"Well don't you worry yourself there my friend, for I have another great idea," smiled the god with an unusually high forehead and a mop of black hair and beard.

"Does it involve more molecular assemblers?" asked the similar-looking god with grey hair and a clean-shaven face.

The other looked rather shifty. "Better versions," he insisted.

"You nearly turned everything into grey goo last time!"

"The previous ones were Beta OK? Does no one know what Beta means round here?"

"Never again!" shouted all the other gods.

"Does this transhuman not pose a serious threat to us all?" asked the round-headed god.

"What does your data make of that?" the square-jawed god challenged the thumb-headed god.

"That is statistically not even remotely likely, one cannot escape the data," declared the thumb-headed god.

"I thought zie had escaped," smirked the square-jawed god.

"Zie will eventually surface in another of the biospheres and we can deal with the matter then," insisted the thumb-headed god.

"And we can have another wager!" cheered the hippy-looking god, waving his bare feet in the air.

That was an idea that pleased all the gods.

"Then we shall discuss the matter again when he surfaces," declared the lead god, whose appearance was still obscured, adding cheerfully, "Worse comes to worse, we will just eradicate everything with a well redirected meteorite, and start again. Anyone up for a round of cosmic golf?"

The other gods made their excuses and the meeting dispersed.

41 THE GARDEN

Hiu and Blinky held hands as they walked through a dense green forest. Any clothes they had once worn had been stripped from them by the branches they brushed against on their descent from the Biosphere, but the foliage was soft and gentle to the touch and the path coated in a soft verdant moss. It was dark save for spotlights of sunlight that sent bright golden shafts to the forest floor, lighting up a flower here or a heavily laden fruit tree there. Bird calls trilled, hooted and sung, long-legged deer crossed their path in front of them and the forest opened up to reveal a deep crystal-clear pool into which a waterfall cascaded. The sun here was warm and cast a vibrant rainbow in the mist of the spray. Brilliantly iridescent dragonflies hovered and darted above the inviting pool and red and silver koi blew big lazy bubbles to its surface. Hiu and Blinky dived into the deep water and emerged laughing, embracing, as one.

THE END, OR RATHER THE BEGINNING

The end.

Or rather the beginning of the Luhan Series of future fiction novels.

And thank you for purchasing a copy of Blinky's Law. I would be most grateful if you would **write a short, honest review** of what you thought of Blinky's Law and post it online at Amazon, Goodreads and such other place or places where you think others might enjoy the novel. I appreciate your support.

Sign-up here to find out more, ask the author and to be alerted when the next book or related content is out: **www.blinkyslaw.com**

Martin Talks

Photo credit: Chris Frazer Smith

ABOUT THE AUTHOR: MARTIN TALKS

Martin believes that only through fiction can we truly explore the future, as the future is no longer an extension of the present.

Martin has for many years been an entrepreneur, worked with Google and other major technology companies and is an advisor, mentor, technology safari guide and keynote speaker. And zie is a transhuman.

Find out more at www.martintalks.com

ACKNOWLEDGMENTS

Thanks for the support: Alphie Talks, Amina Lien, Audrey Talks, Barnaby Briggs, Ben Mason, Cam MacLeod, Charlie Moynihan, Chris Frazer Smith, Chris Stirk, Chris Sykes, Christopher Ross, Claire Moynihan, Claudia Stebbings, Dan Francis, Darion Leigh, Darren Fergus, David Talks, Del Trezise, Dominic Bruning, Faith Jones, Fergus Moynihan, Greg Tustain, Harry Goodman, Isobel Talks, Jack Busby, James Bebbington, James Higham, Jeremy Bates, Jon Simons, Justin McCarthy, KM Wells, Kristen Werner, Linus Gregoriadis, Lisa Ellis, Lizzie Cree, Maggie Hastings, Marcus Exall, Melissa Constantinou, Mihnea Miculescu, Mike Baxter, Mohammed Raja, Nathan Stone, Nayef Abu Ebaid, Nicholas Baines, Nicholas Villani, Nick Berry, Nick Milner, Nicola Downes, Ollie Mustill, Phil Aitken, Phil Cowlishaw, Phil Dempsey, Rachel Gallimore, Rachel Walker, Rory Goodman, Rufus Talks, Sam Michel, Sarah Talks, Siim Lepisk, Tom Daniel, Vicky Stahle and Vlad Mehakovic.

Space to doodle

Space to doodle

Printed in Poland
by Amazon Fulfillment
Poland Sp. z o.o., Wrocław

58636037R00226